A HORSE, A HORSE—MY FATHER IS A HORSE!

"What do you mean, there's a horse in your father's bed?" Sapho achieved after an effort.

"Exactly that," answered her daughter, Hebe, calmly. "Either father has turned into a horse or a horse has turned into father. It comes to the same thing. There's one other possibility. Some horse might have run father out of bed and taken his place or else gone to sleep on top of him."

Together they looked upon Mr. Lamb's bed and beheld a horse. As much of the covers as possible were over this horse, its head was upon the pillows, yet much remained exposed and dangling. Hoofs and legs were eloquently visible. It was obvious that only the most determined of horses would have been willing to sleep in such a cramped position merely for the sake of a bed.

"My God," breathed Mrs. Lamb. "What will the servants say?"

D0037247

By Thorne Smith
Published by Ballantine Books:

TOPPER
TOPPER TAKES A TRIP
THE NIGHT LIFE OF THE GODS
THE STRAY LAMB
*TURNABOUT
*RAIN IN THE DOORWAY

* Coming soon from Del Rey/Ballantine Books

THORNE SMITH

The
Stray Lamb

A Del Rey Book

BALLANTINE BOOKS • NEW YORK

A Del Rey Book
Published by Ballantine Books

Library of Congress Catalog Card Number: 79-55331

ISBN 0-345-28724-X

Manufactured in the United States of America

First Ballantine Books Edition: August 1980

Cover art by Norman Walker

Contents

CHAPTER I

Spines in Transit

MR. T. LAWRENCE LAMB WEAVED HIS LONG, SHAD-bellied body down the aisle, and as one sorely stricken in affliction, crumpled into a seat. He hoped prayerfully that the other half of it would remain unoccupied. He hoped even more prayerfully that if it should be occupied it would not be by anyone he knew even remotely. Every evening he hoped this and almost every evening his hope was disregarded.

Mr. Lamb automatically elevated his knees. Out came his paper and off went the train. All set. Another day smeared.

He sighed profoundly. So far so good. No one had yet encroached upon his Jovian aloofness. Perhaps for a change he would get the best of the break. Adjusting his features in what he fondly believed to be a repellent expression he prepared to concentrate his attention on the financial section of his newspaper. His heart was not in it. Neither was his mind. Lamb was in a vagrant mood—misanthropic, critical, at odds with himself.

"Here we sit," he mused—his eyes darkly contemplating his fellow commuters—"Here we sit, the lot of us, a trainful of spines in transit . . . so many sets of vertebrae, each curved and twisted according to the inclination of its individual owner."

His eyes rested unenthusiastically on a man he heartily disliked, Simonds, a purveyor of choice lots.

"Take Simonds there," he continued to reflect. "That spawn of hell is just a lot of vertebrae all curled up. I myself am scarcely more than a column of vertebrae. And that old lady over there, she's a repository of vertebrae, old tortured vertebrae, no doubt extremely brittle . . . museum pieces."

1

He sighed morbidly over the great age and brittleness of the old lady's vertebrae, and rearranged his own, flexing them deftly between the seat and its back. His knees crept up higher in front of him. His head sank lower. He was gradually jack-knifing into his favorite commuting position.

For some inexplicable reason vertebrae this evening seemed unusually important to Lamb. They were almost getting the best of him. The more he thought of vertebrae the lower his spirits ebbed. There were too many commuters, all trying to contort themselves into the most comfortable, the most restful positions—all striving to do well for their backs after the strain of the day.

Tentatively Lamb peered into his newspaper. He fully intended to wash his hands of vertebrae and to study the details of a new bond issue.

There were newspapers everywhere—evening newspapers. Alluring tabloids with impartially quartered front pages displayed one pair of robust legs, one good corpse, a sanguinary railway accident, and a dull-looking pugilist. What more could any reasonable person crave?

Lamb studied the absorbed readers with detached animosity. Papers were being held at every conceivable angle, some negligently, untidily, others grasped tenaciously as if their owners lived in momentary dread of being deprived of their comfort. Some readers scanned their papers from afar. Others approached them secretively, nose touching type.

"Newspapers and vertebrae," elaborated Lamb, eyeing the suspended sheets bitterly. "That's all we are. That's all we're good for."

In the third seat in front of him sat a dignified old gentleman. He was having tough cerebration assimilating the fact that red ants greatly deplore the existence of essence of peppermint. For sixty-odd years he had managed to struggle through life without the benefit of this information. Now it had become urgent business with him. He must tell his wife about it the first thing. No more red ants for them. Then he tried to remember if they had ever suffered from red ants.

Farther down the aisle was a man whose expression grew bleaker and bleaker. He was following a comic strip. His concentration was almost pathetic. When he arrived at the grand climax he sat as one stunned, gazing hopelessly ahead of him. One would have been led to believe that he had suddenly received a piece of extremely depressing news.

In another seat, crouched like a dog over a bone, an ingrown-looking individual was enjoying a vicarious thrill from the sex irregularities of a music teacher and a casual man of God. Satisfyingly salacious stuff. Shocking. However, this particular commuter would not discuss the sordid affair with his wife. Such topics are better left outside the family circle.

Meanwhile the landscape.

Lamb turned to the window and considered a rapidly receding cow. Then his glance ran through the train. Nobody else was considering that cow. Nobody else was considering anything other than newspapers so far as he could discover. Yet the cow had not been without its points . . . a pleasant, contemplative, square-cut cow. And that brook out there. Lamb wondered idly where it wandered, through whose back yard, through what meadows and woodlands. Lamb himself was wandering now far from the financial section.

No scenery in all God's world, he decided, was quite so unobserved, left quite so utterly flat and to its own devices as those sections traversed by these hurtling slave galleys of progress. For the commuter familiarity with the landscape completely skipped mere contempt and passed into the realms of non-existence.

If that proud home-owner laboring out there on his lawn could only realize how unappreciated his efforts were he would not feel so infernally smug about things. Perhaps, thought Lamb, the man would give up gadgeting about with garden implements and devote his time to disguising the flavor of bootleg gin—a far more utilitarian and artistic pursuit.

Especially this evening, Lamb's thoughts ran on, was the landscape neglected. Eyes looked upon it, but for the most part indifferently, unseeingly. Newspapers were to blame. Lamb worried his own paper. Commuting trains everywhere, he reflected, were more or less spiritually akin. That was the awfulness of it. His feeling of inferiority and sameness deepened. His mood grew more restless. It was gathering in revolt.

What was he himself but a poor doomed commuter, a catcher and quitter of trains? His destiny stood confronting him, smirking at him. Years from now he would be extending a withered and feeble hand clutching a commutation ticket to be punched. He wondered if conductors ever died or grew old. They never seemed to, always stayed about the same—loquacious mummies.

A good Grade A, case-hardened commuter, decided Lamb, would experience but scant difficulty in meeting his soul's brother in any part of the world where commuting trains operated. With this creature he would be able to discuss his favorite topic in his own pet vernacular. Neither of them would give a tinker's dam about the scenery. They would consider it in no terms other than those of building and real-estate development— investment opportunity. With an inner ear, Lamb harkened to a hypothetical conversation:

"That's a neat bit of wooded highland," observes commuter A covetously.

"Yep," says B. "It's just itching to be opened up."

"Wish I had the ready to go in for a proposition like that," replies his friend.

"Man alive," says the other, "if I had the backing, that property wouldn't stay undeveloped long. Give me just six months, and I'd have a couple of paved streets run through and a row of model homes——."

He pauses and frowns masterfully at the hillside.

"And garages," adds commuter A, not to be outdone. "Bang up sewerage and a garbage-disposal plant. That sort of stuff gets the right class of buyer."

The wooded hillside is doomed. Its trees shiver. Trees have a way of knowing about such things. Soon wayward lovers will be seeking elsewhere for stimulating concealment. A neat little garage will have usurped their bower.

"My God!" muttered T. Lawrence Lamb, now thoroughly in revolt against the ordained measure of his days. "I'm a part of the system. I'm all tied up."

Then quite suddenly his attention became riveted on an object.

It was an ear.

CHAPTER II

The Ear Obtrudes

AN UNQUALIFIED FACT. THE OBJECT AT WHICH MR.
Lamb was gazing with such rapt attention was nothing
more nor less than an ear. A small pink ear. A perky
shred of an ear. And this ear in turn was ornamenting
a small sleek head. Exceedingly black hair, closely
trimmed—a severe yet successful bob, becoming only to
about one woman in a thousand.

"That's a mean-looking ear," mused Lamb. "Looks
like a wicked horse's. Snakish sort of a head too, probably filled with all sorts of schemes and misery."

Yet, even as he gazed, Lamb attempted to reject the
existence of the ear. He was not, he assured himself,
actually looking at it. He was merely resting his eyes.
In a moment or so he would return once more to his
newspaper. As a matter of fact, his paper was so held
as to be ready for immediate action. For instance, if
the head to which the ear was attached should chance
to reverse its position, Lamb could instantly take to
cover. Meanwhile, if the ear happened to cross his field
of vision that regrettable circumstance could hardly be
obviated. It was not of his seeking. As he had previously done with vertebrae, he now proceeded to do
with the ear. He washed his hands of it. He firmly set it
aside. That silly-looking ear was really no concern of
his.

Unconsciously Lamb found himself wondering just
how it would feel to bite that ear ever so delicately—
tentatively, so to speak. What would its owner say?
What would she do? Bite back most likely. White
teeth, small active teeth, somehow went with that ear.
A brazen character too, daring and unrestrained. A
thoroughly objectionable female type. Even from the

little Lamb had seen, he considered the owner of the ear a demoralizing influence.

Anyone observing Lamb would not have suspected him capable of such an odd line of thought. Lamb himself was far from being aware of the fact that he was a thoroughly unmoral man, a sort of warmed-over pagan as judged by all standards of conventional morality. Otherwise that ear would not have disturbed him so profoundly, would not have lured him away from consideration of finance and industry.

When the gods were fabricating Mr. T. Lawrence Lamb they were far from being single-minded about it. There had been a certain divergence of opinion, a lamentable lack of harmony. Some had contended, not without reason, that there were already too many commuters cluttering up the earth, too many hard-headed, conscientious home-owners, too many undeviating husbands and proud fathers. Humanity was becoming too stable, too standardized. It needed more highly spiced and less orthodox representatives. Other gods were firmly convinced that in order to allow themselves a few gracious liberties and privileges and at the same to create a favorable public opinion it would be a far wiser thing to keep humanity more or less at a dead level, to make appetites and desires as orderly as possible, and to reduce imagination to a safe and sane minimum. It is to be remembered that these dissenting gods were the greatest hell-raisers on high and that they brought forward their contentions merely to further their own selfish ends and to assure themselves the unexamined enjoyment of their rather indelicate pursuits.

Unfortunately, though outnumbered, these gods represented a small but active minority, and the result with Lamb was an acrimonious compromise, an incongruous blending of strongly opposed elements. Outwardly Lamb looked and acted like a sober, responsible and respected member of the community—one of its more solid members. Lamb firmly believed himself to be every bit of that. But the inner Lamb, the true Lamb, was not quite so good. There was little conformity in him, scant reverence for the established order of things. Consequently Lamb was the seat of much mental and spiritual conflict, of many stray, orphaned thoughts. Within himself he contained an unplumbed reservoir of good, healthy depravity that was constantly threatening to overflow and to spill all sorts of trouble about his feet.

Lamb's face, like his body, was long. His skin was dark and expression somewhat saturnine. His eyes looked out on life always a trifle sardonically. His associates believed him to be a capable serious-minded man, whereas in reality he was filled with a sort of desperately good-natured irony. For purposes of self-protection he was often brusk and caustic. It was just as well for everybody concerned that many of the remarks that sprang uninvited to his lips were quickly stifled. He had a wife who considered herself both artistic and intellectual. Lamb heartily detested these qualities, little realizing he possessed them himself to a high degree.

He enjoyed sitting with his knees elevated and his arms waving vaguely above his head. In this position he gave the impression of a semi-recumbent cheer leader. It was his most effective pose. He could explain things better that way. When customers came to him for financial advice they usually found him in this position, his desk being used solely for the purpose of supporting his knees. As he talked to them, his hands churning about in the air seemed to be juggling the industries and public utilities of a nation. Fascinated, his callers saw golden opportunity dancing before their eyes. Lamb's success as a financier lay in the fact that he was often eloquently inarticulate—staccato. When necessary he could be masterfully blasphemous. His selling talks left much to the imagination. An overhead scrambling of the hands, a tortured oath or so, and a lowering scowl were sufficient to crumble the opposition of the most opinionated investor.

In his dress he somehow always managed to be smartly disheveled, always slightly sprinkled with cigarette ashes. His manners were not good. They were natural. At forty he no longer cared a rap whether or not he ever sold another bond. Like his fathers before him, he was the Lamb of Lamb & Co. Exactly who or what the "Co." represented people had given up speculating. Customers knew that Lamb alone was sufficient. They deferred to his judgment and absorbed his bonds. Lamb had never ceased to be both pleased and surprised by his success. He was conscientious about other people's money. The well-established reputation of Lamb & Co. had not suffered under his management. He was proud of it, but just a little fed up. This he scarcely realized. Fortunately for the business no one ever sensed the lurking instability of the man, least of all Lamb himself.

His wife found it convenient to regard him as an unimaginative plodder—a money-grubber. Lamb no longer bothered his head about her opinion. In his eyes she had long been a matrimonial washout. Occasionally he found enjoyment in annoying her. For years she had been trying to subjugate him, to mold him to her ways of life. Today he was as inexplicable and as recalcitrant as when he had just married her. He was not a satisfactory husband. He knew this and was pleased. He failed utterly to harmonize with Mrs. Lamb's background, yet there he was and there probably he would be always with his long legs and mocking face. Mrs. Lamb often wished she had married an unqualified fool instead of this dark, ambling creature on whom she could make no impression.

It was essential to Mrs. Lamb's happiness that she should always make an impression. She feared Lamb's unuttered observations and never felt quite securely poised in the presence of his enigmatic grin. Lamb was no household comfort. He cramped his wife's style dreadfully. His daughter a little more than liked him. Together they considered life critically, cynically, and just a bit coarsely. With the aid of Hebe, Lamb at times became a jovial vulgarian. It was a relief to him, an outlet. With everyone else he automatically acted the part of the conventional, unemotional, complacent business man he fondly believed himself to be.

And for that reason the ear offended him. Lamb disliked philandering, yet for some reason or other, he felt that with very little persuading he could bring himself to philander with that ear. For several weeks he had been observing it in a casual, detached way. It was such a ridiculously small ear—the merest pretence of an ear. Why should a full-grown man like himself trouble about such a trifle? He was well past the age of foolishness. His own daughter was nearly as old as the ear. Anyway, the whole idea was out of the question. Yet the ear was undeniably a challenge. And that small sleek head so independently perched on a nice-looking neck, that too, was not without its appeal.

Strange to say, Mr. Lamb had never looked on the countenance of the owner of the ear. He had not even tried to push his investigations that far. He had felt it safer to let bad enough alone. He had ideas about the face, vague speculations, but he did not dwell on them. Why should he? Of what interest was it to him? Rubbish!

The train was slowing down for his station. Experienced commuters were already collecting their inevitable packages from the racks. Mr. Lamb methodically folded his newspaper and dismissed the ear from his thoughts—that is, he half rose preparatory to making his way down the aisle when quite unexpectedly the ear turned, and Mr. Lamb sat down hurriedly like one suddenly atrophied. The man was shocked to the core. He felt himself being intimately caressed by a pair of incredibly melting eyes set in a face whose pallor is usually associated with innate vice. There was a mouth too, vivid and terribly defenseless, and at the same time quite capable.

It was one of the most alarming experiences in Mr. Lamb's life. Those eyes. The languor in them. What a way for a woman to look at a man in public! The only word Lamb could think of in connection with those eyes was "voluptuous." They were actually voluptuous eyes, yet strange to say, they were unconsciously so. The girl did not know what she was doing. She could not possibly know.

"A creature with eyes like that," thought Lamb, "should be forced to wear smoked glasses."

She was more dangerous than a floating mine in the path of shipping. Her very innocence increased her potency. For some inexplicable reason Lamb smelled the fragrance of branches heavily laden with blossoms and caught a glimpse of a Chinese print he had once intended to buy.

The girl had turned her face away. Simonds, the bounder, was pausing to talk with her. The girl was smiling a slow, provocative smile, and Simonds, fool that he was, seemed to be ghoulishly pleased.

"She's cooking up something," thought Lamb. "The Jezebel—a regular Messalina, that girl—a she devil."

The train was gradually emptying. Lamb half rose again to make his way out. Then her eyes met his for a second time, and once more Mr. Lamb felt himself transfixed.

This was all nonsense. He rallied and calmly returned the girl's gaze. Then he finished folding his paper, rose snappily and left the train.

"What the hell!" he kept saying to himself. "What the hell!"

CHAPTER III

The Ear Has Legs

STILL NUMBED BY THE HIGH VOLTAGE OF THOSE PAS-
sionate eyes—Mr. Lamb had slightly refined his first
expletive—he made his way down the aisle and mingled
with his kin on the station platform. In his deep ab-
straction he failed to respond with his customary
briskness to the salutations of his friends.

"Lo there, Lamb, how's the boy?" passed unchal-
lenged as did, "Evening Larry, how's tricks?" and
other such innocuous inquiries.

Following the trail of commuters up the circular
stairs, Lamb paused in the waiting-room by the newspaper counter and looked through a window at the glittering array of waiting motors. Some of them were
already pulling out bearing their complacently successful owners homeward through the neat well-ordered
streets of that opulent suburban town.

Ordinarily this massing of wealth, this tangible evidence of purchasing power would have given Mr.
Lamb a comfortable sense of security. It would have
made him feel that all was well with the state of the
nation and that under the beneficent guidance of a cau-
tious administration prosperity was assured. This evening, however, Lamb looked upon the automobiles
without elation. They were mostly being driven by
wives and daughters—smartly togged women for whom
this moment constituted one of the high spots of the
day. Any woman so unfortunate as to be forced to
meet her bread-winner in an outmoded car was the object of some pity and no little secret self-congratu-
lation. Her costume was examined a little more
critically, and questions were asked about her husband.
Did he count or was he unimportant? Why did people

like that try to hold their own in such a well-to-do
community? There were other commuting towns. Nice
little places where they would feel more at home.

The bemused Lamb picked out his own well-
groomed automobile and dwelt on its handsome lines
unappreciatively. There was his daughter at the wheel.
A good girl Hebe, but after all was she really good?
Was any woman fundamentally good? Lamb was none
too sure.

He saw another person standing by his car. A young
man in white flannels, light sweater, and sport shoes. A
well-set-up youngster. Obviously very much absorbed
in Hebe. This youth was leaning over the side of the
automobile, and Mr. Lamb was struck by the lithe,
unconscious grace of the vigorous young body. A fine-
looking pair those two made. A romantic splash of
color and animation. Romance—that was for them.
They still had time ahead. Heaps of it. He was rapidly
running low.

Without realizing how far he was going, Lamb
leaned over the newspaper counter and attempted to
strike an attitude similar to that held by the youth. The
effect was somewhat surprising. The counter was low,
and Lamb was long. As a result of this combination
Lamb appeared to be sprawlingly, jauntily, suggestively
confidential. The newspaper man looked at him with
startled eyes for a moment, then mistaking Mr. Lamb's
motives, approached slowly and leaned tensely forward
across the counter. Unconscious of the man's presence,
Mr. Lamb maintained the immobility of his peculiar
position. Believing that he might be still too far away
to receive the delicate communication Mr. Lamb
desired to make, the newspaper man drew even nearer,
placed his ear to the other's lips and waited expectantly.

For a long moment this odd tableau remained fixed
as if in wax, then the man's curiosity got the better of
him.

"Shoot, Mr. Lamb," he murmured. "Something
good?"

Slowly Mr. Lamb turned. It took a little time for
him to realize the full import of the situation. All he

could see at first was an avid ear. Then he drew back as if stung and gazed blankly at the vendor of papers. Why was the creature so breathlessly expectant? With a shiver of apprehension he suddenly realized the full significance of the situation. He looked down at his unnaturally cascading body and immediately assumed a more normal position.

"What?" he asked, fighting for time. "What's that you said about something being good?"

"Oh, nothing," replied the man defensively. "From the way you were leaning over, I thought you wanted to whisper something. You know, something sort of—er—racy."

The newspaper man had barely avoided the use of the word "dirty." In his substitution of "racy" for it, he felt he had achieved a conversational triumph. Nevertheless, he considered himself cheated—let down. Mr. Lamb regarded him with growing disapproval. He studied the eager eyes and half-parted lips. Sedulously he avoided the ear. That face, he feared, that repellent face would henceforth haunt his dreams.

"No," he replied at last. "There seems to have been some misunderstanding. Those stairs got me. I was merely resting. It must be the weather. Somehow I feel quite worn out this evening."

He turned wearily, his shoulders suddenly sagged, and arranging his body in lines of utter exhaustion he dragged his feet away from the presence of the hateful person behind the counter. Lamb was not cut out to be an actor. His idea of feigning fatigue was far too elaborate. It was arresting but lacked conviction. Mr. Lamb had never progressed in such a remarkable way in the whole course of his life. He looked as if he had been mortally wounded and was blindly making his way toward human aid.

How many others had witnessed his momentary madness, he wondered. How many eyes had dilated at the sight of his humiliating posture? Had the ear chanced to see his breakdown? Lamb was filled with panic.

"Sort of a funny place to pick out for a rest," pondered the mystified newspaper man, looking after the half-crouching figure of Mr. Lamb. "Hope he makes his car before he drops in his tracks."

The object of his solicitude was by this time painfully approaching the automobile. He was relieved to see that the youth he had so disastrously attempted to imitate had departed, but was not at all reassured by the puzzled look of inquiry in his daughter's eyes.

"What happens to have broken down in you, major?" the young lady demanded in a cool, censorious voice. "From that peculiar walk you appear to be practicing, I'd say you needed a hot water bottle and a dose of castor—"

"Don't!" interrupted Mr. Lamb sharply. "You may be right. Perhaps I do, but why advertise my shame to the entire community? Would you like to have people pointing out your father as a man who has or is about to take a dose of castor-oil? Do you desire to drag your own flesh and blood through the dust of these streets? And why do you persist in calling me major?"

"As for the dust of these streets," the girl replied, "you seem to be doing the dragging of your own free will. How came you to get your middle section all bunged up like that? And why are you crouching before me like a jackal about to spring? One would think you'd checked your stomach somewhere. And that agonized shuffle of yours. Why did you embark on that?"

Mr. Lamb looked at his daughter with hopeless eyes. With a deep sigh he opened the door to the front seat and crawled in beside her.

"My stomach got itself that way," he explained briefly. "Don't know exactly how it did it. Had a frightful day in the city. Dog-tired."

Why had he ever attempted to deceive that hellish newspaper vendor with such an obviously artificial walk? It had only succeeded in making matters worse. Now he must somehow save his face. His daughter was regarding him with an undermining look of sympathy. Lamb essayed a groan. Perhaps that might help a little.

"If you go on like that," observed Hebe, "you'll not only be dragging yourself through the dust, but you will actually have to get a prop for your stomach to keep your head from bouncing along on your feet."

"A horrid picture," thought Lamb. Then to keep his daughter's mind from dwelling any longer on the subject, he asked abruptly:

"Just who was that emaciated-looking loafer who was practically swooning all over my car just now?"

"That emaciated-looking loafer," replied Hebe unemotionally, "might be occupying the position of your son-in-law at any minute now. You'd better be careful how low you classify him. I have an idea he was admiring my legs. So many people do."

The physical collapse aroused himself sufficiently to consider his daughter's legs. He had always been interested in legs.

"Is that so?" he remarked. "Well, if he wasn't nearsighted to the point of blindness, he must have got an eyeful."

"Father dear," admonished the girl, "I am still but a child."

"Not with those legs," replied Lamb. "From the way that fellow was peering into the car you would have thought he was trying to learn your legs by heart, or to subject them to the third degree."

"And why not?" demanded Hebe ominously. "What's wrong with the legs?"

"Don't like them," said Lamb. "They're too vigorous. Interminable legs. Do they never come to an end?"

"I wouldn't worry about that," said Hebe. "They're better than Sapho's legs. Not so frank and confiding."

Hebe was alluding to her mother, who had unfortunately been christened Mary, and who because of her penchant for amateur dramatics, had been renamed Sapho by her daughter. The name had been gratefully accepted by Mrs. Lamb. She was strongly of the opinion that she deserved it. Mary Lamb would not have been a livable name.

"You might be right," agreed Mr. Lamb. "Your mother's legs seem to be pretty well all over the place these days. Yours are a little less visible at least."

He paused to consider the subject in all its ramifications. Hebe at times was quite a relief. Only she understood how to treat unimportant matters with academic thoroughness.

"You know," he went on reminiscently. "In spite of Sapho's extreme leggishness, I personally don't seem to see them any more—not as legs, if you get what I mean. But she must have had legs at one time, I suppose."

"Certainly," replied Hebe, "or else I wouldn't be here."

"Logically arrived at," agreed Mr. Lamb, "although your way of putting it has rather indelicate implications. Your parental respect also needs a little brushing up."

They were alone now, the other automobiles having departed, and a new flock was arriving for the next contingent of commuters. Neither father nor daughter seemed to care whether they ever reached home or not. The casual ways of the pair were quite a trial to Mrs. Lamb. They were not popular around the house.

"Speaking of legs," observed Hebe casually, "yon' is an upstanding pair of shafts."

She pointed directly across the street, and Mr. Lamb's eyes followed the direction of his inelegant daughter's finger. The shafts referred to belonged to a pair of arms busily intent on carrying several large bundles from the delicatessen store. Lamb looked on the legs with instinctive covetousness, then, like a frightened rabbit, froze defensively to his seat. They were the legs of the ear.

"Uh-hoo!" bawled Hebe's uncultured voice. "Uh-hoo, Sandy! Over here!"

"Don't!" pleaded her father. "Don't make that awful noise. You sound like some sort of animal."

"Over here!" shouted Hebe with unabated enthusiasm. "We'll take you home."

The legs paused in their progress, altered their course, and came forward attractively in spite of the bundles.

"That ear would have such legs," thought Lamb.

There was something startlingly personal about them. They were vicious legs—suggestive. Lamb decided he had never seen such demoralizingly feminine legs. And Lamb was not elated. He had a premonition of change, of some complication arising to disturb the comfortable regularity of his life. He seriously resented this. He was Lamb of Lamb & Co., a contented, successful man. He was all set—had his own interests. Why should those legs come walking into his life? With characteristic thoroughness he washed his hands of the legs. Nevertheless, washed or unwashed, the legs continued to approach.

"Swarm in," said Hebe urgently to the girl. "Slither over the major and drop your bundles in the back."

"Why do we all have to huddle up here in the front seat like so many immigrants?" asked Lamb inhospitably. "Let me get out. I'll sit behind. Willingly. Gratefully."

In spite of his protest, the legs brushed past Mr. Lamb's knees and arranged themselves alarmingly beside him.

"This is your father—yes?" asked the girl. "Is he a nice father? He doesn't sound very. Is he?"

"He's too long," answered Hebe briefly.

"And drawn-out, perhaps?" suggested the other.

"Exactly," agreed Hebe. "That's just it. He's too long and drawn-out. Take his neck for instance."

"Me take his neck!" cried her friend. "You suggest I should take your father's neck. How amiable!"

Mr. Lamb noticed that her voice was surprisingly deep and rich and that she spoke with an insinuatingly rising inflection. An unwholesomely foreign type, he decided.

"You're mistaken," he hastened to assure the girl. "My daughter didn't mean for you literally to take my neck. She meant for you merely to look at it. She seems to think it's too long."

The girl scrutinized Mr. Lamb's neck avidly. Mr. Lamb thanked God that he was a cleanly man.

"Why, I love that neck!" she suddenly exclaimed, and Lamb was both relieved and outraged. "I think I could neck with that neck."

"What sort of friend is this, Hebe?" asked Lamb. "Something imported?"

His mood was waxing retaliatory.

"Her name's Sandra," replied his daughter, "and in

a manner of speaking, she is imported. Russian on her mother's side. A nice girl but prone to folly."

"Name doesn't sound quite real," observed Lamb. "Does she work in an office?"

"Not Sandra," he was informed. "She's a swell model. Underwear and things."

"You should see me," put in Sandra enthusiastically. "Then I am at my best. Then you would make me much. But to return to the neck, tell me, Hebe, your father doesn't neck,,perhaps?"

"Not sure," said that young lady impersonally. "I doubt it. His sex life is practically nil."

"Well, I'll be damned!" ejaculated Lamb, rapidly changing color.

"Such a big man too," replied the other girl sympathetically. "The poor thing must be starved for some loving."

"Hear that, major?" said Hebe. "What you got to say?"

"I wash my hands of the both of you," came the emphatic response. "Never did I hear such stuff. Do all young women go on nowadays like you two?"

"This is mild," his daughter calmly informed him. "So far, we have respected your feelings."

"But I won't any longer," cried Sandra tragically, "He is trying to go back on himself. He is taking a flat leave of me. I must tell all. For weeks this man has been devouring with hungry eyes the back of my head. Do not deny it, major. I have watched you in my mirror. Today I regarded him with these eyes."

Here she cast these eyes wildly about the automobile, and Mr. Lamb became slightly dizzy. He was glad he was not driving.

"Today I observed him eye to eye, so to speak, and he wilted—wilted before my gaze. Now he would wash his hands of me. Do not let him do that, Hebe. Do not let him wash. I shall not be washed by this long Lamb, do you hear? I shall remain unwashed forever."

On this high note of resolve the emotional young woman paused for breath and gazed magnificently about her. Mr. Lamb was filled with amazement and consternation. The complication had arrived. He was embroiled.

"You may remain unwashed forever, so far as I am concerned," he remarked soothingly. "I shall make no attempt to wash you."

"Good!" she exclaimed with a pleased expression. "I knew you would make me much. And now I depart."

The car drew up before a small, neat-looking home of the modest order, and the girl quickly slipped out.

"Bring him yourself the first time, Hebe," she said. "After that he will come alone."

"By stealth and at night," added Hebe.

"I shall do nothing of the sort," Mr. Lamb retorted emphatically. "Neither alone nor accompanied do I come. The two of you have gone far in depravity. I wash—"

"For goodness' sake, no more washing," protested Hebe. "We're all washed out as it is."

The other girl stood gazing soulfully at Lamb for a moment, then she observed complacently, as if addressing the world at large, "The Long Lamb will come, never fear. I shall have him."

"Stop talking like an adultress in a French farce and go away," urged Lamb. "I want to get home and snatch a drink."

"I shall make you suffer for that," she retorted.

With an emotional swirl of her scanty skirt, Sandra turned and hurried up the walk to the small house. Mr. Lamb in spite of his resolution, followed with his eyes the retreating figure, missing no details of its trim lines.

"Well, major, what do you think of Sandy?" his daughter asked. "Fairly hot stuff, what?"

"Torrid," Lamb agreed. "Does she always go on like that or is this some sort of maidenly pastime you two indulge in?"

Hebe grinned.

"That's for you to find out," she said. "As for me I've discovered the cause of your weird conduct when you left the train just now. Sandy had regarded you with these eyes. Brace up, major. You're a favored man."

"Drive on," growled Mr. Lamb, "and for God's sake don't be an ass."

CHAPTER IV

The Little Russet Man Appears

STRANGELY ENOUGH HEBE HEEDED HER PARENT'S plain-spoken admonition, which both of them knew without saying amounted to nothing less than an abject supplication. One glance at her father's face was sufficient to convince her that his long-repressed emotional arrangements were in a state of fermenting chaos which threatened at any moment to produce revolutionary results of an impredicable nature.

Thereafter she devoted her youth and energy to the business of driving, taking full advantage the while of that great liberality the law extends to the young and not unfavored daughters of prominent citizens of all well-regulated communities. Lamb was too busily engaged in washing his hands of practically everything to notice his close and constant companionship with painful injury and sudden death.

Hebe drove. She drove in the direction of that place in which Mr. T. Lawrence Lamb sought refuge and repose after the comtemplative quietude of a short yet most unprofitable day.

As if preordained by a class-conscious God with an eye to real estate values, this fair mansion was situated on the financially correct side of the tracks.

In most commuting towns of any recognized worth there are always two sides of which the tracks serve as the line of demarcation. There is the right side and the wrong side. Translated into terms of modern American idealism, this means, the rich side and the side that hopes to be rich.

On either side of the tracks there sometimes extends a quarter—a blot—that is not rich, will never be rich, and makes no visible effort to be rich. The blot thrives squalidly amid its fights, sufferings, and enjoyments. It is fundamentally superior to either side of the tracks, because it envies neither, regarding all members of the community as legitimate prey.

Properly speaking, however, those who dwell on one side of the tracks form a separate and distinct race from those who have their being on the other side. The rich side is naturally of finer clay, superior morally, physically and intellectually. And it is the bounden duty of those who dwell on the rich side to defend its borders against the untimely incursions of the financially striving side. Between the two a silently genteel yet none the less bitter guerrilla warfare is in constant progress. No pickets are visible, no orders to halt are audibly voiced, no hostilities are openly exchanged. Nevertheless, there is a certain sense of vigilance. They shall not pass, is the order of the day.

By nature Mr. Lamb was too indolent and skeptical to care a rap about either side. By the accident of birth and inherited wealth he was well above the battle. One side of the tracks was as good to him as the other. He lived where he did, not from his own choice, but because the house had been left to him by those who had gone before after having lived in it themselves and had their fill of it. The modern plumbing and other embellishments were of Mrs. Lamb's contrivance. Like other members of her ilk, she believed, for some obscure reason, that the rich side of the tracks was also the aristocratic side. She was one of those aspiring wives who would have ruined her husband's health, hopes, and happiness in her efforts to drive him across the tracks to the right side, had Fate seen fit to have placed her on the wrong.

If Mr. Lamb was most entirely perfect in the eyes of his friends and associates, it was due solely to his profound disregard of the finer shades of class distinction, his complete indifference as to what was taking place about him in his sacrosanct community. He should have been a civil leader, the chairman of committees, the protector of the established order of things, whereas he devoted most of his time to making a fine art of comfortable if grotesque nitting. This state of affairs, to put it mildly, was most distasteful to Mrs. Lamb. Consequently Lamb enjoyed it the more. Silently, some might say meanly, he observed her irritation. He studied it analytically. He also enjoyed her dizzy attempts to make up in herself for the semi-recumbency of her husband.

Once when Lamb had elevated himself in an endeavor to rid the community of Home Defense lecturers, reformers, and other practitioners of a warped and questionable patriotism, his wife had been so outraged that she had withdrawn to Europe for the duration of three months, much to the peace and gaiety of the entire household. Lamb and Hebe often alluded half despondently to the unguarded naturalness of existence during that pleasant period.

Hebe drove. She drove a winding way along a picturesque, semi-rustic road leading to that desirable eminence from which the abode of Lamb looked down on both sides of the tracks through casements that had framed several generations of watchers, for the ancestral Lambs had always been estate-minded and land-possessed.

Mrs. Lamb objected to the antiquity of the house, but she had to admit the distinction of its location and the advantages of its ample grounds. She had endeavored to make Lamb build. Lamb had studied her darkly for the full space of a minute, and there the endeavor had languished, never to be renewed. He had merely grinned, elevated his knees a trifle higher, and sighted at her over them. That had been quite enough. The subject was definitely closed.

As the car rounded a well-planned curve such as is to be found on the right side of the tracks, Hebe's eyes marked and dwelt on a figure she considered rather unusual. It was a little russet man, as she always afterwards remembered him. A small creature, this person was, appareled in an ancient habit of russet hue. Even the umbrella which he carried with some show of elaboration was of the same color. From the rear, his short plump figure gave one the impression of good living and well being. It was a jolly sort of figure, the embodiment of jocund autumn. Hebe thought of chestnuts and burning leaves, of trees turning and hearths aglow. He was a surprising little man, well poised and suggesting a certain dignity in spite of his odd appearance.

The little man was more surprising still as the car drew near him, for he suddenly stopped, turned deliberately in his tracks and brandished the russet umbrella in a most determined and imperative manner. There was no mistaking the meaning. He desired the car to stop. And Hebe obediently stopped. She noticed the little man's face was also of a russet hue. It was a jolly face, in which sparkled a pair of merry, unfathomable eyes.

"May I try it?" he asked abruptly.

His voice was as clear as a bell. It carried a quality of humorous briskness. Hebe was nonplused.

"You mean—" she began.

"Exactly, my dear," supplied the little russet man as he fidgeted ineffectually with the handle of the rear door. "I mean just what I said: may I try it?"

"Let me help you," offered Mr. Lamb, slightly dazed, as he turned to open the door from the inside. In doing so his eyes encountered those of the little man, and an extraordinary sensation shot through him. He felt as if suddenly he had been discovered, and yet there was a haunting sense of having just failed to remember something he had forgotten so long ago that he doubted ever having known it. The spell was broken at the sound of the little man's clear voice.

"Your servant, sir," he said, and there seemed to be some hidden significance to his words. "Now I suppose one mounts?"

"Just so," replied Mr. Lamb. "One mounts."

After busily podging himself into the automobile, the little man sat down quite unhurriedly and arranged his umbrella in just a certain way. It was his way of arranging an umbrella.

"Now," he said, looking about him cheerfully, "what happens next? Make it do things, my dear."

Feeling much younger and less assured, Hebe put the car in motion as the little man observed her, his eyes alight with great expectations.

"You must understand," he explained in a confiden-

tial voice, leaning over to Mr. Lamb, "in my other—
er—I mean, in my younger days I had no experience
at all with this method of locomotion. How could I?"
he demanded severely. "How could I?"

The question required an answer.

"You just couldn't," agreed Mr. Lamb. "Impossible."

"Exactly!" cried the little russet man on a note of
triumph. "The method didn't exist. Is it—er—er—
quite as you would have it, my dear sir?"

"Not so good," offered Lamb, now knowing himself
exactly how he would have it.

"No," reflected his small passenger judicially. "It is,
as you so laconically put it, not so good."

"Some nerve," remarked Hebe in a smothered voice.

"The expression, my dear, is modern," said the little
man good-humoredly, "yet its meaning is quite clear. I
was merely agreeing with your father, for I presume he
is your father, but perhaps I am in error on that slight
point. It's possible you are his wife, or even better, his
mistress. It is of no importance. As I was just now saying, I prefer to walk. I seem to taste things through the
soles of my feet."

"You must run across some rare dishes," Hebe
threw back jauntily.

The little man eyed the girl with approval.

"Your daughter, sir," he said, "for now I am sure
she is your daughter, appears to possess an unusually
healthy strain of vulgarity. I like it. I myself am vulgar
beyond compare. In my other—er—I mean to say, in
my younger days even strong men were forced to leave
the room. I once remember Rabelais's fainting—the
master vulgarian of them all. That was an achievement.
My highest. Now I am somewhat refined. Not that I
fail to appreciate things."

Mr. Lamb did some vague casting back in his
memory, then became slightly shocked. This strange
passenger must indeed be extremely old, almost too old
to exist at all.

"Did I understand you to say, Rabelais?" he asked
in his most polished manner.

"A thousand pardons," the little russet man hastened to explain. "Rabelais! Certainly not. It must have been a more recent vulgarian. Old fellows like myself are prone to confuse both people and periods. Many years ago, though, I once met you, Mr. Lamb."

"Me," ejaculated Lamb, now thoroughly aroused. "At what time? In what place may I ask?"

"Before you were, in a loose manner of speaking, born," came the quiet reply. "The place does not matter. You would not recall it."

Lamb and his daughter swiftly sought each other's eyes and found therein no helpful revelation. They seemed to be driving on in a dim, wandering silence, almost somnolent.

"From the outset you were destined to conflict," drifted a small, clear, yet distant voice from the rear seat. "It can be rectified. It should be. If I can be of any service—"

Silence. Hebe was driving as those who drive in a dream—automatically, instinctively. Her father seemed to have fallen into some deep quagmire of meditation from which he would probably never be able to extricate himself. Silence still. Higher mounted the road. Had they been driving thus through eternity? Where was the station? Where was the house? And what, exactly, did they matter? Absently Hebe began to sing softly a melody from Tosca. Her low voice was surprisingly sweet, yet for some inexplicable reason an echo voice seemed to be following her today, a stronger voice filled with passion and bitterness, a knowledge and love of life. Lamb kept passing from one brown study to another, each growing browner until the last one threatened to become black. Yet even in his aloofness he listened to the singing and wondered. Something within him responded to it. As Hebe quite naturally slowed down and stopped at the gates to the house before taking the car to another entrance, a clear note rang out and lingered for a moment in the car around them—only them. They started and gazed at each other with bewildered eyes.

"Give over whooping," said Lamb. "What will our passenger think, not to mention the entire neighborhood?"

Hebe glanced back at the rear seat.

"He doesn't seem to be there," she announced unsurely.

"Where the devil did we put the beggar off?" demanded her father.

"Don't know. He's off. That's just all there is to it," replied Hebe. "Perhaps the lunatic slipped out when we slowed down somewhere. I think he is an escaped one—honestly."

"Without the slightest possibility of a doubt," agreed Mr. Lamb. "But do you remember, the devil knew my name?"

"Yes—yes—so he did," said Hebe. "I remember now. Rum, ain't it?"

"No end," replied Lamb with a grin. "This is our show, Hebe, understand?"

"It is. It is," said the girl.

And just as he was leaving the car he asked her as diffidently as he could, "Listen, Hebe, does your friend—what's her name—Sand—"

"Sandra Rush," supplied Hebe helpfully.

"Name doesn't matter anyway," went on her father hurriedly. "Does she always act like that?"

"That's for you to find out," said Hebe.

"Certainly not. No interest," declared Mr. Lamb. "And is it true that she parades in underwear?"

"That's a fact," the girl replied. "An absolute fact. I'll take you to see her sometime."

"God forbid," muttered Lamb, turning up the extensive driveway. "I wash my hands of it all."

CHAPTER V

A Horse in Bed

MR. LAMB RETURNED HOME TO FIND HIS WIFE IN ANother man's arms. The scene would have annoyed if not irritated the majority of God-fearing husbands. Not so Mr. Lamb. It left him cold. To heighten the color of the situation, Mrs. Lamb was clad in what is generally considered an intimate costume—arrangements usually associated with the bed, yet not necessarily with sleep. The costume in which the man rejoiced seemed a bit vague to Lamb. All he could think of was Mardigras, class reunion, and revelry in general. He was not particularly interested.

The couple lay à la Cupid and Psyche upon the floor. At Lamb's entrance Cupid released Psyche with such alacrity that there was the unromantic sound of a thud, Psyche being in the neighborhood of ten stone.

"Ah!" cried Mr. Leonard Gray with a wild wave of his hand and a smile of an uncertain nature. "Croesus home from his mints. How stands the market today?"

Mr. Lamb saw no occasion to reply to this piece of flamboyancy.

"Well, old money-grubber," said Mrs. Lamb, heaving into a more graceful position, "I suppose your hands reek with greenbacks. You're late tonight."

Nor to this remark did Mr. Lamb consider it essential to reply. He merely contemplated the pair at leisure.

"There are lounges," he said at last. "It's merely a suggestion, of course."

"Oh, no, the floor's the place," protested Mr. Gray.

"Not the way I was taught," said Mr. Lamb. "Tilly, where'd you get those funny breeches?"

"Don't be ridiculous, Lawrence," Mrs. Lamb replied

with an attempt at dignity. "They're not breeches. They're—"

"Go on, tell me they're kilts," interrupted her husband. "I'm ignorant. I revel in it."

"You know perfectly well they're your own best silk pajamas," retorted his wife. "I put them on to get a certain effect."

"You'll get a tremendous effect unless you've put them on backwards," Mr. Lamb observed. "I've always had to be careful with those pajamas myself."

"Sapho," put in Mr. Gray hastily, "I don't think I can go on with it now. I can't recapture the mood."

"Try that strangle hold again, young man," suggested Mr. Lamb. "It might do you a world of good."

"Every man must play his part, Mr. Lamb," replied Leonard Gray protestingly.

"But you appear to be playing my part," said Lamb. "Playing it better than I could—far better."

Mr. Gray was the local amateur hero, the focal point of the Woodbine Players. He had once tried to sell bonds in Mr. Lamb's office. It had been a poor try. Even his manly good looks had failed to disturb the stenographers. So, accordingly, he had withdrawn, having failed in all departments. The flappers and married women who had nothing better to do welcomed him back to the fold of the idle, and found him quite a help. Of late he was much to be seen at the Lamb ménage where Sapho and he developed their art.

"Why persist in misunderstanding?" complained Mrs. Lamb. "Leonard and I are rehearsing for Sunday night."

"Then I suppose I should stay away or visit friends?" her husband suggested.

"Don't be vulgar," Mrs. Lamb replied. "You know very well about the Vacation Fund affair."

"When I was a boy," said Mr. Lamb, "such scenes used to be barred in public, especially on Sunday. Why do they close the movies?"

At this point Hebe blew into the room and eyed the weirdly clad couple.

"At it again, I see," she announced. "When will you two ever get tired?"

Mrs. Lamb sighed wearily and considered rising, then thought better of it.

"I'm sure I'll be glad when it's all over," she said. "I'm tired out, and the part bores me to tears."

"I wish I could take it for you," Hebe's voice was deep with unfelt sympathy.

"Child," said her mother, "you'd never understand. It takes—oh, I don't know what it takes."

"It takes a hell of a lot of nerve, I'd say." Mr. Lamb remarked. "Come on, Hebe, I want to desiphon a couple of drinks."

When they had left the room Mrs. Lamb looked questioningly at her partner.

"You shouldn't have dropped me like that," she complained. "I felt so off poise."

"Only thing to do under the circumstances," replied Mr. Gray.

"Perhaps it was," she answered as he helped her to her feet. Then in a lower voice, "I'm afraid we were rehearsing too well, Len. You'll have to be a better boy."

"More careful," he said, equally low.

She nodded.

In the dining-room Lamb was actively caging drinks, being carefully provided for by Thomas and Hebe. Thomas knew Lamb better than Lamb knew himself. He had been in the family longer and was so old that he had grown used to it and was now apparently indifferent to the passage of time. Thomas seemed to feel that he had got so old he could hardly get any older. He had no more room for years. So he cheerfully kept on living and regarding Lamb and Hebe as his last responsibilities. He was far too old for Mrs. Lamb. She was eager to pension him off. Thomas knew this and failed to show the proper amount of gratitude.

Presently Brother Dug came in—Douglas Blumby, Lamb's brother-in-law and pet aversion. Dug always sang the "dead drunk" part in "My Bonnie Lies Over the Ocean," and had never failed to find it amusing. He was about Lamb's own age, forty, and should have been chloroformed some months before his first candle. During the war he had been a camp song-leader and general rouser-up, and ever since that time his one idea in life had been to make people sing. On gala occasions he donned his non-combatant song-leader's uniform and recalled camp life in a loud voice. He did things about Boy Scouts, and they failed to see his point.

Now he entered the room with a "Whoopee, good people! Guzzle's the word. How's tricks, Larry?"

Larry choked so severely over his drink that both Thomas and Hebe sped to his assistance, the one taking the glass from his shaking hand, the other thumping him violently upon the back. When the afflicted man had somewhat recovered he turned a pair of watery malevolent eyes on his brother-in-law.

"I'm not proud of Lawrence," he said in a hoarse voice, "but by God if I'll stand for Larry! Furthermore I don't know any tricks."

Hebe turned to brother Dug reproachfully.

"You've been cautioned enough not to call him Larry," she told him.

Brother Dug was not at all cast down.

"All right, Larry," he replied with a humorours smirk as he patted Mr. Lamb's already flayed back. "I'll not call you Larry."

Thomas and Hebe seized Mr. Lamb's arms and clung to them. For a moment he stood there rigid and straining like a statue of Prometheus chained, then he allowed himself to be placed in a chair and supplied with a fresh high-ball.

Meanwhile Douglas Blumby had drifted away on some merry quest. His booming voice could be heard in the hallway discussing with Gray and Sapho the part that he would play in the Vacation Fund affair.

"Why do you let him live here, father?" asked Hebe.

"God knows, young one," he replied. "Perhaps it's fear of your mother or my final loyalty to her. Another thing, I have a certain duty to society. Bad as I am I could never inflict that ninny on the world. We must keep our troubles in the family."

It was hardly a propitious moment for the entrance of Mr. Melville Long, yet in that young gentleman came without a care in the world, assured of a warm, if not an enthusiastic, reception. Mr. Lamb, gazing at

him with lowering brows, recognized the youth he had
so disastrously attempted to imitate.

"This is Mel Long," said Hebe. "He wolfs with us
tonight, major."

"I know your father," said Lamb, extending a limp
hand. "He works."

"A father's privilege," replied Mr. Long blithely. "I
often thank God he does. If he didn't I don't know
how we'd ever get along."

"You rejoice in your non-productiveness, young
man," observed Lamb.

"I'm not so unproductive," the youth replied. "This
morning I helped a famous dipsomaniac to regain a
part of his health by playing him eighteen holes of golf.
This afternoon I made a sketch of mother that made
the old dear feel fifteen years younger. I'll get a new
car for that. And tonight—well, here I am."

"And I suppose you're going to stay," said Mr.
Lamb rather cheerlessly.

"Until the crack o' dawn," Long replied with a
happy smile. "Golfing makes one hungry."

Mr. Lamb rose wearily from his chair, placed his
half-empty glass on the buffet and walked to the door.

"Well," he said, "if you've settled that, I suppose
nothing I can say would induce you to alter your plans.
At your age I didn't drink—much." He turned to his
daughter and continued: "Hebe you do the strangest
things. Don't drop the decanter when pouring. And
don't wear it out."

With that he left the room. After dinner he retired
to his study, where he sat doing nothing, absolutely
nothing. Once he walked out on his little private
veranda and considered the world at large, after which
he returned to his chair where he continued to do
nothing.

The next day he broke an inflexible rule and jour-
neyed to the city. It was Saturday. There was no sense
to it, yet he went just the same.

As he made for a seat in the train, a slim figure almost tripped him up in its eagerness to crowd past him.

"We shall sit together," breathed the figure."You
and I on a single seat—alone!"

"With the exception of five or six hundred human souls," observed Mr. Lamb, "we are quite alone."

"This is merely the beginning," replied Sandra.

"It is a short trip and I usually read right up to the end of it. That has been my rule for years," said Lamb.

"But now that you've come to know me so well," the young lady continued, "you will have to make a new set of rules."

Mr. Lamb regarded her with a pained expression.

"You get the queerest ideas in your head," he replied. "I hardly know you at all. Why don't you go up there and sit with Simonds? He has no one to talk with, and I doubt if he knows how to read."

"Mr. Simonds!" exclaimed Sandra. "He is a lovely man. He lends me his horse. I ride him tomorrow."

"Why don't you go and tell him about it?" said Lamb curtly. "If I couldn't be a better horse than that clown of his I'd give up trying. At that he's preferable to his master."

"You like him, I see," said Sandra.

"We all do," replied Lamb shortly; then with a quick change of tone, "Tell me, do you really parade in underwear?"

"You mean, march down Fifth Avenue behind a band and Mr. Whalen?" she asked. "Never! I'm too exclusive."

"I didn't mean quite so openly as that," Mr. Lamb explained. "You know what I mean. Don't quibble."

"I have never quibbled," she said with conviction, "and I don't think it nice of you to suggest such a thing. But I do parade in underwear, to say the least."

"I wouldn't put it that way," advised Mr. Lamb, in a fatherly voice. "It doesn't sound nice."

"Oh, I am still unseduced," she replied. "I'm tired of trying to be."

Mr. Lamb looked about him quickly, consternation in his eyes.

"Lay off that," he said in a low, intense voice. "Don't shout the word above the roar and clatter of the train. Confine your unsolicited confessions to this end of the car."

"You misunderstand," she continued earnestly. "I

don't mean that I desire to be seduced. What I tried to convey to you is, I'm tired of having people try to seduce me. You're an exception."

"Let's drop the seduction for the moment," pleaded Mr. Lamb. "Do you like going to plays?"

"Only for the moment will I drop it," said Sandra. "I like going to plays. Take me."

"I will not," said Lamb.

"Dog," said Sandra, and turned to the window.

The conversation languished here. Mr. Lamb opened his paper and endeavored to read. His eyes kept straying furtively to the girl's averted face. Had she caught his glance he would have felt like a thief. The reason was hard to define. Gradually it dawned on him that the girl was looking at the scenery. Actually looking at it. Seeing it. To such an extent, in fact, that he was entirely forgotten. She had dismissed him from her thoughts, if he ever had been in her thoughts. She was out there somewhere, out there in the woods and fields. She was no longer connected with underwear, that is, Lamb hastily amended, she was no longer parading in underwear with commercial intent. Lamb also amended that thought. He did not know quite how to put it, so he gave it up. Anyway she was out there somewhere, and he was left quite behind. He felt injured yet interested.

Suddenly she squeezed his arm.

"Look!" she said. "See the two ponds—the upper one and the lower?"

The ponds flashed past, two brief little bits of metal. She looked at him with cloudy eyes.

"Well, the lower pond is all alone now," she continued. "There used to be swans on it. Such lovely, button-hook-looking swans. Now they're all gone. They're on the upper pond, those swans, and the children play there now. Do you think that the lower pond feels lonely?"

Mr. Lamb considered it a very difficult question. His common sense assured him that the lower pond did not mind in the least, yet somehow, within himself, he felt as did his companion, that the lower pond might feel a little lonely.

"Yes," he said at last, regarding her quite seriously. "I think the chances are that the lower pond feels just a bit out of things. Perhaps it is lying there wondering when the swans will return again . . . and the children."

"I think you're awfully damn nice," she said irrelevantly, and Lamb promptly returned to his paper.

"Just before the train pulled in at the station, Lamb turned to her and asked, "Why do you sometimes speak in such a strange way . . . sort of inverted English?"

"You don't like it?" she asked with a delightfully rising inflection.

"Leave me out of it," he replied. "Why do you do it?"

Then she laughed. She laughed softly, almost inwardly, without regard for either Lamb or his feelings.

"You're so dumb," she said finally when she had pulled herself together. "But just because you've given me such a good time, I'll let you into a secret. Where I work, where I wander around in underwear, the directing gods urge us to talk like that. They think it sounds distinguished, gives the scanty things we wear the stamp of authenticity. Some of the models are much worse than I am. Sometimes I fall into it from sheer habit, at others for the sake of practice. I love to practice on you, you're so—so—gullible, if you get what I mean. Now will you make me much?"

Lamb gave general directions as to just where she could go, and thus they parted, the one to the opulent salons of Fifth Avenue, the other to the thronging defiles of the financial district.

That night Lamb momentarily left his study and stood for a while on his private veranda. In a perverse fashion he was a little nosey about what was going to happen on the following evening and the preparations now under way. Merely because he was so completely out of it. Lamb was that way.

Mrs. Lamb—Sapho—with several turbans around her head, and what he decided must be a romper suit embollished with a scarf round the waist, was temperamentally directing several members of the Woodbine Players in the erecting of flood-lights and the construction of a stage. At times she would pause as if in a trance, one hand pressed to her cheek. And Lamb hated that. He had to look somewhere else whenever she did it. Sapho was also driving Thomas into a long awaiting grave by sending him for something, then not wanting it when the old man had pantingly arrived. Lamb called Thomas to him, and ordered him to bed.

"On your way through the dining-room don't forget to tilt the decanter," he told him.

"I wasn't going to, sir," Thomas assured him, and shambled off with a parting, "I hope we all sleep, sir, in spite of it."

Lamb hoped so. He intended to.

He returned to his study and the charming fabrications of Kai Lung and was getting along quite nicely when he became aware that someone was speaking to him. What he heard was:

"As I was saying, it should be rectified."

Mr. Lamb looked up and saw sitting opposite him, as if he had always been accustomed to occupying that particular chair, the little russet man.

"Can you do anything about it?" asked Mr. Lamb.

"I did not say that I could, sir," the little man replied.

"Then why let's talk about it?" continued Lamb. "From the first, you say, I was destined to conflict. By that, I assume you meant, spiritual conflict. Well, recently I've just realized it. Before that I always imagined I was a singularly contented and fortunate man. I'm not. I don't like things."

"What would you prefer to be?" asked the plump caller, carefully placing his umbrella on the floor beside his chair. "What would you like to do?"

Lamb rose in exasperation. He moved restlessly about the study, poured out a brace of drinks, produced a box of cigars, and finally reseated himself.

"I don't know," he said rather helplessly. "Haven't the vaguest idea when you put it to me straight. One thing I do know, I'm tired of being a human being. I think I'd like to be things if I could—animals, birds, beasts, fish, any old sort of a thing, just to get another

point of view, to keep from thinking and acting always
as a man, always as a civilized being, an economic unit
with a barrel full of obligations constantly threatening
to run up against something and smash."

The little russet man considered Lamb pensively for
a short time over the ash rim of his cigar. Lamb steadily meeting his gaze read a world of understanding in
the little fellow's eyes. To Lamb at that moment he did
not seem little. He seemed large enough almost to be
terrible. Yet the man was not quite terrible. It was his
penetration that gave one a feeling of awe—of nakedness.

"That is all I wanted to know," said the little russet
man emphatically, and put down his glass.

Lamb turned to reach for an extra ash tray. When
he turned back with the tray, offering it to his guest, all
that remained of him was a lazily floating cloud of
cigar smoke. The cigar itself was neatly balanced on
the arm of the chair. Only the glass, cigar, and weaving
smoke gave evidence that he had ever been there at all.

For several seconds Lamb remained in a condition
of suspended animation, the ash tray still extended.
Then he deliberately returned the tray to its place, finished his drink, put his book on the desk, its pages
spread at the place where he had been reading, got up
from his chair and thoughtfully left the room.

It was Hebe's custom to call her father in the morning. Even in the summer-time when most young ladies
lay late abed, especially on Sundays, Hebe was always
hellishly up and prowling.

Mr. and Mrs. Lamb occupied adjoining rooms
though the advantage therein had for some time ceased
to exist. It was through her mother's room that Hebe
gained access to her father's.

This morning as usual, she appeared in a flaming
dressing-gown and softly opened her father's door.
Sapho was still asleep, her temperament entirely abandoned. The girl looked into her father's room
gloatingly. She was going to disturb someone. Then
gradually her expression changed. She cocked her head
on one side like a puzzled dog and continued to look,

her eyes growing rounder and rounder. At last she turned quietly to her mother's bed.

"Sapho!" she whispered. "Sapho! Wake up. There appears to be a horse in father's bed."

CHAPTER VI

Equine Excursions

THERE WAS AN ELEMENT OF URGENCY SHARPENING the edges of Hebe's whisper that penetrated Sapho's vast unresponsiveness to mundane considerations. This woman of many parts and poses sat up in bed and looked upon her daughter as a glacier would regard a rose.

"Your humor, Hebe, is extremely mal à propos," she brought forth.

"Sapho," replied Hebe, "I'm not trying to be funny. Things are funny enough. There's a horse or something very much like a horse in the major's bed."

Sapho still light-headed from a heavy sleep strove to adjust her brain to the reception of this extraordinary announcement. No good. The brain refused to accept it. "What do you mean, there's a horse in your father's bed?" she achieved after an effort.

"Exactly that," answered her daughter calmly. "Either father has turned into a horse or a horse has turned into father. It comes to the same thing. There's one other possibility. Some horse might have run father out of bed and taken his place or else gone to sleep on top of him."

"As if we didn't have enough on our hands with the Vacation Fund affair tonight," Mrs. Lamb complained as she sought for her robe and slippers. "If it isn't a horse, Hebe, I'll be very much vexed."

"And if it is?" Hebe inquired.

"God knows," sighed Mrs. Lamb, tiptoeing across the room.

Together they looked upon Mr. Lamb's bed and beheld a horse. As much of the covers as possible were over this horse, its head was upon the pillows, yet much remained exposed and dangling. Hoofs and legs were eloquently visible. It was obvious that only the most determined of horses would have been willing to sleep in such a cramped position merely for the sake of a bed.

"My God," breathed Mrs. Lamb. "What will the servants say?"

Under the scrutiny of the two women the horse stirred uneasily and opened one eye. It was enough. Mrs. Lamb indulged in a gasp. Hebe was merely interested. Not satisfied with this demonstration, the horse raised his head from the pillows and looked inquiringly at Hebe and Mrs. Lamb. Then his lips curled back in a sardonic grin displaying a powerful set of vicious-looking teeth. He rolled his eyes until only the whites remained and thrust one curved foreleg at Mrs. Lamb, a gesture eloquently suggestive of his intention to inflict some painful injury upon her body and person. Mrs. Lamb hastily withdrew to her bed where she took refuge beneath the covers.

"You do something about it, Hebe," came her muffled voice. "Get the creature out of the house without the servants knowing. It would never do to have them think your mother had a horse in the next room. You know what servants are."

The horse was listening intently, ears pitched forward, and at this last remark he winked slowly and deliberately at Hebe. The girl was amazed. It was her father all over. At that moment she accepted the fact that something strange had occurred.

Then after a few minutes of thoughtful consideration, looking this way and that as if to determine the best way of procedure, Mr. Lamb cautiously got himself out of bed, but not without considerable clattering and convolutions. Hebe watched him with amused interest. She knew it was her father.

"Hurry, Hebe," came her mother's voice. "We can't afford to miss church today—not with that affair on tonight."

Mr. Lamb thought of his best pajamas, and throwing back his head gave vent to a wild neigh. He was feeling rather wild and at the same time a trifle timid. He had often played horses as a child, but never actually been one. Now he tried to recall just how he had gone about it in those early days. He wondered how he looked, what sort of horse he was, and, remembering his full-length mirror, he stepped delicately across the room and, sitting down in a strangely unhorselike attitude, lowered his neck and gazed at his reflection. The effect was not pleasing. He saw a most despondent-looking creature regarding him from the glass. Hebe could not restrain a laugh, and Mr. Lamb turned his head and looked at her reproachfully, then continued his scrutiny.

"I'm not much of a horse in this position," he decided. "There must be some other way of being a horse. Perhaps—"

He rose from his strange position and backed away from the mirror, but was still unable to get the desired view. Bending an eloquent glance upon his daughter, he pointed with his hoof to the mirror. Obediently the girl went over to the mirror and after much shaking and nodding of her father's head, she adjusted it to his satisfaction.

"That's something like," thought Lamb, surveying his reflection with no little satisfaction.

He was a fine body of a horse—a sleek, strapping stallion. Black as night with a star on his forehead. He turned slowly, taking himself in from all angles.

"Rather indecent, though," he thought. "Wish I had a blanket, a long one. Oh, hell! I'm a horse, now. Horses don't mind. Still it doesn't seem quite—well, I just never did it before, that's all." He paused to reconsider his reflection, then continued his soliloquy, "Anyway, if that girl can go about in step-ins and such, I can go about in nothing at all."

He looked at his daughter proudly, and affectionately nuzzled her warm neck. She put up her arms and kissed him, then drew back and looked at him with a half-smile. Lamb solemnly nodded his head, and Hebe understood. Then a pleasant idea occurred to him. He squeezed through the door into his wife's room and quietly approached the bed. Mrs. Lamb was still completely smothered by the covers. Slipping his nose through an aperture, he suddenly emitted a piercing scream sounding like a lost soul in hell. It was as if he had blown the good lady out of the bed. With amazing swiftness covers and all disappeared. Mrs. Lamb found herself on the floor on the other side of the bed, and she felt herself lucky to be there.

"Hebe, dear, for God's sake, what was that?" she wailed.

"The horse," answered Hebe shortly.

"Oh, what a horse!" quavered Mrs. Lamb. She was almost crying. "Can't you get him to go away? There's some Quaker Oats in the kitchen. Perhaps you can lure him out."

Thoroughly satisfied with the results of his first endeavor, Lamb's thoughts automatically turned to his brother-in-law. His spirit of enterprise was fired. He would stir farther afield. Still walking with high-bred softness, he made his way to the quarters of Douglas Blumby. Hebe expectantly opened the door for him, and Lamb, with a courteous inclination of the head, passed through.

Brother Dug was at his shower. He was attacking it as only Brother Dug could. He was literally singing it into silence. Lamb stopped and considered, then gently parted the curtains and thrust in his head. Brother Dug, feeling a draft, reached blindly behind him to reclose the parted curtains. Hs hands encountered the wet nose of a horse. For a moment he fingered the nose thoughtfully. It was not a part of himself, he was sure of that. Then Lamb breathed heavily on his back, and Brother Dug gave up feeling and singing at the same moment. He turned uncertainly only to find a horse confronting him with every evil intent in its eyes.

Mr. Blumby's power lay in his throat, and this organ he now hastened to use with unprecedented vigor. It was a triumph of vocalization. He put his whole heart and soul into it, yet the horse remained. Realizing he could not shout the horse out of existence, Blumby crouched against the wall and held up two shaking hands as if to blot out the horrifying sight. For a moment he thought himself back in bed in the grip of some vividly terrifying nightmare. The horse still remained, water running grotesquely down either side of his nose. Mr. Lamb was killing two birds with one stone—refreshing himself and taking vengeance on his brother-in-law with whom he had never thought he would share a shower. He recalled the weeks, months, years of nausea this creature had caused him by his mere existence, and his anger rose. With one charming foreleg he reached out and pressed down on the hot water lever. Cries of increased anguish from the occupant of the shower. Steam arose. Douglas attempted to escape, but Mr. Lamb implacably pushed him back. By this time Hebe had retired, having no desire to take part in a murder, no matter how justifiable.

Tiring at last of this sport, Mr. Lamb turned from the shower and devoted his talents to the room. This he proceeded to wreck, and, remarking Hebe's absence, gave other effective demonstrations of his scorn.

"Perhaps I shouldn't have done that," he said to himself as he left the room, "but after all I'm a horse; I'm not supposed to know any better."

Hebe met him at the door and suggested a breath of fresh air. Lamb gravely agreed. He was rather nervous and faltering in navigating the stairs, but with Hebe's moral encouragement he finally found himself in the lower hall. The girl opened the front doors and gave him an affectionate pat on the rump.

"That's rather a familiar thing to do even to one's father," Lamb decided.

He turned and subjected his daughter to a reproaching look, then with great dignity passed through the doors and descended the front steps. The Sunday papers had already been delivered. A headline caught his attention. He paused and endeavored to read, but found difficulty in focusing his eyes. Finally he hit upon the plan of using only one eye. This caused him to cock his head in rather an odd fashion for a horse. However, it served Lamb's purpose, and he became thoroughly interested. Having essentially a legal turn of mind, he had been following this murder trial in detail, and this report struck him as being unusually full and intelligent. With a deft hoof he flipped the paper over and continued reading, becoming more absorbed as he progressed.

Suddenly the maid, Helen, came out on the front veranda, hurried down the steps and snatched the paper from under his attentive nose. Lamb started after her up the steps, and the maid with a frightened cry darted into the house. Later she assured her mistress that she had been pursued across the lawn by a wild horse with blazing eyes. Mrs. Lamb was not hard to convince. That horse was capable of anything she thought.

Deprived of his newspaper, Lamb took stock of the world and his altered relations to it. It was a fair world and a brave day. Lamb felt better than he had in years. Nevertheless, he would very much like to finish that newspaper story. Perhaps the Walkers had not risen yet. Maybe their paper would still be out. With this hope at heart, he cantered down the drive and along High Hill Road until he had reached the Walkers' place. Here he turned in and bore down on the front porch as unobtrusively as he could, taking into consideration the fact that he was a stallion of striking appearance obviously on the loose.

Good. The paper was there. Lamb quickly found the exact place in the evidence he had been reading when interrupted and went on with the story. When it came to its continuation on page eighteen Lamb was nearly stumped, but by the happy expedient of applying a long red tongue to the paper, he was able to turn it to the desired page. Just as he had achieved this triumph some inner sense caused him to look up. Walker, clad in a bathrobe, was following his movements with every sign of amazement.

"Well, I'll be damned," said Walker softly. Then he called out: "Come here May, if you want to see something funny—a horse reading the Sunday paper."

"Nonsense," said his wife, coming on to the porch and scanning the moist paper. "The poor fool's been trying to eat the paper, that's all. Such a beautiful horse, too. Wonder whose he is?"

"She called me a poor fool," said Lamb to himself.

"and she's the biggest dunce in town. However, she has sense enough to see that I am beautiful. I am. Very."

He looked at her with arched brows, and Mrs. Walker was visibly impressed.

"He's an odd horse," she admitted. "Perhaps he was, in some strange way, interested in that paper."

Lamb made an approving noise.

Walker, having observed the horse's efforts, studied the page thoughtfully. There was only one continuation on it.

"I'll try him," he said, and he began reading the evidence aloud.

Lamb, forgetting he was a horse, promptly sat down and listened. From time to time, as a telling point was made, he nodded his head, and every time he did this Mr. Walker became so moved that he could hardly continue reading. Mrs. Walker drew up a wicker chair and sat down. She too, became interested both in the horse and the evidence.

It was a strange Sunday morning scene: Mr. Walker comfortably seated on the top step reading diligently and a horse sitting in a weird position listening intently with ears cocked forward. Later when the Walkers attempted to tell the story at the Golf Club, they were jeered into rebellious silence.

Upon the completion of the story, Lamb arose and bowed courteously, so courteously in fact, that Walker in spite of himself, returned the bow with equal elaboration. Thereupon Mr. Lamb walked decently down the driveway and turned into High Hill Road.

"A good sort, Walker," thought Lamb. "I'll remember him if ever I get back to my former self. He believes in taking a chance."

Back on the Walker porch the man turned to his wife.

"Well, that's about the darndest horse I've ever seen," he said.

CHAPTER VII

The Battle of the Church

AN EXCEPTIONALLY INTERESTING TRIAL," MUSED MR. Lamb as he ambled along High Hill Road. "If they can only get someone to corroborate that ragpicker's story the prosecution is going to have tough sledding."

Other considerations occupied his attention. He remembered with a pang that the morning had been lamentably free from any suggestion of bacon and eggs. Few things worse could happen to Mr. Lamb.

"Horses," he continued musing, "seem to get through the day pretty well on grass, but I won't eat grass. It would seem so desperate. What would Hebe think if I ever told her I had eaten grass?"

He looked contemplatively at a near-by tuft. They were about finishing breakfast at home now, well satisfied, gorged no doubt. Smelling agreeably of butter, they were preparing for church. Well, he would miss that in any event.

"That bit there doesn't look so bad," he thought, eyeing the tuft of grass with closer attention. "Suppose I try it just for fun?"

He glanced in either direction and approached the tuft.

"Well, here goes," he said to himself. "Might as well be a regular horse while I'm at it."

He nibbled the grass tentatively, throwing his head back the better to judge its taste.

"Not at all bad," he decided. "Not bad at all. Sort of like a rugged salad."

For the better part of an hour Mr. Lamb continued along the road fastidiously selecting choice patches of grass and experimenting with various combinations of weeds, clover, and wild flowers. Some he found palat-

46

able, others were hard to down. His appetite temporarily arranged for, Lamb bent his mind on other lines of activity. He was not like other horses, content to graze all day. Furthermore, he had come across a cow cropping grass, and this had rather damped his ardor. He had no intention at present of sharing breakfast with a cow. One had to draw the line somewhere. His thoughts involuntarily strayed to Sandra, and suddenly he remembered she had told him she was going riding today on Simond's horse. She had also said some rather silly things about Simonds being a lovely man.

"I'll fix that horse," he muttered or attempted to mutter. "I'll make him rue this day."

With this edifying intention firmly fixed in his mind he cantered off in the direction of Simonds's home. He knew exactly where the horse passed most of its time—in a vacant lot directly back of Simonds's place. A high fence surrounded the lot, and behind this fence Simonds's horse was going about its own business. Mr. Lamb studied the innocent animal with growing animosity. He was the kind of horse Mr. Lamb most detested, a smug, plump horse, exactly like his master.

"He would have a fence to protect him," thought Lamb. "The coward. But I'll settle his hash. Wonder if I can make it?"

He backed off for some distance, gathered his powerful muscles together and made a lunge at the fence, clearing it neatly. Once on the other side he suddenly changed his tactics. Instead of rushing at the horse and demolishing it as he had intended, he decided first to indulge in a little sport. He would be more subtle in his form of attack. He would confound this horse, terrify it within an inch of its life, put it out of commission for Sundays yet unborn.

Accordingly Mr. Lamb did things, things that no horse had ever done before or had ever thought of doing. He lowered his body close to the ground and curved his legs in a most unusual manner. Throwing his head to one side, he allowed his tongue to loll out of his mouth at one corner. With that careful attention to detail that marks the true artist, he flattened his ears and rolled his eyes more unpleasantly.

"Guess I look funny enough," thought Lamb. "Wish I could foam a bit. That would be the final touch."

He tried to work up a convincing-looking foam and succeeded partially. In this manner he approached his unwary enemy.

"Love to have a snapshot of myself," he reflected. "No one would ever believe it."

But several persons did believe it, among them being Simonds himself. He was standing at his bathroom window, and his eyes were starting out of their sockets. A few pedestrians also had stopped and now stood transfixed by the fence. This was more unusual than an appearance of Halley's comet, and years after they remembered the event far more vividly. Simonds, in a thin quivering voice, called to his wife, his son, and his daughter, and together in various stages of disarray, they witnessed the rout and almost total extinction of their horse.

When the horse first spied the strange-looking object creeping up on him he stopped what he was doing and gave his full attention to it. At first he felt no fear. The phenomenon was entirely outside his experience. But as Lamb drew nearer a certain anxiety took the place of curiosity and surprise. And when the horse caught a glimpse of Mr. Lamb's lolling tongue and bloodshot eyes, he realized that here was something that would not improve upon closer acquaintance.

Slowly and deliberately Lamb circled round his enemy until he had reduced him to a state of abject terror. The horse's nerves were shot to pieces. He was trembling in every limb. Then Mr. Lamb, rolling his head drunkenly from side to side, his tongue sliding and slithering revoltingly between his bared teeth, began to close in on the aghast object of his enmity.

"A pretty picture I must make," thought Lamb, as he prepared for the final coup.

Within a few yards of the wretched horse, he paused and horrified the air with a series of heart-searing shrieks. The Simondses drew back from the window, the pedestrians hastily abandoned their points of vantage on the fence. The enemy almost swooned, but some half-numbed instinct warned him that to remain longer in the presence of that animal from hell was certain and painful death. Comparative safety lay only in flight, and flee the horse did. Thrice round the lot he sped, fear increasing his ambition to break all established speed records. Lamb, now at full height, followed just closely enough to keep the edge on the horse's terror.

On the third lap the horse decided that the enclosure was altogether too small to accommodate both of them. He made a dash at the fence. This time Lamb was not forced to jump, the enemy having gone clear through the fence and cleared the way. Out into the streets of the town the chase debouched. Fairfield Avenue swam past Mr. Lamb's vision like a dream. They came to a beautifully kept lawn and tore across it. The enemy rounded the corner of the house and came suddenly upon a breakfast party on the rear lawn. It was either his life, or the party's comfort, decided the horse. The party had to be sacrificed. Too late for turning now. Through the breakfast party the panting animal plowed, scattering table and dishes to the four winds. Lamb noticed as he passed through that one of the ladies had lost her kimono and was rushing about with the table-cloth over her head. He knew the people but had no time to apologize. His interest in the scene had caused him to lose slightly, and he now redoubled his efforts. The ground fairly thundered beneath his hoofs as he dashed down the broad, quiet street at the end of which was situated the stately church he attended. This place of worship had broad doors on either side and a huge main entrance. They were all open to the breezes on this balmy July morning.

The fleeing horse, either mistaking the church for a stable or else deciding as a last resort to seek sanctuary, disappeared into the main entrance, paused in bewilderment, then as if realizing that this was no place for him, made a swift exit through one of the side doors.

Lamb in the heat of the pursuit followed without considering. He found the congregation in a state of wild confusion that was in no wise lessened by the sudden and tremendous appearance of a second and even more terrible horse. Protected by his pulpit the preacher looked boldly down upon his seething flock and for some odd reason began to sing "Nearer My God To Thee." Several women, believing he was summing up the situation altogether too mildly, fainted and lay in the aisles. All of the sleepers were wide awake and convinced that they would never sleep again.

It was at this moment that Lamb's better nature asserted itself. As he surveyed the scene of carnage he had been so instrumental in creating, his conscience smote him and he promptly sat down, hoping thereby to restore peace and harmony to the congregation.

Observing how quiet he was, one of the ushers timidly approached him and attempted to lead him out. Lamb resisted with dignity, and when the fellow persisted, he placed a hoof gently against his chest and gave him a slight push. The usher slid down the aisle as if it had been greased and brought up with a thump against a pew. No more attempts were made to expel Mr. Lamb. He remained quietly seated in the rear of the church, paying strict attention to his own affairs. True, he was breathing hard, but so were many other members of the congregation including the preacher himself.

"This horse," announced the good man, peering at Mr. Lamb with puzzled eyes, "seems to be rather a different type of horse. I don't think he will disturb us and evidently he intends to stay. Who knows? Perhaps he is the first of equine converts."

Lamb's shoulders shook in encouraging mirth, and a polite noise issued from his throat. Several people turned and regarded him with timid reproval, and Lamb waved a placating hoof in their direction. Mistaking his meaning they immediately turned back and looked at him no more.

"Yes," continued the preacher as if in a dream, "a strangely odd horse. Never in my long experience— well, let's get on with the service."

Lamb followed the service closely, rising when the congregation rose and sitting when it sat. His kneeling was an artistic achievement and created such a stir that few people listened to the prayer in their efforts to observe his contortions. Even the preacher became distrait and found himself repeating toward the end of the prayer, "God, what a horse! God all mighty what a horse!"

When the plate was passed for the offering, Mr. Lamb involuntarily reached for his change. The gesture was eloquent but futile. He averted his gaze, hoping no one had noticed his slip.

At the close of the service he was the first one to leave the church and, as was his custom, he waited outside for his family. He had gone this far, he thought to himself, he might as well see the thing through. He little reckoned however, on his reception by Mrs. Lamb. The docility of the horse throughout the service, his obvious reverence and piety, had somewhat reassured this lady. She thought she knew how to deal with any person or creature who actually believed in God and took Him seriously. Consequently, as Lamb followed her and her daughter along the sidewalk, taking his proper place on the outside, she continually tried to "shoo" him, until Lamb in his exasperation gave vent to a piercing shriek.

That settled Mrs. Lamb. From then on Mr. Lamb was perforce accepted as one of the party, much to Mrs. Lamb's humiliation. Time after time she passed acquaintances who in spite of their manners could not refrain from asking her what she was doing with a horse. Mrs. Lamb disclaimed any ownership of or responsibility for the animal. Lamb on his part invariably stepped courteously aside and gave the impression of following the conversation with polite attention. From time to time he nodded his head as if in agreement.

His wife particularly disliked this. It seemed to place her on a social level with a horse, and that was not to be tolerated. However, Lamb asserted his rights, and Mrs. Lamb no longer had the heart to challenge them. Hebe stuck to her father like a soldier, enjoying the situation with a maliciousness not at all compatible with her recent departure from a house of God. Toward the end of their progress the walk developed into a race, Mrs. Lamb endeavoring to leave the horse and Hebe behind, and the pair of them obstinately refusing to be left.

It was at this stage of the game that they encountered Sandra Rush. Mr. Lamb stopped in his tracks and fixed the girl with a triumphant eye. She met his gaze wonderingly for a moment, then turned to Hebe.

"Why, what a peculiar horse you have," she said. "For some reason he reminds me of your father. Something about the eyes. By the way, where is your father, the attenuated Lamb?"

Hebe was startled by her friend's instinctive recognition of the horse. Mrs. Lamb was returning reluctantly to join the conversation.

"I don't know exactly," she hastened to reply. "He's probably trailing about somewhere, or else just sitting. The major's an odd duck."

"A nice duck," said Sandra.

"What's this about ducks?" inquired Mrs. Lamb, as she joined the group in spite of the presence of the horse.

"I don't know," replied Sandra innocently. "I was just telling Hebe that I intended to go horseback riding this afternoon."

"On whose horse?" asked Hebe, and Mr. Lamb became immediately alert.

"That man Simonds's," said Sandra. "I ride on his horse each Sunday. Such a lovely horse."

"Well, he's far from a lovely horse now," replied Hebe sorrowfully. "From the glimpse I caught of him, that horse is a mental case. It will be many a long Sunday before he regains his reason, not to mention his health."

Sandra desired enlightenment, and Hebe told her all she had seen and heard of the chase. At the end of the stirring recital, Sandra turned and let her reproachful eyes dwell on Mr. Lamb. She found him looking noble and unrepentant, but under the pressure of her gaze, the great animal gradually wilted until finally his head hung low to the ground. Mrs. Lamb was outraged to see this demon stallion thus subjugated by this rather questionable friend of her daughter. As a matter of fact Mrs. Lamb resented Sandra's existence entirely. There were so many reasons—all of them good. Sandra was all that Mrs. Lamb would like to be and more than she had ever been.

"Why don't you ride this chap?" suggested Hebe. "It's all his fault."

"I shall," replied Sandra firmly. "I'll ride the devil to death. Simonds will lend me a saddle."

So, much to Mrs. Lamb's relief, the horse followed Sandra and was subsequently saddled and tethered in front of her house. When she came out from luncheon she found him leaning philosophically against a tree, his forelegs jauntily crossed.

"You'll have to cut this foolishness out," the girl said severely. "Only fake horses act like that. Don't make a spectacle of me."

Mr. Lamb turned an idle head and surveyed her long and approvingly. If she was as nice as that in riding togs, he considered, what wouldn't she be in underwear?

When Sandra had released the halter, he crouched close to the ground and peered round his shoulders at her. This proved a little too much for Sandra. The girl began to laugh, and Mr. Lamb shook himself impatiently. It was not the easiest position in the world to hold.

"I'll fix her," he said to himself.

When she finally decided to accept his grotesque invitation, Mr. Lamb crawled hastily forward, and the girl found herself sitting on his rump. She sat there only a moment before she slid slowly but inevitably to the street. Lamb rose to his full height and looked down at the young lady.

"That," she said from the gutter, "was a peculiarly snide trick. I don't know what sort of a horse you are, but if you were a human being I fancy you'd pull chairs from beneath people."

Mr. Lamb executed a neat little dance step and waited. This time Sandra mounted him in the accepted manner, and Mr. Lamb immediately set off backward, looking round from time to tme to take his bearings.

"If you have any gentlemanly instincts at all," said

Sandra at last, "you'll give up all this shilly-shallying and do your stuff like an honest-to-God horse."

Her mind was in a state of confusion. She had ridden all her life and met all types and conditions of horses, but she had never encountered one that had behaved so incredibly as this one. In its very resourcefulness there was something almost human.

At the girl's plea Mr. Lamb reversed his position and went forward majestically through the town. Sandra felt as if she were leading a circus parade. When they reached a dirt road he abandoned his little conceits and settled down to real business. He carried her swiftly, smoothly, and effortlessly over the ground. He was experiencing a sense of freedom and power—a total lack of responsibility save for the safety of the girl on his back. Sandra had never felt so exhilarated. Her mount was self-conducted. She had hardly to touch the reins. Presently they came to a fence that bordered a long rolling meadow. Lamb slowed down and looked back inquiringly at his passenger.

"It's all right with me, old boy," said Sandra. "Can you make it?"

Lamb showed her he could. He landed on the other side of the fence as if he were equipped with shock-absorbers, then stretching his body he streamed away across the meadow. Sandra had a sensation of flying, and Lamb himself felt that his hoofs were touching the ground only on rare occasions. After half an hour of swift running, Lamb came to a halt and sat down abruptly. The girl slid to the grass. When she attempted to rise, Lamb pushed her back with his nose and stood over her. For a moment she looked at the horse with startled eyes, then grinned.

"At it again," she said, pressing a cheek against his silky skin and giving him a small soft kiss.

Mr. Lamb stepped back a few paces and regarded the girl with heavy dignity. He was at a loss to know what to do about it. She had kissed him in broad daylight and made other affectionate advances. A stop should be put to this. Then something, some long restrained impulse seemed to snap in Mr. Lamb, and he began to prance joyously. He performed a dance of great vigor and elaboration after which he went racing round the meadow to give the girl some indication of what he could do when he set his mind to it. When he returned she was calmly reading a book she had fished from her pocket, "Green Mansions," and as Lamb, now adept at reading horsewise, followed several pages over her shoulder, he became absorbed in the narrative and placed a restraining hoof against the margin of the page to prevent her from turning over before he had caught up with her.

In this manner some time slipped by, the horse reading over the girl's shoulder, until at last growing tired of the heavy breathing in her ear, she pushed his nose away and laid aside the book. Thereupon Lamb dropped to the grass beside her and placed his head in her lap, opening one large eye and looking up at her owlishly. Sandra picked up the book and continued to read. Lamb nudged her, and she gave him a sharp slap. He nudged her again and she commenced to read aloud. Lamb settled down to listen. The situation was much to his liking.

An hour later when it was time to return home, the girl had to pummel him to get him to wake up. Still half asleep, he struggled to his feet and automatically reached for a cigarette, then remembering he was a horse, frowned thoughtfully upon his companion. It was all too bewildering Lamb decided, but it had been an altogether satisfactory afternoon. Even while he had slept he had been deliciously aware of the closeness of the girl's body. Lamb was not insensitive to such things.

The stallion's appearance at the Vacation Fund affair that night was not an unqualified success. He first presented himself at the dining-room window where his wife and daughter and the leading actor, Mr. Leonard Gray, were indulging in a late, cold supper. Already the tables on the lawn were occupied. Other points of vantage were rapidly filling up. Cocktails were circulating freely. All those who dwelt on the right side of the tracks knew exactly the class of people for whom the Prohibition Act was intended. They themselves were certainly not meant to be included. That went without saying.

Mr. Lamb announced his presence by thrusting his head through the window and unloosing a piercing scream. The dining-room was filled with horror. . . . It took several minutes to find Mr. Gray, and several more to induce him to crawl from under the grand piano where he had apparently taken up permanent residence. Mrs. Lamb herself was none too well. When she and her leading man attempted to resume their dinner, their knives and forks clattered so violently against their plates, it sounded as if they were playing at beating the drum. The situation was saved by Hebe. That young lady of infinite composure, gathering up practically all the salad, made a quick exit through the window and led her father round behind some box bushes that encircled the field of activity. There was a convenient opening in the bushes at this spot through which, unobserved, Lamb could get an idea of what was going on.

Lamb thought the salad delicious. He had never tasted anything quite so whole-heartedly satisfying in his life. And when Hebe returned with a cocktail he felt that life was opening up indeed. A slight difficulty arose here, however. Lamb was unable to drink from so small a glass. He spilled most of its contents. His daughter with admirable resourcefulness thereupon fetched a bucket, a bottle of gin, some ice and oranges. While Mr. Lamb looked on approvingly, she mixed this mighty cocktail and placed it before him. Lamb speedily inserted his nose, swallowed several cupfuls and sank back with a sigh.

"All set now?" asked Hebe.

Lamb nodded enthusiastically.

"When it's empty, I'll fill it up," she assured him. "Sprawl here and get an eyeful. I'll send Mel around with a tray of sandwiches. This affair is going to be a riot."

At the time she little realized the remarkable accuracy of her prognostication.

When Melville Long appeared with the sandwiches he found Mr. Lamb nose-down in the bucket, which from the sucking sounds that issued from it he judged to be empty. Mr. Lamb withdrew his head and received his visitor graciously. He literally beamed upon him, extending a hoof which Long seized and shook vigorously.

"A nice chap," thought Lamb. "One of the best. Wonder if he could mix me another cocktail? Every one else is having a good time."

With the aid of an eloquent nose he drew the young man's attention to the dispiriting state of the bucket. The youth was not long in catching Mr. Lamb's meaning. With a curt "We'll fix that," he hastened away. When he returned he was carrying two bottles of gin and an armful of oranges.

"Hebe's bringing the ice," he explained as he poured the gin in the bucket and rapidly squeezed the oranges. "Didn't have room myself."

Together the young people arranged Mr. Lamb satisfactorily, then left him to his own devices, their presence being required elsewhere. Mr. Lamb was feeling remarkably well-disposed. He thrust his head through the aperture and eyed the lawn. At the unexpected appearance of the head an elderly lady jumped with the agility of a girl.

"God bless me!" she cried, spilling her cocktail down her dress. "Did you see that, Helen?"

Helen, her daughter, fortunately had not seen. She regarded the hole in the bushes nervously. It was empty. Turning back to her trembling mother, she endeavored to sooth her, but the old lady had been profoundly shocked. Mr. Lamb did not like this old lady nor was he exceedingly fond of her daughter. Arranging his face in its most demoniacal expression, he bided his time. When the two women were once more gazing nervously at the hole he suddenly popped his head through with instantaneous effect. Clinging to each other for support, mother and daughter cut a swath through the lawn party, uttering frightened little cries in their flight. Not until they were safely ensconced in their limousine and being driven rapidly home did they release their hold on each other. Then they sat up very erect and kept tapping their hands distractedly.

"I never saw such a face in my life. What was it?" asked the mother.

"Those eyes," intoned the daughter, and tightly closed her own.

Mr. Lamb's next opportunity to annoy someone came when a gentleman moved his chair close to the aperture and carelessly tossed his cigarette through it. The still lighted cigarette fell on Lamb's nose and burned it just a little. It was quite enough for Lamb. He promptly shot his head through the hole again and took a good look at the offender. Lamb did not like this man either. In his present state of liquor, Lamb hated the very sight of him. Therefore he withdrew his head and, thrusting a long leg through the hole, placed it against the chair and gave a tremendous shove. Man and chair parted company, but continued in the same general direction. The chair knocked the legs from under an innocent bystander, and its erstwhile occupant, passing completely through a group of ladies, came to rest on a rosebush. Extricating himself from this he hurried back to the hole and looked about for an enemy. None was to be found save an old gentleman quietly observing the colorful scene.

"Did you do that?" demanded the man in a hostile voice.

"Do what?" asked the old man amicably.

"Give me a clout just now," replied the other.

"Go away," said the old man deliberately. "You're drunk—drunker than you realize."

The assaulted man had reason to believe him, and quickly withdrew from the party. He did not feel quite drunk, but he imagined he must be. Those cocktails. They were strange concoctions. Just the same someone had given him a clout. There was no denying that. Drunk or sober, he knew when he had received a clouting.

This supine activity, in spite of its pleasing results, began to pall on Mr. Lamb. He yearned for larger fields. Taking another swig at his monolithic cocktail, he rose and, finding a gate in the box bushes, mingled with the party on the lawn. Although a trifle unsteady, he managed to maintain his dignity. He conducted himself as he conceived a gentle and unobtrusive horse should. The guests were rather surprised, some even alarmed, but after a short time they accepted him as a part of the evening's entertainment. Mrs. Lamb was so advanced.

From afar Mr. Lamb observed two particularly pretty girls in intimate conversation. Approaching the girls quietly he nipped one of them in an extremely ungentlemanly manner. The girl gave a startled exclamation and, heedless of the onlooker, tenderly rubbed the injured spot. Then she turned and saw the horse looking at her roguishly.

"My dear," she said to her companion, "you should know what that horse just did. Why, the creature's almost human."

When Lamb next tried this unmannerly trick the afflicted lady gave the gentleman she was conversing with a resounding slap in the face and followed it up with a piece of her mind. The poor man looked thoroughly mystified and wretched. The husband of the lady hurried to the spot, and upon learning what had occurred, drew back mightily and knocked the man down. He was literally dragged out. Today he is still wondering why.

Sapho had more than a suspicion that all was not going well with her party. The Vacation Fund affair was threatening to become a shambles. It was all the fault of that hell-born horse. Nothing could induce it to go away. She decided to put on the final act—the *pièce de résistance* of the night. Her act. In the meantime, having become bored with his surroundings, Mr. Lamb sat down and, leaning against a tree, fell into a light doze.

When he next opened his eyes the curtains had been parted on the flimsily constructed stage. His wife in his best pajamas was wallowing about in the arms of Leonard Gray, who was saying something about being "far from my own glade," in a high complaining voice. This bored Lamb beyond endurance. With a shriek of utter abandon he galloped toward the stage. Mr. Gray cast one horrified look at the speeding horse, then with amazing expedition got even farther from his own glade. Sapho also left at once, virtuously clutching the pants of Lamb's pajamas.

Springing to the stage, Lamb gave a drunken exhibition of a horse's idea of clog dancing. The audience was in confusion. In the midst of his hurricane efforts the stage collapsed, and Lamb disappeared beneath a small avalanche of scenery, planks, and trappings. Those who lingered to look back saw only a horse's head projecting from the ruins. The horse was either dead or asleep.

Later that night Lamb feebly dug himself out and sought his bucket. Someone had thoughtfully replenished it. He drank avidly and made his way to the front of the house. He had some vague idea about sleeping in the hammock, but failed to retain it. Resting his head on the first step, he draped himself across the lawn and drifted off.

Mrs. Lamb was awakened the next morning by the maid announcing that a passer-by had stopped to inform her that there was a dead horse on the lawn.

"I hope to God he is," said Mrs. Lamb, as she pulled the covers more securely over her head. Her only regret was that the animal was not buried and well out of sight.

CHAPTER VIII

What Happened to the Horse

AFTER SEVERAL OTHER EARLY COMMUTERS HAD IN-
formed the maid that a horse had passed out on the
lawn Mrs. Lamb decided to look upon the gratifying
sight herself. But when she reached the veranda the
horse was no longer there, and the good lady was just
as glad.

Lamb had awakened dizzily and made a tour of the
ruins he had created. Vaguely only did he remember
the events of the night. The little he did recall was sufficient to make him wish to forget.

"I'd better get the hell out of here," he said to himself. "There'll be no living within a mile of Tilly for
some time to come."

He cantered off to the station and hung about there
for a while, getting in the way of hurrying commuters
and keeping an eye out for Sandra. When that young
lady undulated into view he trotted up to her and
stopped. So did Sandy. She put her arms round his
neck and gave him a good morning kiss. Lamb became
a horse of stone. Dimly he heard an insistent honking
of horns, but paid little attention to them. He had lost
all traces of his headache. Sandy had kissed them
away. He glanced about him and discovered he was
blocking the way of two motors, the drivers of which
were far from resigned. Stepping aside politely, he
looked after the retreating figure of the girl.

"She shouldn't have done that," thought Lamb, "but
I'm not altogether sorry she did."

At this point a state trooper tried to do things about
the horse. Lamb reared back on his hind legs and
pawed at the air. The trooper hurried elsewhere and
returned with a long noose rope.

"Thinks he's Will Rogers," said Lamb to himself, as he watched the trooper out of the tail of his eye.

Craftily anticipating the man's fell purpose, he took immediate steps to outwit him. Carelessly Mr. Lamb maneuvered himself alongside one of the town's most revered citizens, Mr. Robert Bates, fat, fifty, and influential—a factor in local politics. As the noose came swishing through the air Lamb crouched close to the ground and ovserved the rope neatly pinion Mr. Robert Bates's arms to his sides. Feeling the rope grow taut, the trooper tugged with a mighty effort and succeeded in pulling Mr. Bates completely over the back of the crouching horse. After that there were no impediments to bar the rapid progress of Mr. Robert Bates across the road.

The trooper wound the rope round a telegraph pole, secured it firmly, and turned to survey his prize. His prize lay struggling at his feet, emitting a long succession of unpleasant sounds terminating with "I'll break you for this, my man."

Naturally this little episode had neither gone unnoticed nor unappreciated. It was a pleasure to many to see Mr. Bates thus handled. It was no pleasure to the state trooper. The humor of the situation escaped him; but Mr. Bates did not escape. He would be with him always, the trooper feared. Mr. Lamb with a triumphant neigh left the poor fellow explaining to the sizzling first citizen that the unfortunate occurrence was entirely due to the horse, and thunderingly cleared the town. Thereafter all that remained of the horse was a not unblemished reputation.

Mr. Lamb was next discovered straining his neck to reach a particularly delectable blackberry on the edge of the woods. Several children, shepherded by an elder sister, were regarding the enterprising horse. They had never seen a horse pick blackberries. The children decided that he was a "funny horse" and made a jubilant noise about it. Mr. Lamb, with a start of surprise, beheld his admiring audience and immediately fell to cropping grass in the conventionally accepted manner. The children then drew near the horse and patted him with small adventurous hands. The horse did tricks to amuse them, and they brought him a wild flower to smell. Amazingly the horse smelled it, rolling his eyes to show his appreciation. He was enjoying himself more than he had for years. Presently the horse took leave of the children and once more sought the road. The children returned home to hamper their mother's activities by telling about the funny horse.

After this pastoral interlude, Mr. Lamb continued cheerfully on his way. Many miles now separated him from Sapho. He regretted the absence of Hebe. A pity she too, could not have turned into a horse. The little russet man was responsible for it all. Had Lamb only realized it at the time of their last conversation he would have arranged things differently—introduced an element of order. However, the little russet man had given him no chance. Now Lamb did not know how things stood, whether he was to be a horse permanently, or when he would stop being a horse. All such details should have been considered.

Mr. Lamb had taken to the more unfrequented roads and was now in a territory unknown to him. He was decidedly on the loose. He came to a meadow in which several sleek-looking mares were grazing. To Mr. Lamb they seemed quite girlish. Without further ado he leaped the fence and swaggered up to the mares. His unexpected arrival created quite a sensation. The mares were all a-twitter. One began to tremble nervously from an excess of sex consciousness. The stouter of her girl friends merely gazed at Mr. Lamb with an expressively submissive look. The third, however, was a mare of another color. She looked at Mr. Lamb for a long moment with a bold, appraising eye and seemingly found him to her liking. Then she trotted off to a secluded part of the meadow, occasionally glancing back at Mr. Lamb and tossing her head prettily.

This mare interested Mr. Lamb strangely. At the same time something urged him to proceed with caution. There was no good in that mare. Mr. Lamb followed her. There was something on his mind. He was trying to remember the image the mare evoked. Something about the eyes. Whose eyes were they?

When he reached the mare's side he peered into her eyes thoughtfully. The mare returned his gaze languorously and rubbed her nose against his. Mr. Lamb started back offended. Then he remembered. This passionate creature had the eyes of Sapho when she was developing her art in the arms of Leonard Gray. Undeterred by the rebuff of her first effort, the mare circled round Mr. Lamb, gradually closing until she again stood at his side. Suddenly she turned and bit his neck, then sped away.

"Well, if she thinks I'm going to follow her," thought Mr. Lamb, "she has another think coming. They're all alike the world over. This mare is determined to get me into some compromising situation."

He spent the remainder of the afternoon alternately grazing and repulsing the mare's advances. Her two friends looked at him hopefully from time to time, but were ladylike enough to leave him to his own devices. Finally the mare, disgusted with this aloof, dignified, and apparently unemotional stallion, abandoned her attempts to seduce him and contented herself with gazing at him scornfully. She joined her companions and the three of them put their heads close together. Occasionally they would lift them for a moment and look steadily at Mr. Lamb, then resume once more their intimate conversation. Lamb, growing uncomfortable under the continual scrutiny of the horses sought another section of the meadow, but the mares, as if fascinated, followed him at a respectful distance and discussed his every move.

The situation was becoming intolerable, and Mr. Lamb was heartily thankful when at sunset the three mares trotted off to one end of the meadow and waited there expectantly. Lamb followed them at a casual amble, and when a sleepy-looking farm-hand presently plodded up to the fence and opened a gate, Mr. Lamb slipped by unnoticed with the other horses and continued with them across the field to the stable.

"This is what might be termed crashing the gate," he said to himself, as he entered the stable and sought refuge in an empty stall.

He would have been perfectly satisfied with the oats

the farm-hand had provided had not the shameless mare kept thrusting her head over the partition in order the better to observe him crunch. Eating oats was a new experience to Lamb. He would have preferred to have practiced it alone, but every time he glanced up, the mare's large eyes were fixed upon him with such unabashed curiosity that Lamb immediately suspended action and pretended he had finished.

Apparently the acquisition of a strapping new stallion meant nothing in the life of the sleepy farm-hand. He closed the stable doors and went his way, and Lamb to escape the prying eyes of the abandoned animal in the next stall, lay down, placed his head on a bucket and prepared to sleep. After the indulgence of the previous night, he was too tired to ponder over the radically altered circumstances of his existence. But before he took leave of consciousness Mr. Lamb once for all washed his hands of the inquisitive mare, who was moving restlessly about in the next stall.

Mr. Burnham was not quite so unobservant as his handyman, the name being in this instance strictly a courtesy title. When he discovered the sleeping stallion the next morning his heart was filled with wonder and admiration.

"Why didn't you tell me of this, Sam?" he demanded of the farm-hand.

"Didn't rightly notice it myself," replied that individual. "He acted so natural-like, seemed he must belong."

"And if a cavalry regiment had quartered here last night," observed Burnham, "I dare say it would have meant the same thing to you."

He looked at the three mares suspiciously and hummed under his breath.

"I wonder—" he continued as if to himself, then catching the look of disgust in the brazen mare's eyes, he shook his head and returned once more to the sleeping stallion.

"Funny way for a horse to sleep." Mr. Burnham drew his right arm's attention to the horse's head resting on the bucket. The right arm also had failed to notice this. He agreed, however. It was a funny way for a horse to sleep.

Mr. Burnham then applied a foot with insistent pressure to the stallion's rump, and Mr. Lamb looked up with sleepy indignation. Gazing for a moment at the two strange faces, he replaced his head on the bucket and closed his eyes.

"Get up, sir!" commanded Mr. Burnham, and this time the application of the foot was slightly more vigorous.

"If this sort of thing is going to continue," thought Lamb gloomily, "I might as well abandon all thoughts of sleep."

He rose, stretched his great body and stepped out of his stall. The two men followed his movements in silence. Lamb walked out into the stable yard and, seeing a large trough full of water under the pump, plunged his head deep into it. Very busily he put in his front legs and twirled his hoofs around. Picking up an empty flour sack, he tossed it about his head until he was partially dry. After this Mr. Lamb felt considerably refreshed. He lifted his head proudly and looked down at the silently watching men. Even the farm-hand had been able to detect something out of the ordinary in the actions of the horse.

"Well, Sam, what do you think of that?" asked Mr. Burnham, inhaling a deep breath.

Thinking was one of Sam's most vulnerable points. He was unable to put into words his confused mental reactions.

"It ain't right," was all he said.

"If nobody claims that stallion," declared Mr. Burnham, "I'm going to enter him in the show this Saturday. He's the finest body of a horse I've seen in years."

At this Mr. Lamb set himself and paced gallantly round the yard. He fully intended to earn his meal ticket. Sam eyed the horse with growing suspicion. His imagination was at last aroused.

"Feed him," said Mr. Burnham, "and keep him well groomed. I'm going to make inquiries. This seems like a gift from heaven. Those mares need entertainment."

Burnham made inquiries throughout the course of the week, but could find no claimant to the stallion. Those who had seen the horse, or who had even heard remotely about it, declared they would have nothing to do with it. They did not want that horse. As a result of his investigations, Mr. Burnham had no scruples in attaching the horse to himself. And Mr. Lamb was well pleased to be attached. He was living on the fat of the land, and Sam, in spite of his mental deficiencies, was proving himself to be an entirely satisfactory valet.

On Saturday Lamb was taken to the show. It was a semi-bucolic affair, a thing of barter and trade, but more than a thousand horse-lovers were present and assembled about the field. Mr. Lamb was placed in a shack and carefully guarded by Sam. The stallion seemed greatly elated. Mr. Lamb was really anxious to win a prize—to establish a name for himself and Mr. Burnham.

It was a gala day for Sam. Lamb noticed that his valet was not too dumb to indulge copiously in corn whisky, a great bottle of which was reposing on a table in the shack. As time passed, Lamb began to grow nervous. He hated waiting. When Sam stepped outside to view the world, Mr. Lamb quickly elevated the bottle and drained its contents. His nervousness immediately left him. He knew he would win a prize. Nothing now could stop him. Sam returned and looked at the bottle with an injured expression.

"Someone's been in here," he muttered. "Like to catch 'em at it."

He departed again and presently returned with another bottle, which he uncorked and sampled appreciatively.

"Watch that bottle," he told the stallion when he next left to mingle with the throng. "And if anyone tries to get at it kick 'em through the shed."

Mr. Lamb made sure that no one would take liberties with the bottle. He introduced the fiery fluid into his system and felt even more convinced that he was certain to win practically all the prizes.

A few minutes later, when he was taken out to be judged, the whisky was taking full effect on him. Mr.

Burnham was so keyed up himself, he failed to remark
the staggering gait of the stallion. However, the judges
and spectators noticed it as Mr. Lamb was led thrice
past the stand. When he endeavored to prance bravely
he got all tangled up in his legs.

"How many legs have I?" he wondered. "Seem to
have grown an extra pair."

"That horse seems to think he's imitating a drunkard," observed a judge. "What on earth does he think
he's doing?"

When he was brought up to be looked over at closer
range Mr. Lamb almost fell over one of the judges. He
succeeded in regaining his balance, only by stepping
heavily on that shocked dignitary's foot. To make matters worse Lamb was seized with a violent attack of
hiccoughs which he was unable to control. There was a
strong smell of alcohol in the air. The judge regarded
Mr. Burnham suspiciously.

"Got to do something to make up for all this," Mr.
Lamb said to himself. "Wonder what I can do—some
sort of a stunt—something a little different."

An idea grew and flourished in his dizzy brain.

"I'll be a hobby-horse," he said to himself. "That's
the very thing. I dare say nobody ever saw a live
hobby-horse before."

He thought for a moment, then stiffening his legs
and placing his hoofs close together, he began to rock
forward and aft, gaining momentum with each swing.
Every eye in the multitude was riveted on Mr. Lamb.
The judge stepped back and regarded him indignantly.
This animal was making a fool of them—taking their
horse show altogether too lightly. Cheers of encouragement broke from the spectators. They went to Mr.
Lamb's head. With gratified expression he redoubled
his efforts. Mr. Burnham looked on helplessly, disgust
written in every line of his face. He felt as if he had
been betrayed. Mr. Lamb turned his head and winked
at his owner as if to say, "We'll show these hicks something new in the line of a horse."

He did. Each rock was bringing him nearer to the
ground. Finally, in an excess of zeal, Lamb made one
supreme effort. He pitched recklessly forward, held his

position for one breathless moment, then nose first continued to the ground where he remained with eyes tightly closed.

"I won't look," he said to himself. "This is the end. I'm disgraced."

"Will you please take that thing away?" asked one of the judges, turning to the humiliated Burnham. "We don't want it at this show."

Burnham tried to raise his crumpled horse—the heaven-sent—but Mr. Lamb refused to budge. One of the judges knelt down beside him and sniffed.

"How crude!" thought Lamb dreamily. "These judges!"

"Why, this horse has been drinking corn whisky," the judge announced rising. "The animal is actually dead-drunk. Disgraceful, Burnham, I say. Never heard of any such a thing in my life. Take him away."

Burnham, regarding the stallion, wondered exactly how the judge expected him to take his entry away. He certainly could not carry the besotted horse from the field in his arms. Nothing less than a derrick would be required to lift that body. The judges apparently were of this opinion, too, for they removed themselves to another section of the field and continued with the show. Lamb remained recumbent, gently snoring, in the center of the field. A circle of admiring spectators had gathered round him.

Before the day was done Mr. Burnham had sold the heaven-sent to a fancy truck farmer. The price given had reflected no credit on the value of Mr. Lamb. The truck farmer had turned in his own horse as a part payment.

Darkness had fallen by the time Mr. Lamb had recovered sufficiently to be driven away. When he came to his senses he found himself harnessed to a light farm wagon. He was being driven along a country road.

"Sold down the river," he mused to himself. "Parted from family and friends."

Monotonously the fields and trees moved past. Lamb began to recognize the road. He remembered certain landmarks. They were going in the direction of his

home. Presently his new master drew rein and getting
down from his seat, began to search in the back part of
the wagon. Lamb fell into a light doze. When the farmer returned he found a man clad only in pajamas
standing where just a moment ago his recently
acquired horse had stood. The man seemed a bit dazed
and was pulling at the shafts. At first the farmer was
afraid to approach, then indignation got the better of
his timidity. He strode up to the white-clad figure and
looked at it wrathfully.

"What are you doing there?" he demanded.

Lamb started and looked down at himself.

"By God, I'm back," he said under his breath; then
turning to the farmer, he replied, "Just fooling with
these shafts."

"And what did you do with my horse?" continued
the farmer.

Mr. Lamb dropped the shafts and seated himself by
the roadside. The farmer followed his example.

"What could I have done with your horse?" asked
Mr. Lamb. "Do you suppose that I tore him limb from
limb and scattered his parts to the four winds?"

"No," said the man after a thoughtful pause. "You
couldn't have done that."

He paused and considered Mr. Lamb with thoughtful eyes.

"Then you were the horse," he announced in posi-
tive tones. "You must have been the horse."

"What, me?" exclaimed Mr. Lamb. "You're crazy,
sir. Do I faintly resemble a horse?"

"Not now, you don't," replied the man with conviction, "but a minute ago you did, and what's more, you
acted like a horse—not a very good horse, but enough
of a horse to get along with. Now you're no earthly
good to me."

"Well, I'm relieved you recognize that fact," said
Mr. Lamb. "What are we going to do about it?"

"Listen," said the man, as if endeavoring to explain
the strange occurrence to himself. "This business isn't
as simple as it seems to you. This evening at the show
I bought you for a horse. You were dead-drunk on the
field in front of hundreds of people. In spite of that I

bought you and gave you another chance. I was going to give you a nice home and keep you away from drink. I've been over the ropes myself. Don't object to a little fun within reason, but—"

"It's all right about that," put in Mr. Lamb. "Go on with this remarkable yarn."

"It does sound crazy when I hear myself telling it," admitted the man. "But it's true just the same, every word of it. I got you sort of sobered up and started off home with you. Everything was getting along nicely. At this spot I got down from my seat and turned my back on you for a minute. When I turned back—no horse. You were standing between the shafts pulling like the devil. Now answer me this," he continued in a reasonable voice, turning full on Mr. Lamb. "A minute ago there was a horse, or the dead image of a horse, standing between those shafts. If you weren't that horse, who was the horse or what was the horse? Answer me that."

Mr. Lamb did not want to answer him that. He realized that the man—any man—was mentally unequipped to be told the true state of affairs. He himself was reluctant to admit the terrible thing that had happened to him. It was too far removed from the kingdom of God as generally conceived. It was too mythological. Only a pagan would believe and understand. And back of it all, Lamb knew, was the little russet man.

"Well, I'll tell you," said Lamb slowly. "It was like this: when I was a very little boy I just loved to play horse. That's a fact. I played horse so much and so long that I was never able to break myself of the habit. To this day—would you believe it?—I still play horse. It's a weakness—a failing. It's like strong drink to other men."

Lamb halted to see what impression he was making on his erstwhile owner. The man seemed absorbed in the story. Lamb himself was beginning to believe it.

"Well tonight," he continued, "I gave a bit of a party, and I guess we all had a little too much. I remember after going to bed that it struck me as being rather a good idea to get up and play horse. I slipped from my bed, you understand, quiet as anything so as not to wake up my wife, who suffers from insomnia just like her mother, and whose brother has lumbago, poor chap. Without making any noise I crept downstairs, turned the key in the front door lock and ran down the road. I ran and ran and ran. After a while I came to this wagon and crawled in between the shafts, then you came along. That's how the whole thing happened."

The climax seemed rather smeared for a good story, but it was the best that Lamb could achieve at the moment. He looked at the man hopefully and regretted to see that the farmer's face had fallen considerably. Apparently he had lost interest in the story.

"It's all right," he said, "but it doesn't explain what became of my horse."

"There really wasn't ever any horse at all, was there?" asked Lamb, evasively.

"No," replied the farmer with elaborate sarcasm. "I was dragging this wagon along by myself just for exercise."

There followed an uncomfortable silence.

"Well, I'm sure," said Mr. Lamb at last, as he rose and stretched himself wearily, "I can't imagine what can have happened to your horse. You can see for yourself that I'm not anything like a horse."

"But I'm not so sure," the farmer replied, "that you weren't a horse a little while back. There's something queer about all this."

"All right, have it your way," said Lamb with a yawn. "I'm not your horse now. Have you any old bags in that wagon you don't need?"

The farmer tossed him a couple of sacks which Lamb draped about his long body.

"What am I going to do about the wagon?" demanded the farmer in a gloomy voice.

"Wait here for that horse," said Lamb. "He's sure to come back if he ever existed at all. I begin to fear he was not alone in his cups."

The farmer watched Mr. Lamb trudge off down the road, then seating himself once more on the moist leaves and grass, he thought over the strange events of the day until his head began to swim. Dawn found him still sitting there waiting for a horse that would never return.

"Why," Lamb asked himself, as he climbed quietly through one of the lower windows of his own house, "why, if that little russet chap took my silly outburst seriously, does he insist on making a practical joke of it?"

Like a thief he stole upstairs and crawled into bed. Someone was sleeping beside him. Switching on the light he gazed on the face of his neighbor. It was Mr. Leonard Gray. Lamb grinned and quietly got back into bed after turning off the light.

"These rehearsals are getting better and better," he thought as he composed his limbs for slumber.

CHAPTER IX

The Height of Tolerance

MR. LEONARD GRAY WAS NOT HABITUALLY AN EARLY riser, but some extra special instinct urged him to be up and doing this morning. Perhaps, after all, the instinct was not so extra special. It may have been due merely to his sense of touch and Mr. Lamb's whiskers which were extremely hardy and assertive. Tough, stubbly whiskers were the last things in the world that Mr. Gray expected to encounter. They had not been included in his plans. Consequently when it was borne in on him that he was tenderly stroking a cheek abundantly provided with a week's growth of knifelike hair he opened his eyes with no little interest to see wherein he had erred.

Nor had Mr. Lamb expected to have his whiskers stroked either tenderly or otherwise. In fact he had forgotten all about whiskers and imagined he was still a horse. He, too, opened his eyes and looked uncomprehendingly into those of Mr. Leonard Gray. Lamb drew back his lips and exposed his teeth in a most disagreeable expression, then suddenly realizing he was no longer a stallion, he controlled his natural impulse and grinned pleasantly at his companion. It is difficult to say whether the snarl or the grin did the most to upset Mr. Gray's delicately organized nerves. It came to the same thing in the end. With a stifled gasp the splendid fellow gave Mr. Lamb the entire bed and dartingly began to dress.

"Where's the fire?" asked Mr. Lamb easily. "No need to pop off like that. There's plenty of room in this bed. Lie down and get your beauty sleep."

"Only wish I could," the young man faltered, briskly slipping his arms through the legs of his trousers.

74

"Must run along. Worked to all hours last night on the books of the Woodbine Players . . . got so fagged I couldn't go home. Crawled right into your bed and slept like a top."

"One of the most active gadgets I know," observed Mr. Lamb.

"That's so too," agreed Mr. Gray, grittily getting into his shoes. "Tops are active, aren't they?"

"Very," said Mr. Lamb, "when on pleasure bent."

This point having been settled there seemed to be nothing left to talk about. Mr. Lamb lay quietly back in bed and watched Mr. Gray at his toilet, his eyes following every movement of the desperate youth. This was terribly trying to Mr. Gray. Dressing to him was a ritual which he preferred to perform in private.

"Don't you ever wash in the morning?" Lamb asked at last, unable to restrain his curiosity.

"Oh yes," said Mr. Gray quickly. "Always wash in the morning, always."

"Well, you're not washing this morning," continued Mr. Lamb argumentatively.

"I will though, I will," the young man explained hastily. "When I get home I'll tub it."

"That will do you no end of good," said Mr. Lamb. "I say, your collar's all rucked up in the back, and for God's sake do something about those trousers. You can't face the world in such a confiding condition."

Mr. Gray with a convulsive movement tried to attend to himself in two different places at once. Lamb continued to observe him with quietly brooding eyes. An old saber was hanging on the wall near the bed. Lamb lazily reached up and took it down. Mr. Gray redoubled his efforts as he watched his languid host delicately test the blade then thoughtfully transfer his gaze to him.

"Do you know something?" observed Mr. Lamb. "This old saber is very sharp. It would snip that head off your shoulders as easily as slicing cheese."

Gray gave an hysterical little laugh and continued his dressing in a far corner. Suddenly, Lamb half rose in bed and darted the saber at him. With a strangled cry Gray looked helplessly about him.

"Your vest," said Lamb. "Your vest. It's buttoned all wrong."

With dancing fingers the pride and joy of the Woodbine Players readjusted his vest, snatched up his coat and moved warily toward the door. If he could only make it life would be just a little bit more secure. The saber flashed out and barred his path. Gray shrank back.

"Before you leave," said Lamb, "I'd like to ask you a question, just one question."

Gray feared that question. Why had his torturer reserved it to the end? Suppose Sapho, unaware of her husband's return, should enter the room at this minute with some shockingly revealing endearment? Gathering his histrionic abilities for one heroic effort, he half looked at Lamb and smiled. His face gave the impression of a wax figure that had partly melted in the sun. Lamb was studying his neck intently, and Mr. Gray was unhappily aware of his gaze. Also he was not forgetful of the presence of the saber. Was this to be the end of what he had fondly believed to be a picturesque career?

"Throw back your head," said Lamb abruptly, poising the saber in his hand.

Gray as if hypnotized elevated his chin and awaited the stroke of doom.

"If you think there's been anything—" he began, but Lamb cut in on his last-minute perjury.

"Tell me," said Lamb, his eyes still fixed hungrily on Mr. Gray's neck, "where do you buy your ties? I want you to get me some."

Gray almost collapsed. So that was the reason for Lamb's long scrutiny. He snatched at his neck and tore off the colorful decoration, tossing it to the man on the bed. "Here," he said hurriedly. "Take this one. Piles of them at home. I'll send some over."

"Bring 'em," suggested Lamb.

"I will," breathed Gray. "I will. First thing."

He left Lamb reclining on his bed happily inspecting the necktie. Sapho was sleeping the gloating sleep of a successfully unfaithful wife. Gray tiptoed past her door with face averted. No time to warn her now. Safety, assured bodily safety, was the first consideration. Never had life seemed so sweet. The fresh morning air fanned his face. He passed an unsteady hand across his forehead and found he had been perspiring profusely. Then the reaction came. He began to laugh softly—secretively. Lamb was such a fool, so ridiculously unaware of his horns. These husbands! They were all alike. And their wives. They were all alike, too, or almost all alike, if you pressed your campaign in a certain manner. By the time he had reached his home Mr. Leonard Gray had thoroughly convinced himself that the joke was on Mr. Lamb. In the meantime that gentleman to whose head he had so adroitly affixed horns was falling blissfully asleep with the saber held lightly in one hand and Mr. Gray's necktie in the other.

Hebe took a long chance that morning and quietly sought her father's room. She was surprised and delighted to find him there asleep, but a little puzzled by the playthings he had taken to bed with him. Mrs. Lamb had failed to announce to her daughter the presence of a visitor. If the truth must be known, she had entirely forgotten to tell anyone at all about it. The household had been unaware of the great honor Mr. Leonard Gray had conferred upon it. So far as Mrs. Lamb was concerned it would continue to remain unaware. Hebe thought there was something not distantly familiar about the necktie.

"The major must be getting childish," she said to herself as she gently closed the door.

"Sapho!" she whispered, and Sapho woke up with a startled cry. "Father is sleeping in his own bed for a change."

In utter consternation Mrs. Lamb looked at her daughter. Her frame of mind was not to be envied.

"Hebe," she said after a long pause, "I told you distinctly never to come near this part of the house on Sundays. Since that Vacation Fund affair and the strange disappearance of your father my nerves have gone to pieces. I must have repose. You know it."

"But the major's back," replied Hebe. "Come and look."

"That was just what Mrs. Lamb most objected to

doing at that inauspicious moment. As she gazed
blankly at her daughter a keen realization of the situation ominously grew within the lady.

"Have you seen him?" she asked, after a moment's
hesitation.

"With these eyes," responded Hebe.

"Did he look—er—as usual?" Mrs. Lamb was
growing confused.

There was something mysterious about that room.
First her husband turned into a horse, then her lover
turned into her husband. Peace and security seemed to
have departed from the world.

"The picture of himself," answered Hebe, "only
there was something sort of strange about him. He had
a saber in one hand and a necktie in the other."

Mrs. Lamb gave a start and smothered an exclamation.

"What sort of necktie was it?" she asked.

"That's the funny part about it," said Hebe in a
puzzled voice. "It didn't look like the major's at all. I
have it! It looked exactly like Leonard Gray's."

"O-o-o-oh!" The sound came fluttering from Mrs.
Lamb's lips. The color had left her face. So that was
all that was left of Leonard Gray, only a necktie.

"Was the sword frightfully bloody?" she asked, fascinated by the horror of the situation.

"I didn't notice," said Hebe, looking strangely at her
mother, "but I seem to think it was."

Once more the low cry issued from her mother's
lips. She sank weakly back on her pillows and closed
her eyes.

"Leave me," she said to her daughter.

Already she was picturing herself playing a most important role in a fashionable murder trial. Too bad
about Leonard, though. Mrs. Lamb then considered
her husband. She was more than a little suspicious of
Lamb. A well-nigh unbelievable conviction was form-
ing in her mind. For the past few days she had dismissed it, fearing it might unbalance her reason. There
was no getting away from the fact, however, that it had
been a strangely acting horse . . . so like her husband
in many ways. The whole thing was mad, wild, impos-

sible, but—but—if she were really married to a man who even occasionally turned into a horse, surely the courts could do something about it. Everything was altogether too much for Mrs. Lamb. It was not a successful Sunday morning. Her life should have been so different—so much larger and more magnificent. What sacrifices she had made in marrying that man! She was overwhelmingly sorry for herself and only a little bit sorry for Mr. Leonard Gray, indubitably deceased.

Later in the day Hebe was having a business meeting with Melville Long. The meeting was held on the veranda and presided over by a decanter of Scotch.

"There is only one of two things to be done," the young lady began briskly. "Either you'll have to ruin me or else start bootlegging."

"Why not do 'em both," suggested Long, "and thus make assurance doubly sure?"

"Might be something in that too," admitted his fair companion, "but the way I see things at present one or the other must be done."

"Well, I draw the line at ruination," declared Long in a more serious voice. "I'm off that ruination idea entirely."

"There's something in it," Hebe went on. "We won't dismiss it altogether. If you ruin me and I actually find myself with child—"

"*Enceinte* is the way nice people say it," Mr. Long corrected.

"Don't interrupt," said Hebe impatiently. "It all comes to the same thing in time. As I was saying, if I were actually beyond doubt that way I know the major would do the handsome thing. He'd see us safely married and give us a chunk of cash. He's got no end of money. Sapho would be annoyed at my carelessness, but the major would fix her. You see, then we'd be all married and everything."

"Yes," agreed Mr. Long. "Particularly everything. With the head start we'd have you could easily be a grandmother before you were thirty-five. Then again, there's an element of amateurishness about ruination. People might get the idea I didn't know my way around. Wouldn't like that. Bootlegging is better. I'd feel more independent."

"All right," said Hebe impartially. "Why not try that? We could make enough money in a year to start out on our own. Ruination can easily wait."

"I know a guy down in the slum district," Long continued meditatively. "He's a nice guy, and I know he'd start me off right—get me the stuff and all that."

"And we could use one of our cars," put in Hebe. "The big one. That would be slick for deliveries."

"We've certainly got to do something if we want to get married," the young man went on broodingly, "Honest work takes too long. Painting won't net me a red, and the old man absolutely refuses to come across until, as he puts it, I've proved myself. He goes on about me as if I were a problem in geometry. Always asking me to prove myself."

It was here that Sandra put in an appearance, and the edifying alternatives were explained for her consideration.

"I think," said Hebe on concluding, "that ruination would be the best and safest, don't you?"

"It would be by far the most agreeable," Sandy decided. "Also the most effective. Bootlegging though is pretty exciting. I'd like to try it myself. And Mel has a lot of rich friends. He could poison them for a long time before they actually died or lost their sight."

"By the way," said Hebe, changing the subject for her friend's benefit, "the major's back."

Sandra brightened visibly, and Long looked startled.

"That's so nice," said Sandra. "Is he tired of being a horse?"

"Don't know," replied Hebe. "Haven't spoken with him yet. He was pounding when I last saw him."

During Mr. Lamb's absence the three young people had discussed him earnestly and had come to the conclusion that, as incredible as it seemed, he had been the horse. All had advanced their reasons, and they had seemed incontrovertible. Hebe had even related her father's experience with the russet man and his strange behavior. This had clinched matters. Mr. Lamb had been and probably still was the horse. There was no getting around that amazing fact. Not being so far removed from fairy tales themselves they accepted Mr. Lamb's metamorphosis without much difficulty.

At this moment the subject of their conversation blithely entered the room. He was resplendent in Mr. Gray's tie.

"Good afternoon, ladies and gentleman," he said amiably, then turning to his daughter. "Did you get my letter Hebe?"

"Yes, indeed," replied Hebe with undisguised sarcasm. "And all your telegrams and that lovely box of candy."

Mr. Lamb sat down and considered the three young people with an affable expression.

"I forgot to tell either you or your mother," he continued, the lie coming with surprising readiness, "that I have an important deal on in Philadelphia. I might have to pop off at any moment. Probably open an office there."

"Why not a livery stable?" suggested Hebe.

Mr. Lamb favored his daughter with a false laugh.

"Why a livery stable?" he asked daringly.

"Honest to God," spoke up Sandra, "tell us something. Weren't you that horse? You're among friends."

"Suppose I should say yes?" parleyed Mr. Lamb.

"Then I'd say that you were one of the worst and best horses I've ever ridden," replied Sandra.

Lamb considered the situation for a short time. He realized that these three young people not only thought he was the horse, but also knew he was the horse.

"What do you think?" he asked turning to the tactfully mute Melville Long.

"Well," said Long, "no natural-born horse could have consumed cocktails the way that horse did. Never saw anything like it. And the sandwiches—it must have had human blood in its veins."

Lamb was regarding Sandra closely. What would she think if he came out and admitted that he had been the horse? She could never possibly afford to associate with a man who turned into things. At the moment he heartily regretted ever having had anything to do with the little russet man. He bowed his head and unhappily studied the extreme tips of his shoes.

"I guess I was that horse," he said at last in a low voice. "I don't know much more about it than you all do. It just happened. There I was—a horse. But I'm not a horse now," he added hopefully.

Hebe went over to her father and gave him one of her rare kisses. Sandra sat as close to him as possible without sitting on his lap.

"Do you remember," she said, "I kissed you?"

"I might be a horse again or something worse at any moment," Mr. Lamb looked at her warningly.

"How does it feel to be a horse, Mr. Lamb?" Melville Long's voice was replete with interest.

"Remarkable," began Mr. Lamb and stopped.

A motor was fussing up the gravel in the driveway. Mrs. Lamb came in and sank down exhausted. Even the sight of her husband failed to revive her. Then she saw the tie. She sat up, an expression of horror marring her features. All day long she had been searching for traces of Leonard Gray, hoping against hope that he might have escaped with only a wound. Here was the person who had done her lover—perhaps her last—to death, callously conversing while his victim's necktie, like a trophy of war, hung flauntingly from his neck.

Mr. Lamb went through all about Philadelphia again. Mrs. Lamb scarcely heard him. Her eyes were fixed on the colorful tie. Hebe, noticing the direction of her mother's gaze, also looked on the necktie and became uncomfortably interested in it.

"That's a terrible tie, major," she remarked. "Where did you get it?"

"Ask your mother about that," replied Mr. Lamb easily. "She knows more about my neckties than I do."

"Murderer!" Mrs. Lamb had been unable to restrain the accusation.

Mr. Lamb sat up appalled.

"Have I killed someone?" he asked. "This is the first I've heard of it. Hebe made no mention of a murder."

Mrs. Lamb, now beyond control, came close to him and extended a tragic finger.

"What did you do with the body?" she demanded in a low vibrating voice. "And all the blood. What became of that?"

Mr. Lamb was no more startled than were Hebe and her friends. Their round eyes regarded the murderer wonderingly. Mr. Lamb pulled himself together and returned the accusing gaze of his wife.

"What did you do with the body first?" he inquired. "That would be more to the point."

Mrs. Lamb turned away and walked to the window. Her face was safe from scrutiny. At that moment Mr. Leonard Gray himself saw fit to arrive.

"Here they are!" he cried, placing a package on Mr. Lamb's lap. "All new. Went into the city and picked them out myself. If you like the tie you're wearing, you'll go crazy about these."

"Meet my chum, everybody," said Mr. Lamb quietly. "We're roommates now. Thanks for the ties, Len."

Mrs. Lamb with a distracted look about her, fluttered her hands above her head and left the room. Leonard Gray followed. The murderer threw himself back in his chair and favored Sandra, Hebe, and Mr. Long with a benign smile.

"And they all lived happily ever after," he said.

"Let's have a look," urged Hebe. "Mel could use a new tie."

Mr. Lamb obligingly opened the package.

CHAPTER X

Lamb Takes the Air

SUPPOSE I SHOULD TELL HIM I'VE JUST GOTTEN OVER being a horse?" Lamb mused to himself, as he politely eyed his customer, an aged person of many motheaten millions. "I guess the old blighter would drop those bonds and close his account on the spot."

He resisted the temptation to experiment with the old gentleman and thereby materially added to his own not inconsiderable wealth.

When his customer had departed, Lamb summoned his secretary to him and told her all about Philadelphia. He had already told her about Philadelphia, but this time he told her better. He shrouded his future movements in tantalizing mystery. Lamb was taking no chances. God only knew what the little russet man had in store for him, and Lamb very much doubted if he had taken even God into his confidence. He would have liked to have had a short conversation with the little russet man, but he knew of no way to get in touch with him.

All that week Mr. Lamb had been hearing about the horse. He had gleaned impressions from many unexpected sources. The stallion had created no end of excitement in the town and surrounding countryside. An enterprising reporter had strung together a story which the city people laughed at and dismissed, little realizing that it was the most conservatively handled piece of news in the paper. Simonds was the most voluble about the horse. Also the most bitter. He had sent his own horse away for a change of scene. The poor animal was actually pining away in its lot, constantly fearing a return of that diabolical stallion. The state trooper had lost his easy post. He no longer postured about the station, a target for the come-on glances of women who with a sigh of relief had seen the last of their husbands for that day.

Lamb was highly edified by what he heard. He had been a horse among horses. His exploits would be remembered. Whenever Mrs. Lamb referred viperously to the Vacation Fund débâcle he would thoughtfully finger his necktie and look at her significantly. Mrs. Lamb quickly changed the subject. Leonard Gray's neckties were constantly reminding her of a most disturbing interruption of what had started out to be an unusually diverting week-end.

"Wonder what we're going to be next?" Hebe speculated one evening, entering into the situation with the enthusiasm of her years. "How'd you like to be a giraffe?"

"God forbid," said Mr. Lamb quickly. "I hope the little chap feels that he has sufficiently convinced me of the unwisdom of unconsidered wishing."

But the little russet man did not feel that way about it, and when Lamb woke up one morning he found himself perched precariously on one of the four posts of his bed. When he attempted to stretch, as was his wont, he heard an unfamiliar swish in the air.

"I'm something else," he said to himself. "Wonder what it can be?"

Fluttering lightly to the floor, he observed himself in the mirror. His excitement was intense. What he saw was a smoky-looking seagull with black rings round its eyes. The effect was that of detached thoughtfulness. Mr. Lamb spread his wings and looked with approval on their snow-white lining. He was a good gull.

"As gulls go," he admitted to himself, "I dare say I'm about as good as they come. Wonder how it feels to fly? Don't know the first thing about it."

He went to the table and looked at his watch. Sandra would be taking the usual train. He had plenty of time.

"No use disturbing the household," he thought, hopping to the open window and balancing himself on the edge. "Well here goes for a Lindbergh. Hope I don't foul a tree."

Lamb extended his wings and took the air. He landed in some confusion among the box bushes, but managed to beat his way out with the loss of only a few unimportant feathers.

"Must do better than that," he commented. "I'd best try a couple of take-offs."

He gave himself a running start and left the ground. This time he flew with gathering confidence and landed on Hebe's window, upon which he tapped gently. That young lady woke up without effort and immediately let him in. She had schooled herself to be surprised at nothing and to be prepared for anything. She looked at her father with admiring envy.

"Golly," she said. "I wish I was in your shoes."

Lamb extended one claw and emitted a peculiar crackling noise intended to be a laugh.

"How does it feel to fly, major?" his daughter continued.

The gull gave an exuberant hop expressive of much enjoyment, and Hebe understood.

"How about grub?" asked Hebe. "I suppose you don't fancy a couple of succulent worms?"

The gull shuddered and almost twisted its head off in the violence of its opposition to this revolting suggestion.

"Well, come along," said Hebe, slipping into her dressing-gown and quietly opening the door.

Mr. Lamb, skipping lightly behind his swift-footed daughter, followed her to the pantry where she set before him a bowl of puffed rice and cream. When he had eaten his fill of this he delicately polished his beak on a convenient napkin and spread his wings gloriously for the benefit of his daughter. After this he left the house and made his way to the station.

From a great height he saw Sandra leaving her house to start off for the station. Swooping dizzily down the air lanes, he circled round her head, then came to rest at her feet. Without a moment's hesitation, for Sandra had also been warned to be prepared for anything, she picked him up and held his head against her warm neck. Mr. Lamb was so elated that he freed himself and tried to loop-the-loop. This enterprising endeavor resulted in a small disaster. Mr. Lamb found himself flat on his back in the gutter. His claws were busily churning the air. It was a ludicrous sight, and Sandy laughed at the gull. Lamb adjusted himself with as much dignity as he could summon to his aid and after a certain amount of necessary preening, preceded the girl to the station in a more orderly if not so spectacular manner. As he planed along the platform he took occasion to knock off Simonds's hat and had the satisfaction of seeing it roll to the tracks, where its usefulness was destroyed by the thundering arrival of the city-bound express.

When no one was looking Mr. Lamb slipped into the baggage-car and hid himself behind a trunk. Later when he had made sure that the conductor was several cars ahead, he made his way on foot through the train. He was searching for Sandra. As the gull swayed cautiously down the aisle of the first car heads popped out from behind newspapers and amused eyes followed his progress. Mr. Lamb was uncomfortably aware of the interest he was creating.

"Why can't they mind their own business," he thought, "instead of staring at me?"

At the end of the car he turned and favored its occupants with a hoarse cry, at the sound of which several heads darted back behind the newspapers.

The other half of Sandra's seat was unoccupied. Mr. Lamb quietly hopped up to it and sidled as close to her as possible. She spread her paper accommodatingly and together they read the news of the day. From this Mr. Lamb looked up in time to discover the approach of the conductor. Mr. Lamb wanted no trouble. He was too large a gull to hide, too large to creep under the seat. Then a brilliant idea occurred to him. With one swift, insinuating look at Sandra he fell down on the seat and allowed his head to dangle over it. The head swayed distastefully with the rhythm of the train. To all intents and purposes the young lady was carrying a dead seagull to the city. Sandra after some quick thinking fathomed Mr. Lamb's intention and ordered her actions accordingly.

The conductor, arriving at her seat, looked down at

the seagull with an expression of disgust. Years of service had inured him to all types of commuters. He had seen them carrying all sorts of surprising packages from vacuum cleaners to French pastry. He had never, however, previously encountered a commuter carrying a dead seagull.

"That's a strange thing to be lugging about with you," he informed Sandra.

"He just died," replied the girl sadly. "I'm taking him to be stuffed. The poor old thing has been in our family for years."

She picked Mr. Lamb up by his legs and dangled him convincingly before the conductor's eyes. Although Lamb felt a rush of blood to his head, he continued to act the part of a dead gull. The conductor seemed convinced, especially when the bird flopped limply against his face. The remainder of the trip was uneventful, and when the train reached the station Sandra once more seized Mr. Lamb by the legs and carried him out with her. He was very much squeezed and rumpled. Once when a stout lady backed into him he was forced to resort to rather brutal tactics in order to induce her to remove a large portion of herself from his face. With an indignant expression, the stout lady looked suspiciously about her, then hewed a path through the crowd.

By the time he had been carried to the street Lamb was literally almost a dead gull. He cocked his head up as well as he could and looked pleadingly at the girl. She took him in her arms and smoothed his feathers. Lamb felt better. Then to the astonishment of many onlookers he rose in the air and circled above Sandra's head. The onlookers glanced at the girl questioningly. They had seen an apparently dead seagull come to life and fly away. Sandra was unconscious of their gaze. Higher and higher mounted the gull. All he could see now was the white face of the girl straining up to him. Impulsively, she raised one hand in farewell and something white fluttered in the air, then she faded from view.

For some reason, when Sandra turned away, her

eyes were just a little moist. She wondered if he were lonely up there and if he would ever come back.

"He doesn't know the first thing about being a sea-gull," she said to herself. "Anything could happen to him up there. Might even run into an airplane."

All that day Sandra was a greatly preoccupied young lady in underwear. She kept remembering the excited throbbing of the bird's heart as she had held it in her arms. Mr. Lamb was rapidly becoming a problem seriously to be considered. His sardonic grin and long lean body drifted across her vision. She was very much afraid she loved this man who happened at the moment to be a bird floating somewhere about in the sky. One of the reasons that made her more than suspect she loved him was the fact that she so thoroughly detested his wife.

"Have you any knowledge of your father's movements?" Mrs. Lamb asked her daughter that night.

"Not the slightest," answered Hebe truthfully, "but if you'd taken the trouble to look you'd have seen there's been a bird in his room."

Mrs. Lamb was slightly revolted. If she were only sure. If she could only get absolute proof. She thought of life with Leonard Gray and chewed her steak with abandon.

That night Hebe put a bowl of puffed rice on the back steps. At three o'clock in the morning she was awakened by a series of wild cries, and going to the window, saw a large bird chasing a cat round the yard. When she came down to breakfast, all that remained of the combatants was some fur and a few feathers. Hebe picked one of the feathers up and examined it attentively. It was smoky-gray with a dash of white on the inside.

"The major's been here all right," said Hebe, half aloud, as she collected the rest of the feathers and carried them to her room.

CHAPTER XI

An Aerial Interlude

MR. LAMB HAD BEEN A SEAGULL FOR SEVERAL DAYS and had become a thoroughly experienced flyer. Since his defeat of the cat he had stedfastly refused to return home. He was going to be a seagull up or down to the last detail, but in doing so he was becoming an extremely hungry bird, not being able to accommodate his appetite to raw fish and the cast-off bounty of ocean liners. Once he had brought himself to nibble at a fair-looking piece of grapefruit sliding along the waves, but had swallowed so much salt water in the attempt that he had been forced to abandon the object of his desire.

Today he had been feeling rather light-headed as he swooped and circled over lower Manhattan. His sharp eyes looked down into the dark cañons of stone pierced by many windows. He thought about the office buildings. He considered them from a new point of view. Hitherto he had looked on them as outstanding examples of American industry and progress. To have things to do with them had always given him a feeling of accomplishment—a comfortable sense of regimentation. Today he was not so sure.

"Millions of souls in those buildings," he mused, sweeping close to his own. "There's a good-sized town in that building of mine alone. And they're all working. Thousands of them loafing . . . just getting by. Poor pent-up devils! Suppose the little russet man had turned them all into gulls instead of picking on me. What a remarkable sight it would be. Trails of gulls issuing from every window. The air filled with the beat of many wings . . . all released!"

Lamb pictured the scene to himself. He was weary and painfully hungry. Still he soared—alone.

"Scissors dropped," he continued. "Pens rolling off abandoned desks. Stocks and bonds and crisp clean bank-notes suddenly left unguarded."

Lamb, in his reverie, saw the sky growing black with gulls. Birds pushing their way to freedom, crowding on one another. He painted a mental picture of a little group of conscientious gulls, still held by habit, poising on window ledges and peering back into their offices to make sure that all was in order before they took to the air. What a sight! A river of gulls, following the precedent of years, homeward bound across the bay to Staten Island. Another river flowing uptown, and a turbulent one into Brooklyn. A bridge of gulls passing over the Hudson. It would split at various commuting tracks and grow thinner at each suburb. Gulls everywhere pecking at windows, vainly trying to get their wives to understand that something unusual had happened to them—actually to them, their time-tabled husbands.

Lamb's thoughts were growing wilder as his hunger increased. He saw dense masses of gulls flocking to the subway stations, impelled there by habit. The dark tunnels would be filled with several counter-flying columns of frantically surging wings. Gulls trampled on in trying to get out, when they might just as well have been flying in the open air. And the busses, too. They would be packed to the top rails. Birds swaying in close ranks. All going home—home to their wives. Mostly men.

The girl gulls wouldn't go home. Not they. . . . They would be far too enterprising. Down to the Island for them. Snatching free rides on the scenic railway, no doubt, and keeping their eyes peeled for boy friends they had never met. Some of them would infest chop-suey joints and flutter about to the tune of an automatic piano. Others would just hang round soda shops and giggle and wait for something to happen. But the fact remained, the girls would be pleasure-bent—sex-driven, alert, seeking—they wouldn't go home. Lamb could hardly blame them. He wasn't going home either. He was going to swoop around and pity the slaves in the office buildings below. He was—

"Oh, hell!" he broke in on his thoughts. "This isn't getting me anywhere. Must have food. I'll take a chance and try it."

He coasted down from his high place and landed in a narrow street before the doors of a restaurant in which he had usually taken his luncheon. The restaurant at that hour was crowded, but the smell of food and the hospitable clatter of plates were irresistible to Mr. Lamb in his famished condition.

"Well, here goes," he said to himself as he waited his opportunity and sidled unobtrusively into the restaurant.

Mr. Lamb's unusually sharp eyes picked out a table at which one man was sitting. This gentleman's head was completely hidden behind his newspaper and on the opposite side of the paper, between it and Mr. Lamb, reposed a plate of chicken and French-fried potatoes. The waiters were in a fever of activity. Everyone was in one way or another occupied with food. The presence of the seagull passed unnoticed. The sight of the French-fried potatoes was too much for Mr. Lamb. Being a bird himself he decided that it would be rather indelicate to partake of the chicken. However, the potatoes would suffice. With the utmost caution he mounted the chair opposite the reading gentleman and, protruding a stealthy neck, fastened upon one of the potatoes. This swiftly disappeared. Once more his competent beak shot forth and another potato was done in.

By timing his forays judiciously, Mr. Lamb was getting along quite nicely—making a meal for himself. The table was a secluded one and was partly concealed by a railing. But all good things must come to an ending, and Mr. Lamb's luncheon was rudely interrupted. The man lowered his paper and looked with some surprise upon the seagull. The seagull froze in the chair, a portion of potato still protruding from its beak. The bird returned the man's stare unwinkingly. This man, Lamb decided, was a mild man. There should not be much trouble. Of course there would be some. No matter what happened it would be impracticable to try to deprive him of the potatoes he had already eaten. The gentleman neatly arrested the progress of a hurtling waiter.

"I say," he said, looking thoughtfully at the waiter. "Don't you cook your food any more? Am I expected to swallow that thing feathers and all?"

The waiter, regarding the motionless bird, almost dropped the tray.

"I don't know how it happened, sir," he said. "It never did before."

"There's always a first time for everything," continued the gentleman patiently. "And by the way, you seem to be stuffing it from the wrong end."

"That gull's been stuffing hisself," replied the waiter and, quickly putting down his tray, seized upon Mr. Lamb, who just managed to gulp down the remainder of the potato before he was carried from the restaurant.

"Be gentle with him," admonished the gentleman. "That bird is rather an innovation in the line of gulls."

Mr. Lamb sent him a parting look of gratitude.

"Well," he said to himself philosophically, as he was cast into the street, "this is the first time I've been given the bums' rush since the halcyon days of Jack's."

He arranged his feathers and watched some pigeons picking something on the street corner. His first instinct was to swoop down on them and appropriate their food. Then he thought better of it.

"I haven't come to that," he decided. "Damn if I'll bully pigeons yet."

A brilliant idea was shaping itself in his mind. He knew of a seafaring cafe on the river front that rejoiced in a number of stuffed birds. He had always considered them as rather dusty and repellent decorations, but somehow they seemed a part of the place. If he could only succeed in insinuating himself into this café he might be able to pass himself off as one of the stuffed birds and thus pick up some choice bits. The place as he remembered it still sported a free-lunch counter. Prohibition had left it undisturbed.

Mr. Lamb put his plan into action. It was not difficult, because most of the occupants were standing at the bar with their backs to the free-lunch counter. This consisted of a huge buffet with a long, low shelf upon which were displayed various ornaments which the proprietor seemed to feel were essential to the esthetic contentment of his guests. Lamb saw a boat in a bottle, a framed flag done in silk, some particularly ghastly part of a fish, and a neat little group of extremely unlifelike glass flowers.

Awaiting his chance, Lamb sprang lightly to the shelf among this weird collection and immediately poised his wings. Directly facing him over the bar was a stuffed owl and out of the corner of his eyes he could see a moth-eaten-looking hawk. He studied the technique of these two birds carefully. There were several others in the room, but he could not bring them into his range of vision without turning his head which was thrust slightly down and forward over a dish of dried herring. This in his present state appealed to him greatly.

"I hate bolting down food," he thought, "but this is no time nor place to observe the niceties of table manners."

With a lightning-like dart of his head he snatched up one of the herrings and, cramming it into his mouth, once more became a stuffed bird. Only a slight tremor around the throat gave evidence of the activity that was going on within him.

Mr. Lamb made three more successful snatches before an interruption occurred. The interruption took the form of a stout gentleman with thick horn-rimmed glasses. Detaching himself from the bar, this individual lurched sleepily over to the lunch counter and leaned against it. He sampled a herring, then half turned to the bar the better to observe his friends.

"This bloated man is likely to camp here all day," thought Mr. Lamb dejectedly. "And if his friends come over and get into action they'll clean the place out."

Slowly moving his head as close as possible to the plate, he made a short, swift snatch. The herring was his, but the man had noticed something. He turned and looked hard at the gull, then transferred his eyes to the plate. Removing his glasses, he polished them deliberately and once more inspected the gull. As he walked over to the bar he stopped suddenly and looked back.

Mr. Lamb was prepared for the move. He looked fixedly back at the man and just before he turned away Lamb slowly closed one eye. The man stopped in his tracks, swayed back to the gull and, getting his face very close to it, studied the bird for a full minute.

"Well, I give up," he muttered at last. "It must be the grog, but I didn't think I was as drunk as all that."

He hurried back to the bar and called for a double brandy. With this comfortably inside him, he returned once more to the gull.

It was unfortunate for the complete success of Mr. Lamb's luncheon that he was discovered in the act of consuming the largest herring of them all. He could not possibly hope to get the entire fish into his mouth. Realizing the fuddled condition of the man, Lamb had decided that he would retain no clear impression of what he saw. Therefore he leisurely finished off the fish before the man's bulging eyes, and resumed his inanimate position. The drunkard clutched the edge of the buffet and held on.

"Tell me," he demanded thickly. "Are you a stuffed bird or not? For God's sake be one or the other or I'll go potty."

Mr. Lamb returned the man's pleading gaze with a cold, dead eye. Only one herring remained on the plate, and Mr. Lamb had his heart set on that. He was determined that the inebriate should not have it. Watching the gull closely, the man moved his hand slowly toward the last herring. Lamb allowed him to pick it up, then shot out his hand and tore it from his fingers.

"That settles it," said the man aloud, stepping hastily back from the buffet. "When stuffed birds begin to snatch food from customers' hands I'm through."

He lifted up his voice and demanded the immediate presence of the proprietor. That worthy party, bearing a mug of beer, joined him.

"What's wrong here?" he asked good-naturedly. "Not enough food?"

Still clinging to the buffet the man pointed a none too steady finger at the gull.

"Is that a stuffed bird?" he demanded. "Because if it is it must have been stuffed alive."

"Why, damn my eyes," said the proprietor, looking intently at the gull. "It must be a stuffed bird, although I don't rightly remember this one."

He paused and thought for a moment, then his face cleared. His mind insisted on explaining the presence of that bird. Unconsciously his imagination helped him.

"I remember now," he said. "We had a sort of a blowout last week, and one of the boys must have brung him in. That's it. That's just how it got here."

The other man looked at the proprietor with a pitying smile.

"Did you ever hear of a stuffed bird polishing off a plate of fish and fighting for the last one?"

"Did that bird do that?" asked the proprietor.

"That and more," declared the other. "The damn thing had the nerve to wink at me."

This last statement settled the proprietor's doubts. His customer was seeing things. That was all there was to it. He took the man by the arm and attempted to lead him away.

"Come on over," he said coaxingly. "I'll stand the drinks. After that you'd better go home."

This irritated the other considerably. He reached up and, seizing the gull by the feet, carried him to the bar. Mr. Lamb stiffened his body and awaited developments. He caught an inverted view of a cuspidor and a floor covered with sawdust before he was roughly hauled aloft.

"Gentlemen, I ask you," cried the stout man. "Is that a stuffed bird?"

Mr. Lamb was passed from hand to hand along the bar. He was minutely examined. His feathers were parted and skin inspected. In the course of his journey up and down the bar his head was dangled conveniently over several glasses of beer from which he drank with avidity, the herring having made him thirsty.

"Of course it's a stuffed bird," one of the men said at last. "What do you think it is? No live bird would let himself be handled like this without putting up a hell of a squawk."

"Jim's right," put in another voice. "Sure it's a stuffed bird."

"What do you mean, stuffed?" asked a skeptical individual. "Look at that bird's skin. It's altogether too fresh to be stuffed."

Lamb's skin was again examined and prodding fingers were thrust into various parts of his body. The wear and tear was beginning to tell on him.

"This is no go," he said to himself. "Those drunkards will make a wreck out of me."

"Well, put him down and let's have a drink on it," a reasonable voice suggested. "What do we care whether he's stuffed or unstuffed? It's all the same to me."

Lamb was placed at the end of the bar and allowed to get his breath. The gentlemen returned to their drinking.

"I earned that luncheon," he said to himself, thirstily watching the glasses. "I'd better be shoving off now before they're at me again."

He kept his eye fixed on the original cause of the investigation and, when that tippler's head was tilted back, leaped upon it and fastened his claws in the thick hair. Flapping his wings violently, Lamb strained his throat in a piercing cry and pulled with all his might. The man's cry was as piercing as the bird's. He staggered across the room and crashed to the sawdust, leaving in Mr. Lamb's claws several tufts of hair. Thoroughly interested now, Mr. Lamb swept down the bar, overturning glasses in his flight. Most of the investigation committee had taken refuge behind chairs and tables. With a final scream of triumph Lamb circled the room and made his exit through a conveniently open window.

"What did I say?" demanded the prostrate man in an injured voice. "I told you it wasn't a stuffed bird."

"Well, what in hell was it?" someone asked. "It wasn't a regular seagull. No normal bird has sense enough to act stuffed."

"I'm glad we all saw it," said a third, "or I'd be feeling awful now."

The gentlemen emerged from their various places of shelter and returning to the bar looked up at the owl suspiciously.

Lamb, dropping the hair in some innocent bystander's face, flew out over the harbor and settled himself on a wave. Here he was presently joined by a venerable-looking seagull who, without any form of salutation, plopped himself down beside him. Lamb regarded him respectfully as a gull much older than himself.

"How do you do," offered Lamb.

"What?" almost snarled the ancient.

"What?" repeated Lamb blankly.

"Yes," scolded the other. "How do I do what?"

"Oh, nothing!" replied Lamb. "I was just saying hello."

"You weren't saying hello," the old gull snapped. "If you'd said hello, I'd have heard, hello. You asked me how I done. Don't think I'm deaf."

"Did," corrected Mr. Lamb.

"See!" cried the gull. "You're wrong again. I always use done."

"Then you always say it wrong," said Lamb, his irritation getting the better of him. "You're an insufferable old fool and you don't know you're alive."

"There you go," retorted the other. "You're always wrong. If I wasn't alive I wouldn't be here."

"And I wouldn't miss you," replied Lamb.

"The sea is large," the old gull suggested. "Why don't you hop off?"

"I was here first," said Lamb.

"I'm always first wherever I am," his disagreeable companion announced. "And besides, you've drifted half a mile since you lit on the water, so you're not the first because you're not there any longer and I—"

"Oh, for God's sake," interrupted Lamb, "you win. Have it your own way."

"Of course I win," said the gull complacently. "I always win. I can argue you down on anything. Say something and I'll bet you're wrong."

Mr. Lamb made no reply. He abandoned the conversation as hopeless. Besides he did not care for the old gull's rasping voice. The sea was rough at this spot, and Lamb was beginning to feel far from well. The choppy motion of the waves was seriously disturbing the herring. He looked over to see how his companion was standing it. The old bird was stolidly bobbing up and down apparently lost in some exasperating line of thought.

"Do you ever get seasick?" Mr. Lamb ventured.

The gull looked up irascibly.

"Put it properly," he rasped. "If you mean, do I ever get sick from or because of the sea, my answer is no, certainly not. On the other hand, if you are trying to ask, do I ever get sick of the sea, then that's altogether different."

He paused and looked broodingly at the sky.

"I'm fed up with the sea," he continued. "I'd like to retire and settle down. Build a nice little nest somewhere—nothing elaborate, you understand—and take life easy. I've been following the sea all my life and now I'm about through with it. I'd like to pass my few remaining years on shore. It's a dog's life for a gull."

"Why don't you retire?" asked Mr. Lamb. He was almost sorry for the old bird.

"Got to get my living, gotten I?" snapped the other.

"Haven't I," Mr. Lamb suggested mildly.

The old gull made an unpleasantly sarcastic noise.

"You're starting in again, I see," he observed with a hint of a threat in his voice. "I said 'gotten I,' and I mean 'gotten I.' No good trying to trip me up, I know."

Mr. Lamb once more relapsed into silence. There was nothing to be gained by arguing with this opinionated old bore. Time passed and the sun began to consider the Jersey hills. It had had a full day making the city sweat. Now it was time to close up shop. The old gull stirred and looked at Mr. Lamb.

"Want to go inshore and eat fertilizer?" he asked.

Mr. Lamb shuddered and clung to the herring.

"Thank you, no," he replied when he had a little mastered his nausea. "I've already dined."

"It's swell chow," said the old bird, "but suit yourself. More fertilizer for me. I love it."

He clapped his beak together with repulsive anticipation.

"Well, we'll probably run into each other sometime," he continued. "A big liner goes out tomorrow. Lots of first-class garbage. Probably see you with the mob. So long."

He rose from the water and streamed away inland. Lamb watched him out of sight.

"What an uncouth old devil," he mused.

That night when Sandra was undressing for bed she looked up from her garters and saw a large gull sitting on her window-sill.

"You low-down old loafer," she said, deliberately pulling down the shade. "And I was actually feeling sorry for you."

A loud, ribald squawk clattered in the air, but when she went to the window the gull was gone. She sat for a long time that night looking into the darkness.

CHAPTER XII

Mr. Billings Removes His Clothes

THE NEXT DAY MR. LAMB PUT TO SEA. IT WAS ENtirely unexpected. One of those unplanned excursions that turn out so excellently.

He had been hanging about the three-mile limit all day, idly sniffing empty bottles and recalling his vision of Sandra; when along toward three o'clock a big liner came stepping swiftly on her way to Europe.

Mr. Lamb had never crossed. It was one of those things one promises oneself and keeps on promising until the tomb puts an end to the hoary illusion. He was fond of ships. He felt that he could do well on a ship. The only thing wrong with Europe was that his wife had been there. He was not so fond of Europe for this. It should have been out when she called.

He tagged along with a motley throng of gulls in the wake of the ship. His companions were greedy for garbage. He most disliked their squawks of disappointment and satisfaction. One little gull who, in spite of her frantic efforts, was getting almost nothing, he helped out. She appreciated the half-filled banana peel hugely, but immediately began making improper advances, and Lamb had the time of his life convincing her of his chastity. It was all new to her. She returned to the garbage a much puzzled bird. She was more hurt than annoyed.

Then Lamb boarded the ship. He was going to see for himself. With a stealth that was now well developed he slipped into the scuppers of the main deck and made his way forward to the smoking-room. From his point of vantage there were many legs—forests of legs. He averaged them up on his way and decided they were far from bad. Good, satisfactory legs, well-hosed and frankly displayed for all the world to admire. He thought of slave markets where women were sold nude, and he wondered why the pictures always showed them cringing. Why, just show these women a slave market, and they would be racing to see who could strip first. Lamb was not a nice man. He did not think in nice ways. Mrs. Lamb had found that out.

His reception in the smoking-room was a great deal better than he had either hoped for or expected. The minute he thrust his serious, bespectacled head into the door a man in the corner began to laugh quietly to himself. From then on Lamb was a made gull so far as the smoking-room was concerned. He was accepted as one of the boys.

It all started from the man in the corner feeding him with bread soaked in wine. From then on things went from bad to worse. He was borrowed by various tables and urged to indulge. That is hardly correct. Lamb needed no urging. When a pretty woman held him in her arms and temptingly offered him a sip from her own cocktail he saw no reason to make a display of himself. He sipped and continued sipping. After dinner he did things with liqueurs. Exactly what he did with them he never quite remembered. However, a certain highball lingered long in his mind . . . that highball and a slanting deck, then an open door and a bed. Life became a comfortable hiatus.

When he next visited consciousness he was pecking irritably at a soft but firm object that was seriously disturbing his slumber. Several times beneath his pecking the object moved convulsively. Then suddenly the object was removed and the lights flashed on. When the coverings were pulled back, Lamb found himself frowning up into the face of a seriously perturbed young lady auspiciously attired. Now it so happened that this young lady had mastered only one cry of alarm that she considered suitable for shipboard. This cry she made all haste to utter.

Rushing from the room, she shouted at the top of her extremely robust lungs a warning that is feared and heeded on all the seven seas.

"Man overboard!" she announced with an earnestness that lent conviction. "Man overboard!"

The cry was automatically caught up by the stewards and passed forward to the bridge.

"Where?" demanded an officer, seizing the distracted young lady by a well-bared arm.

"Don't know," she half sobbed, "but I think it's in my bed. It bit me."

Too late now. The ship lost headway, then went into reverse. Doors popped open, and half-clad figures rushed to the decks, all of them cheerfully shouting something about a man being overboard. The scene was as giddy as a college rush.

During this refreshing interlude Mr. Lamb found an opportunity to remove himself to another stateroom, and to make sure there would be no misunderstanding this time he deliberately perched himself on the back of a chair.

"Well, that's doing pretty well for a mere seagull," he thought dreamily as he took up his sleep at the point where it had been disturbed.

Upon the bridge the skipper, when he learned the true state of affairs, was credited by his officers for inventing an entirely new language—something more concretely awful than they had ever heard before.

When the occupant of the stateroom Mr. Lamb had selected for the remainder of the night returned he glanced at the chair and averted his eyes. Then he rang for the steward.

"Steward," he asked when the man had arrived, "does there seem to be a bird on that chair in the corner?"

"There is, sir," replied the steward. "It's a seagull."

"Is the bird alive or dead?" continued the man.

The steward approached Mr. Lamb and scrutinized him closely. "He seems to be more asleep, sir," said the steward. "I'll chuck him right out."

"No," said the man. "No, steward. Let the damn fool sleep. I merely wanted to find out if we saw the same thing. I know exactly how he feels."

The steward withdrew, and the man, after a sympathetic survey of the gull, quietly prepared for sleep. He omitted dropping his shoes that night—a sleeping gull should not be aroused.

Mr. Lamb woke up a wreck. He had a confused memory of confusion. Impossible to put things together. He was sure, however, that the skipper did not want him on the ship. As a matter of fact, when the skipper had received a fuller report of various happenings aboard his ship he had said, "Find the ——, ——gull and wring its——, —— neck." Instinctively Mr. Lamb knew that the skipper would be snooty enough to issue an order like that. Lamb had heard about skippers.

Therefore, with a parting look of interest at his cabin-mate, he hopped to an open porthole and abandoned ship. As he wheeled high in the heavens he saw smoke on the sky-line. Soon he was able to make out the lines of a ship heading in the opposite direction— New York bound.

"I guess I'll have to hitch-hike it," he decided, stumbling over an air pocket and almost losing his balance. "In my condition I could never make port on wing."

Before he finally left, however, he flew back to his own ship and secretively introduced himself into the skipper's quarters where he succeeded in arousing the weary man by patiently toying with his hair. Then at a safe distance, close to a porthole, the gull arranged himself and listened while the skipper made all the noise. Mr. Lamb wished he had a stenographer present to take down many of the wonderful words he heard. The skipper went into his parentage, dwelt on various irregularities of birth, and gave specific evidence showing that Lamb was a nameless, immoral scavenger of the sea, the scum of all feathered things. Then Mr. Lamb took up the burden of the conversation and cursed the skipper vilely but impartially, as only a seagull can.

The air was filled with a wild clattering sound. The skipper listened for a while to the cursing gull with truly professional interest, then relost his temper. There were a great number of bells in his room. The skipper rang them all. When practically the entire crew had been assembled the skipper gave it explicit instructions just what to do with the gull. To have done all the things the skipper commanded would have required a lot of gulls—one gull could never have lasted. Mr. Lamb waited politely until the man had exhausted his supply of unpleasant suggestions, then poising himself in the porthole, rebuked him roundly for his lack of self-control. The crew had never heard the skipper so severely addressed. It was panic-stricken. It advanced on the cursing bird with extended hands. Lamb watched the determined men with an ironical eye, then dropped out of sight forever. After putting his crew on half-rations, the skipper cleared his cabin and returned to his bed, where he did not sleep.

When Lamb dropped down on the inbound vessel he dropped in a place where he would be free from intrusion, and there remained recuperating until the ship had passed the Battery. Then he sought the quiet waters of the Upper Hudson and drowsed peacefully round a battered old hulk until the lights began to appear in the windows of the apartment houses looming up high on the banks above him.

About five o'clock in the morning Mr. Lamb made up his mind that he was thoroughly sick of being a sea-gull. He had seen enough and done enough. If the little russet man insisted on his being things, Lamb wanted to be something else. He flew down Wall Street and turned into Broad Street. The financial district was deserted. Remarking that one of the windows of his office had been left open, he skimmed through it and sought his own private room. Everything was clean and in order. A large pile of slit envelopes was neatly stacked in the unfinished business basket. Perching himself on the edge of the desk, he closed his eyes to think and continued right through to sleep.

Time did not stay for Lamb's slumbers. It continued evenly about its business. The office staff made its appearance, and Billings, the treasurer, quietly entered Mr. Lamb's room. The old gentleman halted in the doorway and considered the sleeping gull long and thoughtfully. It was not his nature to be surprised. The moment he saw the gull his mind automatically leaped the events leading to its presence and occupied itself with devising schemes best fitted to relieve the office of its uninvited guest. Gulls did not buy bonds. Therefore gulls had no place in the scheme of things. It was all plain sailing to Billings.

He closed the door gently and returned to his desk the better to perfect his plans. This was a situation he had better handle himself. The ejecting of a seagull from the chief's private office would be too much of a treat for the lamentably frivolous members of the staff. He selected a long basket designed to hold ticker tape and once more entered Mr. Lamb's office, closing the door behind him. He hoped the gull was still sleeping.

But the gull was not still sleeping. The gull was not there at all. In its place squatted Mr. Lamb on the extreme edge of the desk. Mr. Lamb was clad only in pajamas, and to Mr. Billings this fact was more to be regretted than the existence of Russia and the popularity of Al Smith. Those phenomena were inexplicable, but the conduct of his chief would have to be explained, and Billings greatly doubted if a satisfactory explanation could be found. He fervently thanked his God that there was no smell of liquor in the air. Mr. Lamb must have left the bottle outside. He had the sense at least to do that.

Billings was about to close the door and lock it, feeling it wiser to let his chief finish his sleep, when Mr. Lamb woke up and began to flap his arms against his sides in a singularly birdlike manner. Billings, remembering the gull, gasped as a shocking suspicion entered his mind. The flapping was the cause of more trouble. Mr. Lamb lost his balance and fell with a crash to the floor. The fall and the sight of the familiar face of his treasurer were sufficient to give Mr. Lamb a comprehensive realization of his predicament. He looked down at the pajamas, then smiled cordially up at Billings.

"Morning, Billings," he said. "Would you mind taking off your clothes. I have an extremely important engagement."

For only a moment did Billings hesitate, then he slowly began to strip. It was up to him to see that Mr. Lamb kept that engagement. A cool million might hang in the balance. Who could tell?

At this intimate juncture Miss Helen Wilson, bearing the morning letters, came swiftly into the office and, to the relief of both gentlemen, went swiftly out again. The expression on her face was enough to collect an interested group.

"The boss is in there in pajamas," she quietly told the girls, "and Billings is undressing."

"My Gord!" breathed a snappy-looking stenographer. "What do we all have to do, go to bed?"

A few minutes later Mr. Lamb, clad in a suit several sizes too small for him, came smilingly from his office and greeted his demoralized staff as if nothing unusual had occurred. And a few minutes after his departure Mr. Billings summoned his assistant to him and shortly appeared wearing a suit several sizes too large for him. With an air of deep preoccupation he flopped across the main office, then flopped from view behind the protection of his own door.

What steps the assistant took to cover his nakedness are not known. It is to be assumed that Mr. Billings did not permit him to go home in Mr. Lamb's pajamas.

When Lamb presented himself at his home his arrival created a small stir. Even Thomas was quietly edified. Mrs. Lamb was not amused.

"That's rather a dashing little ensemble you're wearing, major," Hebe observed, looking up from her plate. "Do you feel that we need to be diverted?"

"I sort of fancy it myself," said Lamb, taking his place at the head of the table. "It's Philadelphia's latest. Do you like it, Sapho?"

"Where have you been?" asked Sapho. "And what am I to understand by these mysterious disappearances?"

"Flying," said Mr. Lamb enigmatically; then as if it were an afterthought he asked: "Would it be quite convenient for me to retire to my room after luncheon? I want to save this suit for Sunday."

Mrs. Lamb refrained from asking further inconvenient questions. Her husband ate more than usual.

CHAPTER XIII

A Lapful of Sandy

"WHY MUST I BE CARRIED INTO THE CITY?" MR. LAMB complained, as his daughter spread disorder among the traffic in upper New York. "I just came from that wallow of vice and corruption."

"I'm going to spend money, I told you," his daughter patiently explained, "and I want you to watch how I do it. You see, major, at any moment now I might get married or something very closely related to getting married. From now on I've got to be always on the alert."

"There's an infinity of space between getting married and something very closely related to getting married," Mr. Lamb mildly observed. "Then of course there remains the relatively unimportant question of the morality of the thing."

"There you have me," replied Hebe. "I've always been backward on morals, but I do know how to dress appropriately for any given occasion, and that's more than half the battle."

"You may be right," her father agreed. "My own morals are undergoing a severe strain at present. They seem to be almost undermined, although thus far I am still intact. As a seagull I slept with a lady, but not very comfortably nor very long. I made an impression at that. It is a question in my mind if that lady ever sleeps again. She will certainly never sleep with a seagull."

Hebe parked the car in a side street and, taking her father's arm, directed his steps to a magnificent shop just off Fifth Avenue.

"This place is obviously not designed to improve one's morals," Mr. Lamb remarked as he looked about him. "I can hardly understand how a woman with such remarkable contraptions on underneath can refrain from discarding her outer garments and displaying herself demi-nude."

"All women cherish or have cherished that pious desire," Hebe replied wisely. "Your mind operates too crudely to understand the finer feelings of women. Anyway, here comes madam."

Madam having been introduced to Hebe's father and the young lady's wishes having been made known in a low voice, the couple were ushered into a private room and offered ridiculously inadequate gilt chairs.

"If you weren't my daughter," said Mr. Lamb, "I'd be leaving at just this point. What goes on here? The presence of that sofa over there is not reassuring. Am I expected to ring for drinks?"

"I wouldn't have a mind like yours for the world," his daughter told him. "It's so utterly evil—so bad."

"Do you mean to sit there and tell me—," Mr. Lamb began, but he never finished the sentence.

The door opened and a girl clad in what Lamb considered next to nothing came slithering and swaying into the room. The girl was Sandra . . . impersonal, aloof, and unsmiling. Her eyes glittered dangerously, Mr. Lamb thought, when they occasionally met his.

"Get an eyeful you old roué," she gritted as she swept close to his chair.

Mr. Lamb started back.

"Hebe," he said, "I think I'd better be going. My morals as I have already told you are almost undermined."

"Is it not chic?" Madam demanded. "Is it not *ravissement?*"

While Hebe was agreeing with madam that the garment was both chic and *ravissement* Sandra once more glided past Mr. Lamb.

"Nasty," she muttered. "Nasty old man."

Mr. Lamb leaned close to his daughter and actually brought himself to whisper, so great was his indignation.

"She just called me a nasty old man," he told her. "You staged this party—not I."

Hebe patted her father's arm with a soothing little hand.

"Don't mind her," she replied in a low voice. "You are nasty, but you're not so very old."

"Well, I'll be damned," breathed Mr. Lamb, and fastened his eyes on the exact center of the rug.

"What do you think Mr. Lamb?" asked madam, fearing that the source of revenue might be growing bored. "Would not your daughter wear well in that?"

"What?" said Mr. Lamb with a slight start. "Wear well? Oh yes, of course. She'd wear splendidly if she didn't wear out altogether."

"Your father is droll," laughed madam. Come, I have something to show——," and taking Hebe by the arm, she led the girl from the room.

"Un moment, monsieur," drifted back to him through the closing door.

Then things began to happen. When the click of the latch assured Sandra that was she alone in the room with Mr. Lamb, she took instant advantage of their privacy. With one spring she was on his lap, her arms twined tightly round his head. To Mr. Lamb it seemed that Sandra's unexpected demonstration was more in the nature of an assault than an expression of tender emotions. Suppose he should be discovered in this compromising position? Lamb grew frantic.

"Get up," he mouthed, his vowels being muffled by a quantity of ineffectual lace. "Get up at once—this instant!"

Then madam and Hebe made their appearance. Madam uttered a shocked cry and covered her eyes, but Hebe studied the situation with her usual detached interest.

Sandra wriggled off the knees and took refuge behind madam.

"It was a veritable assault, madam," she chattered with every appearance of terror. "The moment you left the room that nasty old man on the chair looked at me and said, 'I'm going to get you,' and with that I was seized—you saw."

She embellished this lying statement with a volley of extremely convincing sobs and shudders. Madam put her arms around the girl and did her best to quiet her maidenly alarm.

"Let me explain," Lamb began, but Hebe interrupted.

"Madam, said she, "I think I'll take several sets of that small thing she's wearing."

Madam was delighted. She even regarded Mr. Lamb with sympathetic eyes.

Mr. Lamb walked out of the shop and allowed Hebe to guide his faltering steps at random.

Hebe knew of a place and thither she led her father. For the remainder of the afternoon she dutifully fed him highballs until his belief in the ultimate wisdom of God was partially restored. He was even able to smile ruefully over the memory of Sandra's assault.

At a late hour that night he was still drinking highballs and running up a commendable check at a night club for the benefit of Sandra, his daughter, and Melville Long. Mr. Lamb had danced with more diligence than grace. Now, however, he was past dancing. In fact, if the truth must be known, Mr. Lamb was rapidly disappearing, the top of his head being level with the table cloth, and in a few minutes even the little of him with which he saw fit to grace the table was withdrawn from public view.

Observing the reluctance of her father to remain in an erect position, Hebe called the waiter and asked for the check. Presently he returned with a beaming face in anticipation of a heavy tip, but as he was on the point of proffering the final reckoning he suddenly became transfixed in his tracks, his eyes riveted themselves on the floor, and the beam slowly melted from his face giving place to an expression decidedly unnerving to behold. The party looked down and saw what the waiter saw—a long, large, tawny tail protruding from under the table. The waiter felt sure that even to look at such a thing was not included in his salary. He tiptoed away carrying the check with him. Let more intrepid spirits collect it if they could. His duty lay with his family.

The two girls looked at the one remaining man, who himself was not so crisp.

"What's on the other end of it?" asked Sandra.

Hebe bent over and thoughtfully contemplated the tail.

"Search me," she said at last, "I don't rightly remember ever having had any dealings with a tail like that before."

"Perhaps it's an altogether new and better animal," Mr. Long suggested enterprisingly.

He pulled a flask from his hip pocket and passed it to the ladies. The situation called for a drink.

"That," said Hebe, sweeping the back of her hand across her mouth, "endears you to me for life."

At this moment Mr. Lamb decided to relieve the tension of the situation. A long, sleek head with a pointed snout appeared above the table, slid onto the rumpled cloth and looked moistly at the three young people. In the due course of time the head was followed by a body, which slumped back awkwardly in its chair.

"I don't want to be hasty," said Hebe, "but roughly speaking, I think my father and our host leans toward kangaroo. What will we use for money now that he has gone?"

Once more Mr. Long was enterprising.

"Mightn't he have a pouch?" he asked. "I seem to remember something about kangaroos and pouches."

The kangaroo laughed foolishly and beat on the table with his short but powerful forelegs. Hebe cast her lover a smile of infinite commiseration.

"For one I'd prefer not to look for it," she remarked. "You see, darling, he's not that sort of a kangaroo."

"I beg your pardon," said Mr. Long. "It was merely a suggestion."

"Rather an indelicate one," observed the girl.

For some minutes Sandra had been looking with growing disgust at the obviously inebriated kangaroo, who had been fatuously trying to hold her hand.

"Now, I ask you," she demanded. "What are we going to do with that? You just can't leave a kangaroo to shift for himself in a city like this."

"He'd be safe so far as women are concerned," observed Melville Long, surpassing himself in optimism.

The kangaroo received this remark with a giggle of appreciation.

"I don't know," said Hebe. "He's not such a bad-looking kangaroo."

"He's a terrible-looking kangaroo," declared Sandra. "Look at him there, all slouched over. Why can't he sit up properly?"

Mr. Lamb favored her with a scowl.

It seems unfortunate that at this state of the conversation a gentleman in executing an ambitious dance step should have descended heavily on Mr. Lamb's tail. It seems doubly unfortunate that Mr. Lamb had not sufficient restraint to withhold the vicious upper cut he immediately delivered upon the point of the gentleman's chin. From that time on everything seemed increasingly unfortunate.

The dancer retaliated with a left hook to Mr. Lamb's jaw, and Sandra, as if guided by an infallible sense of balance, sprang upon the man's partner and partially disrobed her.

"Touch a hair of his head," she shouted, "and I'll strip you clean."

Several ladies rushed to the assistance of the assaulted woman, and this quite naturally brought Hebe into the fray. One thing led to another, and presently Melville Long found himself engaged in biting the ear of a perfect stranger while kicking another diligently in the stomach. On all sides it was an earnest, hard-breathing little engagement that did not lose one whit of interest because of the fact that only a few of its participants had the vaguest idea of what it was all about.

In the meantime the kangaroo, highly excited by all that was going on, was leaping from table to table and impartially smiting both friend and foe whenever the occasion offered.

The room was not quiet nor the scene restful. Several men, as if preferring not to trust the evidence of their eyes, were sitting motionless at their tables, their heads buried in their arms. When Mr. Lamb's head managed to get itself through a snare drum, retaining the frame round his neck, it seemed high time to think about going home.

Hebe, Sandra, and a shockingly tattered Mr. Long cut a path through the whirling mass and joined the kangaroo at the door.

"Cut and run!" cried Sandra. "The car's round the corner."

The four of them burst so compactly from the place that two arriving policemen were heavily borne to the pavement. There they sat and blew their whistles, then lurched in the direction of the flying wedge. They were trailed by a waiter wildly waving a check.

"Off again," thought Lamb to himself, as he leaped along beside Sandra. "My universe of late seems to be in a disconcertingly unsettled condition."

As they swarmed into the automobile a motorcycle policeman came into view and calmly took the number of the car, which by this time was gathering speed, then with a satisfied grin, settled himself down on his machine to show these people exactly where they got off.

At Columbus Circle another officer tried to hold them up when they were forced to slow down in traffic, but a hairy arm shooting out unexpectedly from the rear seat of the car, landed him in the gutter.

"What sort of a mob is that?" he wondered, vividly recalling the strange-looking arm that had so bewilderingly altered his plans.

Melville Long was at the wheel, and Hebe was sitting beside him. On the back seat Sandra was clinging to the kangaroo and laughing softly at the festive appearance he made with the rim of the drum round his neck.

When they were well out of the city the motorcycle policeman, who had not forgotten them for a moment, telephoned ahead to the next fair-sized town and gave full particulars and an adequate description of the merry little party. They were all laughing now, save Mr. Lamb, who showed a strong inclination to doze off on Sandra's shoulder. Melville Long's merriment was the greater because of the skillful manner in which he believed he had eluded pursuit.

The flight came to an end at the railroad tracks of

the next town. The bars were down, and it was here that the reception committee waited.

"Damn," said Melville Long under his breath as several dark figures emerged from the shadows and manifested their presence in other unpleasant ways.

"You big stiffs," said Hebe. "Why didn't you call out the army?"

"That's all they are," agreed Sandra unhesitatingly. "They're just great, big, liver-footed stiffs—morons!"

"That talk ain't going to help you a bit," one of the officers warned the ladies.

"Aw, shut up," said Mr. Long. "We're not asking you for a lesson in polite conversation."

The officer was about to attend to the young man for this remark, when a terrible, grinning face was suddenly thrust into his. He started back with a cry and had to be supported by two of his brother officers. But this was Mr. Lamb's last effort that night. He had no recollection of being driven to a station house and half carried to a cell in which he was locked up in company with his prospective son-in-law. The two girls, still busily insulting every uniform in sight, were given a barred apartment of their own where they sang and jeered themselves to sleep.

When Judge Gibson arose next morning he made up his mind to give all prisoners brought before him whom he could not sentence to painful death at least a life term at revolting labor. In this cheerful frame of mind he repaired to his court and proceeded to spread dread and dismay among the ranks of evil-doers. When Sandra, Hebe and Melville Long were lined up against the rail he kept them waiting a considerable time before he looked up from a paper he had been studying with growing interest. When he did look up his expression was almost happy. Here was something he could get thoroughly enraged about. Convulsing his face into a small bunch he slowly considered in turn each youthful face looking bravely up into his.

"Good morning," he said in a suspiciously pleasant voice. "Can you think of anything you haven't done?"

"Rape," replied Sandra promptly.

"Arson and pillage," added Hebe.

"Treason," was the best that Long could achieve.

The Judge was a little taken back by the nature of the snappy replies. Evidently these young people were not so soft as they looked. He would have to deal with them astutely.

"Well, I have you down here for about everything else," he continued, referring to the paper. "I'll select a few charges at random just to give you an approximate idea of how very long you are going to be with us."

He cleared his throat efficiently and carefully adjusted his glasses.

"A mention is made here of driving while under the influence of spirituous liquor, of demolishing a restaurant and refusing to pay the check, of assaulting, maiming, and wounding upwards of half a hundred innocent persons, of speeding and violating every known traffic regulation in the most flagrant and callous manner, of having in your company and possession a dangerous wild beast, of attacking several officers of the law, and of being in possession of a flask of whisky. Your evening seems to have been industriously spent in disturbing the world at large."

"I'll bet you love to read the weather reports that say 'Rain and increasing cold,'" observed Sandra with her most disarming smile.

The judge was not annoyed. He looked at the girl a long time as if trying to fix her image forever in his memory.

"Where you are going," he told her distinctly, "you won't have to worry about the weather. It will be all overcast to you."

In spite of herself Sandra shuddered at this unemotional announcement.

"Your honor," put in one of the policemen. "They also used bad language and called us a bunch of big stiffs."

The judge looked at the policeman with a shocked expression, then turned his eyes to the prisoners.

"How did you find that out?" he asked.

"You can see for yourself, your honor," replied Hebe.

"I know," agreed the judge, "but we've been trying

to hush it up. Don't go giving us away every time you get run in."

The judge paused and once more considered the document.

"It refers here," he continued with a new note of interest in his voice, "to a dangerous wild beast. Where is this wild beast at present, Donovan?"

"He's locked up," replied that worthy.

"Did you capture it last night?" asked the judge.

"The four of us, your honor," said Donovan modestly. "Officers O'Boyle, Burk—"

"Quite right," the judge interrupted." Then I assume the beast was neither dangerous nor wild."

"It gave us a terrible start, your honor," Donovan got in. "An awful sight it was with the drum around its neck, and all."

The judge looked up quickly. This was all news to him.

"It must have been dreadful," he remarked with elaborate solicitude. "But what's this about a drum? It says nothing here about a drum."

"Yes, sir, it was wearing a drum," said Donovan.

"And you say this drum was around the neck of this alleged wild beast?" continued Judge Gibson. "What sort of wild beast does it happen to be?"

"The doctor just came in on a case, sir, and claims it's a kingaroo," the officer replied.

"Kangaroo, Donovan," corrected the judge.

"Yes, your honor," Donovan continued, "but Sergeant Brophy says it ain't a kingaroo, because kingaroos don't act that way."

"In what lies the eccentricity of this unknown wild beast's behavior?" demanded the judge now thoroughly interested.

"Didn't get your honor," said Donovan.

"What's wrong with the thing?" snapped the judge, then turning to his prisoners added politely, "You'll pardon me I hope before I put you away. I must get Donovan to tell me all about this kingaroo."

"Certainly, your honor, we'll pardon you if you will pardon us," replied Hebe.

"Very good," said the judge with a ghastly grin. "You were going to say, Donovan?"

"I hadn't intended saying anything," replied Donovan.

"Well, go right ahead and say it," urged the judge patiently. "I think you can confide in us. What's wrong with this wild beast?"

"Well, your honor," replied the officer with every sign of hesitancy. "The last I saw of the thing it was humming 'Me and My Shadow' and dancing around in its cell."

"What!" the judge almost shouted, leaning far over his desk; then, sinking back, he added, "Don't say any more for a moment, Donovan. I need to think."

The prisoners before him were leaning on the rail, their faces hidden from view.

"I wish I could laugh," said the judge gloomily. "Never have I been forced to listen to such an involved and successfully obscured narrative."

He picked up a newspaper and read for several minutes, occasionally stopping to look penetratingly at Donovan until that intrepid limb of the law began to grow more than a little reflective.

"What did you say the name of that song was?" the judge asked at last.

" 'Me and My Shadow,' " Donovan replied.

"Is it a pretty song?" continued the judge. "Do you know it?"

"I couldn't sing it myself, your honor," said Donovan, fearing the judge's next request, "but I know it when I hear it."

"I'll buy you a record, your honor," offered Sandy. "It's sweetly wistful like so many of your clients."

"You won't be near any store," said the judge.

"Oh," said Sandy, "that's too bad!"

"Sounds like a criminal record," observed the judge. " 'Me and My Shadow'—shadow, you see. Good! Everyone gets 100 but Officer Donovan."

The judge folded his papers with a snap and sat up abruptly.

"Enough of this," he said briskly. "Donovan, bring

in that singing kangaroo. Let's all have a look at it. Perhaps we'll be able to agree on a name."

"He's not such a poisonous judge," murmured Hebe to Sandra.

"Not at all," said Sandra. "Quite a human being."

"Wait till you see what he does with us," Melville Long whispered behind his hand, his optimism vanished.

The kangaroo was not entirely sober when Donovan, holding a rope, the other end of which was secured around his neck, brought him before the judge. The animal covered the ground with a peculiar gliding motion that gave him the appearance of skating. He was still humming under his breath in a preoccupied manner. Greeting his friends with a casual wave of a relatively short foreleg, he bowed to the judge.

At this point several sleepy reporters came back to life and began to ask each other questions. Here was a good story. They collared an attendant and obtained full details. The few remaining spectators also displayed signs of returning interest. The judge leaned forward and listened intently, one hand held up for silence. A strange noise was issuing from the kangaroo's lips. Observing the judge's strained attitude the kangaroo obligingly increased the volume of his humming, and the room was filled with what the kangaroo fondly believed to be a song.

"You've a better ear for music than I have, Donovan," said the judge, settling back in his chair. "Is he still harping on his favorite song?"

"That's what he thinks he's doing," answered the officer. "It ain't so bad, your honor, considering he's a poor, dumb, soulless beast."

Mr. Lamb looked pensively at Donovan.

"Where's his drum?" asked the judge suddenly.

"He refused to come out of his cell until I'd taken it off for him," Donovan replied.

"Too bad," observed the judge. "I'd like to have seen that." Then turning to Hebe, he asked, "Miss Lamb, where did you get this singing kangaroo?"

"My uncle found him in the bush," said Hebe.

"What bush?" asked the judge. "Try to be specific."

"The Australian bush," replied Hebe. "He's been in our family ever since he was a pup."

The judge continued to question the girl about the kangaroo until Mr. Lamb grew bored. He was also becoming extremely sleepy. The liquor was wearing off. Slowly he sank down and fell into a gentle slumber. The judge looked over the edge of his desk.

"Donovan," he ordered, "wake that kangaroo up. Neither man nor beast sleeps in this court."

A violent jerk on the noose brought the kangaroo erect like a released spring. He made a side swipe at Donovan, but, luckily for that officer, failed to land. Then, as if suddenly realizing his surroundings, he looked apologetically at the judge.

A strange feeling was taking possession of Mr. Lamb, a feeling not entirely due to his overindulgence. Some sort of chemical revolution was taking place within him. He was unable to shake off his drowsiness and confusion. As he drifted off to sleep again he had a vague idea that the judge was asking Donovan whether the poor soulless beast had been given a cup of coffee that morning.

A loud discussion in the back of the courtroom between two heavy-faced, unhatted ladies stoutly defending the smirched reputation of their respective husbands presently to be tried on a charge of jointly attempting to put an end to each other's lurid careers, created a momentary diversion. All eyes were turned in their direction, and by the time the belligerent ladies had been voluminously ejected, another diversion had arisen to mar the tranquillity of the judge's morning. When he next peered at the kangaroo he found himself looking into the dark eyes of a tall, fashionably clad gentleman of distinguished manner and sober bearing.

"Hello!" exclaimed the judge in some surprise. "Where the devil did you spring from?"

Mr. Lamb presented his card and explained his presence in the court. Having learned indirectly about the escapade of these young people and being the father of one of them and an old friend of the parents of the other two, he had hastened to help the judge to show them the error of their ways.

"You are just in time to see the last of them, Mr. Lamb," Judge Gibson informed him. "And by the way, how did you manage to get that noose about your neck?"

Mr. Lamb's hand flew to the rope. For a moment he appeared to be crushed. His companion of the night gazed at him with dismayed eyes. How could he lie himself out of this? Then a bland smile touched Mr. Lamb's lips as he looked up at the judge.

"I just found it lying there on the floor," said Mr. Lamb, "and I thought I'd try it on."

"Are you in the habit of trying on nooses?" asked the judge.

Sandra was leaning against Mr. Lamb. Her face was crimson, and a handkerchief was crammed in her mouth.

"That's the most deflated lie I've ever attended," breathed Hebe.

"No," replied Mr. Lamb in reply to the judge's question. "It is not one of my hobbies."

"I'm glad to hear it," the judge remarked. "One of the nooses might stay put sometime."

Mr. Lamb laughed politely.

"Donovan," continued the judge, "where has that kangaroo gotten himself to? Is he still sleeping or what's he think he's doing?"

When the judge's eye gathered in Donovan, he imagined the officer was giving every appearance of shell shock. Donovan was staring at Mr. Lamb with frightened bewildered eyes.

"Why, that gentleman's the kangaroo!" he faltered. "The rope ain't never been out of my hand, your honor."

"No, Donovan," replied the judge. "Mr. Lamb is not a kangaroo in spite of his eccentric conduct. You've tried to convince me of many strange, unbelievable stories in the course of our relations, but I refuse to be convinced that this gentleman is a kangaroo."

A hard light came into the judge's eyes, and he leaned far over his desk again.

"Now, Donovan," he rasped. "You go out and find me that kangaroo. Take some of your fellow incompetents with you. Bring that animal back to me. I want him to teach me that song."

"I beg your pardon, Judge Gibson," Mr. Lamb put in, "but I think I can help the officer out. As I was coming in a kangaroo burst from between two excited women who were evidently being put out. The creature almost knocked me over in his eagerness to go somewhere. He turned to the left and jumped into a passing van heading away from the city. That's the last I saw of him."

"Search for that van, Donovan," said the judge. "And don't forget to beat every bush. He likes bushes. So far it seems you've made a mess of the case. There's not a witness here in court to support a number of your charges. I don't even see a plaintiff."

Donovan left with one last fascinated look at Mr. Lamb, who immediately after retired with the judge to his private chamber. When he returned he smiled encouragingly at the delinquents. The judge brushing his lips with a handkerchief also smiled upon them.

"What your various parents are going to do to you will be plenty," he said happily. "You will come to wish I had put you in prison forever. I've just had Mr. Long on the wire, young man, and he actually pleaded with me to sentence you for life. He said something about being able to prove yourself in jail. In view of the approaching unpleasantness I am letting you off with a suspended sentence. Get them out of my sight, Mr. Lamb. They've taken up my entire morning—they and that kangaroo."

Back in the automobile Lamb collapsed. Sandra nestled against him.

"I hope this will teach us all a lesson," he said piously. "It will all come out in the papers."

"T'will make erotic reading for Sapho," replied Hebe. "I think we had better go away somewhere."

"I know I had," said Long moodily. "There'll be no living at home. I've proved myself conclusively at last."

"Ruination?" suggested Hebe.

"We're ruinated enough as it is," said Long.

Sandra's hand crept in to Mr. Lamb's.

"You're such a nice, long, lovely liar," she murmured.

Mr. Lamb was looking at her ear.

"That thing," he said, pinching it slightly, "was the start of all my troubles."

"Kiss it," urged Sandra in a low voice.

Mr. Lamb looked coldly at the girl.

CHAPTER XIV

Sapho Tries to Murder a Fish

MR. LAMB HAD SPOKEN CONSERVATIVELY. THE REPORTers got it. The papers printed it. Yards of it. In spite of the vast multiplicity of detail, in spite of the unscrupulous embellishments, the callous innuendoes, the gentlemen of the press were still heavily befogged as to the actual facts of the affair. Mr. Lamb appeared in print, but not in his true rôle of a converted kangaroo.

One story in particular disturbed the overtaxed equanimity of its central character. The author of the story in question had seen fit to treat his subject facetiously, which when one comes to consider its nature seems about the best way to treat it. One can hardly work up a spirit of profound indignation or grow morbidly melancholic over a humming kangaroo. A few morons exist who perhaps could, but these singleminded gentlemen were, as usual, too busy suppressing books, collecting unpleasantly reminiscent picture postcards or putting disturbing factors behind the bars to worry about Mr. Lamb and his companions.

Nevertheless, Mr. Lamb would have wrung this individual reporter's neck quite cheerfully and thoroughly had the neck conveniently offered itself. However, the necks of reporters are not always the easiest things in the world to establish contact with, save through the medium of a bottle containing any fluid remotely alcoholic including varnish and rub-down preparations.

Sitting this evening in the quietude of his study with his old friend Kai Lung safely balanced on one long, thin knee, Mr. Lamb delayed for a moment the pleasure of having this engaging Oriental unroll his mat in order to peruse for the fifth time the far less engaging inventions of some obviously depraved occidental newspaper reporter.

These inventions were in part as follows:

THE STRANGE BEHAVIOR OF MR. T. LAWRENCE LAMB

APPEARS IN COURT WITH A NOOSE ROUND HIS NECK
JUDGE GIBSON REFUSED TO HANG HIM

Apparently anticipating the worst, Mr. T. Lawrence Lamb of Woodbine N.Y., a well-known and, just previous to this writing, conservative investment banker, presented himself before Judge Gibson in general session today with a noose neatly arranged round his neck—this in addition to a tie of unusually lurid color.

In full justice to Mr. Lamb it must be stated that his appearance in court was due to no moral lapse of his own. One can only ascribe Mr. Lamb's unconventional neck adornment to a desire to offer himself in vicarious atonement for the sins of his daughter, Miss Hebe Lamb, and her two accomplices, Miss Sandra Rush and Mr. Melville Long, all active members of Woodbine's younger set.

That these young people were a little more than active on the evening of their arrest and subsequent incarceration is evidenced by the fact that no less than fourteen serious charges were lodged against them and that their trail of destruction extended from the dead center of New York's night-club district to a spot some forty miles distant from the city.

Additional interest is added to the mad progress of these young people through the presence of a singing kangaroo, or, as Officer Patrick Donovan prefers to call it, kingaroo. Whether this convivial animal was a kangaroo or a kingaroo is difficult to establish at this moment, due to the unfortunate fact that whatever the creature was it successfully thwarted retention and is still at large. According to Judge Gibson it is probably in some bush. The judge never offers an opinion without some good reason.

An element of mystery is introduced here arising from the inexplicable coincidence that the noose so unsuccessfully used to restrain this night-club-loving animal was the identical one that so nattily adorned Mr. Lamb's neck.

Mr. Lamb has stated that finding the noose on the floor he picked it up and slipped it on merely through lack of knowing anything better to do with it. To his way of thinking, a noose obviously required a neck, and not wishing to intrude upon the neck of some perfect stranger, he quite logically put it on his own.

In view of the gentleman's social position and well-established conservative leanings, this is an explanation difficult to believe. It can only be assumed that Mr. Lamb's mind suddenly broke down under the shock of his daughter's conduct and that temporarily the man was not anyway near himself.

Evidently this was the charitable view that Judge Gibson took of the situation, having been somewhat shocked himself by the sudden appearance of an otherwise normal gentleman wearing a noose round his neck, and to all intents and purposes willing to pay the supreme penalty for his erring daughter and her no less erring friends.

Apparently the sight of Mr. Lamb, together with the sincerity of his bearing, touched some hitherto successfully concealed spring of tenderness in the judge, who released the youthful offenders on a suspended sentence after what is believed to have been a pleasant conversation in his chambers with the sacrificial Mr. Lamb.

Miss Sandra Rush, an underwear model of no mean proportions, is often seen in one of the many Lamb automobiles. This is, of course, due solely to her close friendship with Mr. Lamb's daughter. The singing kangaroo, it is believed, is still caroling his ribald songs in some secluded bush.

It was on this high note that the story came to an end. It was also as this note sounded that Mrs. Lamb entered her husband's study. Once entered, she stood still and tragically awaited his acknowledgment of her presence. Fearing that the acknowledgment might be indefinitely delayed, she altered her pose at last and slanted an accusing finger at the newspaper now drooping from Mr. Lamb's hands.

"What are you going to do about it?" dropped gloomily from her lips. "I suggest you resign from everything and live somewhere else under an assumed name."

Mr. Lamb elevated his knees, skilfully retaining control of Kai Lung, and looked at his wife as if he were trying to place her in an extremely feeble memory. Presently he unlimbered, rose and vaguely offered her a chair which she in turn spurned, overacting the part in doing so.

"Ah yes!" murmured Mr. Lamb. "It's Sapho—my Tilly. You were saying? . . ."

"I was saying," Sapho put in, "that you should drop out of sight and live under another name."

"Couldn't I grow a beard?" Mr. Lamb asked mildly. "I might even dye my hair and continue to lurk here as one of your inspired friends or a conveniently acquired uncle from Australia. They say here in the paper that the kangaroo or kingaroo—I prefer the latter version—came from the bush. And to think that we both shared the same noose. This paper also says that he sang. I missed that part. Can't have everything, I suppose. Do you believe he actually sang, that kangaroo?"

"You should go to your underwear model or to your own daughter for such information," was Mrs. Lamb's crushing retort. "The light attitude you are now assuming seems in the worst of taste to me. Once more I ask you, what are you going to do about it? I cannot afford to be associated with a laughing-stock. My life—what modest talent I possess—was never intended to be shackled to a personality so—so coarse and

unsympathetic as yours . . . so utterly self-centered
and lacking in the finer shades and vibrations of emotion. My life should be led with a larger, a higher
vision. Everyone recognizes that fact."

"The word that I have in mind," said Mr. Lamb
slowly, "the only one I consider a fitting reply to your
bathetic remarks, is frequently applied to wives by less
delicate husbands than I. It's too honest a word for
your ears, so I'll exercise your limited imagination.
Consider the word as said."

He looked thoughtfully at some cigarette ashes that
had fallen on his knee, started to brush them off,
then deciding the effort was too exhausting, gave it up.

"Still there is something in what you say," he remarked at last. "That Vacation Fund affair, from what
I heard of it, provided enough laughter to last this
community for years. If both of us become laughing-
stocks the general merriment might provoke an epi-
demic of hysteria."

"I absolutely deny I was a laughing-stock," said
Mrs. Lamb. "A horse was responsible for all that . . .
a low, vicious, yet strangely human horse in some of its
more objectionable actions. In many ways that brute of
a horse reminded me of you. Even now I shudder when
I think of him."

"Another point I share in common with this horse of
yours." Mr. Lamb grinned good-naturedly.

"I did not come here to discuss my emotional reactions to you," Mrs. Lamb answered coldly. "I hoped
that we might be able to arrive at some understanding—some civilized arrangement. Since the appearance
of all this scandal in the papers my nerves have been
uprooted. It will take years to get them anyway near
back to their former condition. They'll never get back
entirely. You don't know what a thing like that does to
me."

Mr. Lamb, still grinning, seemed to be considering
things. His wife did not care for the grin. She recognized it. Also the light in his eyes. Something particularly disagreeable always followed these facial
manifestations. She was not disappointed. Something

unpleasant did—something surpassingly disagreeable, a real accomplishment for Mr. Lamb.

"Here's an idea," he said quite nervously. "Suppose I should give you the use of my room over week-ends? What would you think of a clubby little scheme like that? Sort of ménage à trois, one member being absent. . . . I have a little pride."

Mrs. Lamb did not express an opinion of her husband's little scheme. She did not even deign to meet Mr. Lamb's eyes. The mental process of this crude man was altogether too antiquated to deal with the complex sex impulses of a modern woman of genius. In bringing up that phase of the situation he was once again displaying execrable taste. She had come to his study to discuss his affairs, not hers. She was her own woman, but now since the newspapers had published such full reports of his actions in court, his affairs were public property.

"A long week-end," she heard Mr. Lamb urging. "From Friday to Monday night. How about it, Tilly?"

She turned to the door, fully intending to go through it, when Mr. Lamb's voice recalled her.

"I have one more suggestion to make," he said. "Suppose I should retire from business and write a book entitled 'Wild Animals I Have Been'?"

This suggestion was sufficiently arresting to move Mrs. Lamb to change her mind and to accept the once rejected chair. Arranging herself becomingly she regarded her husband with what she fondly believed to be a disarming smile.

"Then you have been animals," she remarked conversationally. "How interesting! Tell me all about it. I knew you were that horse of course, and I suspected you of being the bird, although I never saw it, or rather you. Were you also the kangaroo?"

"Why this sudden interest in animals?" asked Mr. Lamb. "I never noticed it before save perhaps in that worn-out dishmop you occasionally defile our presence with—that snug harbor for jaded fleas. And suppose I should admit I turned into animals and things, I dare say you'd keep my guilty secret from the entire world with the possible exception of the law courts and a se-

lect multitude of your strolling players. You'd love to
see me arrested as an escaped kangaroo. Your present
mood of sweet confidence—wifely interest—amuses
me."

With a burst of determination Mr. Lamb brushed
the ashes off his knee, spilled some more on his vest
and continued.

"Well, strange as it may seem," he said, "I'm going
to tell you right here and now to your exceedingly false
face that recently I have acquired the habit of turning
into animals, both wild and domestic. At this very moment I might become some extremely deadly reptile
and do you in with fangs filled with horrid poison. I
wouldn't squeeze you to death because even snakes
have some self-respect. Frankly I'd like to fang you. I
feel like doing it, but unfortunately the choice does not
lie with me. I might become a panther instead or an
anteater or a rat or a butterfly—God knows what I
might become."

Lamb paused and regarded his wife darkly. She was
not a thing of beauty. Terror failed to improve the arrangement of her features. Standing in the doorway she
returned his gaze with eyes of glass, so fixed and polished was the expression in them.

"I'm taking the trouble to tell you all this," Mr.
Lamb went on evenly, as he followed her into the dining-room, "because I don't give one shrill hoot in hell
how you spread the news. No one would believe you
anyway. You'd only be making a bigger fool of yourself than you have already, if such an enormous
achievement is possible—which I very much doubt."

Mr. Lamb was thoroughly aroused now. For so
many excellent reasons he found himslf weary of this
woman and all her false standards of life. He was
standing by the goldfish aquarium looking down absently at its four occupants, three fish and one diminu-
tive but aged turtle.

"Doesn't that damned old turtle ever budge himself?" his subconscious mind was asking, while quite
consciously he continued deliberately on with his wife.

"And here's another thing to worry about," he
heard himself saying "It's highly possible for me to re-

turn home some morning in the early hours in the guise of a famished tiger, an undernourished wolf, a man-eating shark, a wild boar, a—a—" He paused to give himself time to think of some particularly disagreeable animal. "—a crocodile," he resumed triumphantly. "And if that frail lily of yours should chance to be in my bed I'd gnash him up like that and gladly pay for the subsequent nausea his presence in my belly would cause me. How'd you like to come vamping into my room in that decrepit way of yours to find all that remained of Mr. Gray was only a couple of corns dangling between my jaws? A pretty picture? But a possible one, and you'd be responsible for the death of the Woodbine Players' worst actor just as sure as I'm standing here."

The picture of Leonard Gray's corns dangling between the dripping jaws of a crocodile proved too much for Mrs. Lamb. She turned her back upon her terrifying husband and covered her face with her hands. A sudden liquid plop startled her into reversing her position. Mr. Lamb was no longer there. Amazingly, the potential crocodile had vanished. His last words, she remembered, had been, "just as sure as I'm standing here," but the man was not standing there, and Mrs. Lamb seriously doubted if he ever had stood there.

The confused woman was about to hurry from the room when her eyes were drawn to the aquarium where a fourth and larger goldfish was chasing the other three round the tank in frantic circles.

Recalling the liquid plop she had heard, Mrs. Lamb slowly and thoughtfully left the room. A sweet, womanly little plan was buzzing in her mind. As she prepared herself for bed she wondered idly how Lady Macbeth undressed while engaged in perfecting one of her many dirty tricks.

While this dramatic disrobing was in progress Mr. Lamb, with an exasperated nose, was busily budging the turtle over the floor of the aquarium. When the little russet man had taken a sudden fancy to change him into a goldfish there still had been a number of things on Mr. Lamb's mind he had wanted to say to

his wife. Now he was taking his irritation out on the
turtle.

"Never thought of a goldfish," Lamb said to himself.
"From a crocodile to one of these made-up
sardines. . . . What a let-down!"

He gave the turtle an especially vicious budge.

"Get a move on," he muttered. "Shake a leg, you
old scrow. Show us what you look like inside. Out with
your head."

After many disturbing budges, the ancient turtle protruded his neck and, looking resentfully at Mr. Lamb,
gave utterance to the equivalent of:

"What in hell, may I ask, do you think you're trying
to do with me? This is a private home. Flip on."

"I won't flip on," replied Lamb. "And I'm going to
budge you to my heart's content. Are you so con-
founded thick-shelled you don't know when you're
being budged?"

"I know when I'm being budged, all right," retorted
the turtle, "and I know when I'm not being budged,
but what I don't know is what purpose all this budging
is going to serve. I never have dealings with goldfish.
We're not on the same level."

"No," replied Lamb, "you're on the lower level."

"Now low enough for you," said the turtle.

"You should be delighted I even budge you," answered Mr. Lamb.

"I'm not delighted," said the turtle. "And I hate ostentation."

"I'm only a goldfish pro tem," offered Mr. Lamb.
"Tomorrow I may be a zebra."

"There's no such thing as a zebra," the turtle retorted. "It's all a lie—the whole sordid story."

This fruitless conversation did not serve to restore
Mr. Lamb's good humor. The turtle, he decided was
just about as opinionated and ignorant as the seagull
who had so revoltingly invited him to eat fertilizer.

"Don't make a display of your vast ignorance," said
Mr. Lamb. "I myself have seen any number of zebras."

"Show me only one," challenged the turtle.

"There aren't any zebras here," replied Mr. Lamb.

"That proves it," said the turtle with a nasty laugh.

"That makes a liar of you. The first thing I know you'll be trying to tell me there's such a thing as a lion."

"Got you!" cried Lamb exultantly. "If there aren't any lions, how did you know their name?"

"I didn't say I did," replied the turtle. "Good night. I loathe a liar."

With this he withdrew not only his head but also his four feet.

"Budge and be damned," came through the slit in his shell. "I'm going to sleep."

"You've never been awake," Mr. Lamb threw back, as he flipped himself to the surface of the tank.

"All goldfish are living lies," the turtle shouted after him, popping his head from his shell. "There's not a gram of gold in the whole silly mess of 'em. Just try to spend one, and see how much change you get back . . . not even a slim sardine."

Lamb dived swiftly back and made a vicious snap at the turtle's head, which was neatly withdrawn.

"I hope your stomach turns up before dawn," he bubbled through his shell.

"I'd like to meet you in a plate of soup," was the best Mr. Lamb could offer on the spur of the moment.

Still in an evil mood Mr. Lamb swaggered up to the goldfish now huddled in a corner and, singling out one of them, addressed himself to it.

"What sort of fish are you?" he demanded truculently. "Male or female?"

"Female," snapped the goldfish, "for all the good it will do you."

"Hold on, baby," said Mr. Lamb. "I'm a fast and ruthless worker. No morals at all. I take my fun where I find it, and I find lots."

"Well, don't feel funny round here," the other retorted. "Go somewhere else and grab off your fun."

Mr. Lamb regarded her broodingly for a minute.

"The lot of you get out of this corner," he said at last. "I sleep here."

He chased the goldfish to the other end of the tank and swayed moodily off to sleep, thinking disagreeably about his wife. He strongly suspected that the good lady was planning something, that if she could only muster sufficient evidence to prove that he turned into things she would try to obtain a divorce. It would make a pretty case, one of the most unusual in the history of that splendid institution. Mr. Lamb did not object to being divorced. To him it was an end highly to be desired. But he did object to being divorced on the grounds of being a kangaroo or a horse or a seagull. That would be just a trifle too sensational for him.

His life as a goldfish was not a constant round of revelry, and he was forced to resort to various little devices to keep himself from being too oppressively bored.

His first effort in this direction was extremely elaborate and gave him no little satisfaction. He had discovered that by rubbing his nose against the side of the tank he was able to trace a clear impression which would, under favorable conditions, remain visible for a few minutes. This opened up rare possibilities. Mr. Lamb wondered why other goldfish had not hit upon the idea before. He began by tracing letters much in the manner of a sky-writer, and at last succeeded in mastering the art of writing backwards. After much practice he became highly proficient, so much so, in fact that he felt himself qualified to give a public demonstration.

One evening when Leonard Gray was dining at the house for the further development of his art, Hebe called the attention of that gentleman and her mother to the strange behavior of the new goldfish, which Mrs. Lamb for purposes of her own, claimed to have purchased.

"Why, that new goldfish is actually tracing letters on the side of the tank," announced the acute Hebe. "Look, everybody! It seems to be trying to write something."

Everybody looked, including Thomas and one of the maids. All eyes grew wide with surprise, some even with consternation, when they spelled out the boldly written word:

ADULTERER

It is perhaps not edifying to record that the youngest person present was the one least shocked. With amused eyes Hebe looked from one face to another.

"Now I wonder," she said musingly, "just who that fish is panning. Are you by chance an adulterer, Thomas?"

Thomas looked really pleased.

"While my wife was alive, Miss Hebe," he explained, "she was a just but exacting woman. I had neither the time nor the energy, miss."

"I understand and sympathize, Thomas," the girl continued. "Well, how about you, Nora?"

"Why, Miss Hebe," Nora faltered, quite red but undismayed, "you know very well I'm not married."

"You win on a technicality," said Hebe. "Neither am I married, so a little possible adulteration lies for us in the future. Leonard, you don't need to be married, so that leaves only—"

"Hebe!" cried Mrs. Lamb, her voice well out of control. "Please bring this farce to an end. Immediately!"

Mr. Lamb, seeing that his efforts had not gone unrewarded, cut jubilant capers across the surface of the tank and before the dinner was over achieved the following cryptic warning:

KEEP OUT OF MY BED

Again Hebe made sure that this feat, though clearly unappreciated by her mother and Mr. Gray, did not pass unread by them.

From this point on, conversation became a matter of eloquent silence pierced by furtive glances. It is to be doubted if either Mrs. Lamb or her leading man was aware of what they were eating. Mechanically they masticated, sedulously averting their eyes from the tank containing the loquacious goldfish.

Later that night when Sandra Rush and Melville Long dropped in, Hebe introduced them to the remarkable goldfish, who with great speed and celerity traced on the side of the tank:

JAILBIRDS

He also attempted to flip some water in Sandra's face with his tail, but only succeeded in spotting her dress.

"It's the attenuated one all right," replied Sandra, "but very much compressed. I recognize his feeble sense of humor. Let's take him out and make him gasp a bit."

She made a snatch at the goldfish, but some clever fin work sent him to the floor of the tank where he remained craftily alert. Hebe stood considering the goldfish with an unusually serious expression. Long, taking note of this novel manifestation, asked the reason for it.

"Sapho says she bought him herself," replied Hebe. "Wonder why she claims that?"

Sandra looked at her quickly with large, comprehending eyes.

"Perhaps she intends to do in earnest what I suggested in fun," she said. "You'll have to stand guard over that goldfish, Hebe. Perhaps your little russet friend didn't foresee such a possibility as this. The attenuated one is quite defenseless now."

Sandra, too, was a little more serious than was her wont. For a long time she stood looking down at the goldfish lurking at the bottom of the tank.

"How long do you suppose this animal stuff is going to continue?" she asked of no one in particular. "It would be nice if he remainded himself for a while, so that a person could get to know him."

The following evening Mr. Lamb arranged still another little diversion for the edification of his wife. When she put in an appearance for dinner she found him floating gruesomely with his belly prominently displayed for all the world to see. The other goldfish, huddled in a corner, seemed to be regarding the corpse with frightened eyes.

An expression of gratitude to God escaped the lips of the fish's wife. He had spared her the annoyance of being a murderess. The happy woman raised up her voice and called for aid.

"Hebe!" she cried. "Nora! My poor goldfish is dead."

When these witnesses had been summoned to her side Mrs. Lamb proceeded to do a thing that revolted her every instinct.

"See," she said in a voice of anguish as she dipped her hand in the water, "the beautiful thing must have died. What a pity, and what a darling he was!"

"You'll look swell in mourning," observed Hebe, closely scrutinizing the goldfish. "Are you going to give it a church funeral?"

"Don't be silly, Hebe," she replied casting her daughter an uneasy look. "This is no time for humor."

To hold the fish either dead or in the full flower of youth is not one of life's most reposeful moments—not for the vast majority of normally constituted persons. Mrs. Lamb, though not normally constituted, felt far from well when she fished the slithery body of her husband from the water.

"Nora!" she cried. "Get something to put him in . . . the garbage can."

"Him?" inquired Hebe mildly. "Do you know that fish's sex?"

It was at this moment that Mr. Lamb decided it was about time to stop playing dead. He had sacrificed for his art practically all the breath he could well afford to lose. If he ever got into the garbage can he felt sure he would sacrifice his entire quota. Therefore, with an artful wriggle, he flipped himself from the delicate grasp of his wife and plopped gratefully back into the water.

When Nora returned with a coffee-strainer held diffidently in her hand she had the joy of seeing the goldfish sporting briskly about in his temporarily natural element.

Mrs. Lamb was not able to dine. She was revolted as well as disappointed. When she attempted to express her profound pleasure at the restoration of the goldfish to its former good health and spirits her voice choked with the insincerity of her emotion.

Naturally this altogether uncalled-for conduct on the part of a goldfish did not pass unnoticed by his colleagues in the tank. Their first attitude of fear passed to one of pity, for they felt that the poor fish was indeed a child of God, more than a little cracked about the gills. This attitude, however, soon gave place to one of admiration when they realized that there was a method behind the apparent madness of this resourceful companion of theirs. The lady goldfish, taking Mr. Lamb at his word, gave evidence of the sincerity of her admiration by suggesting the production of goldfish on a modest scale. Mr. Lamb toyed with the idea, but realizing he might be a bull or a zebra by the time his progeny were goldfish, the incongruity of the situation robbed it of its attractiveness.

He succeeded in teaching them to swim in formation like airplanes, putting them through loops, nose dives and tail spins. The servants could hardly be driven away from the tank so great was their interest in these aquatic displays. The climax was reached one morning when the four goldfish were discovered solemnly swimming backwards round their tank. There was no ostentation about this performance, no suggestion of a desire to please or to attract attention. It was as if overnight the fish had come to the decision that it was about time to reverse the order of things. They merely swam backwards with a naturalness that would have led one to believe that fish had always swum backwards from the infancy of Noah.

It was difficult to serve breakfast that morning through Nora's inability to keep her attention fixed on her ordered duties. Even the impeccable Thomas seemed a trifle vague and preoccupied. Mrs. Lamb endeavored to ignore the goldfish, but Hebe's cheers of enthusiasm made it hard to pretend that all was not as usual.

The turtle was disgusted. When Mr. Lamb with pardonable pride asked him what he thought about it he replied that it was "Silly damn rot," and that no good came from going against the laws of nature.

With the turtle Mr. Lamb could find no point of agreement. They began to argue and bicker whenever they tried to converse. The turtle insisted on criticizing the furniture and appointments of the dining-room. He was particularly sarcastic about the design of the rug. Mr. Lamb naturally took this to heart, the dining-room being more or less his, and although he was not responsible for its arrangements he found himself defending them with the fervor of a zealot. To hear him argue with the turtle one would have thought that Mr. Lamb had personally selected each article of furniture in the room. Relations between the two were finally broken off when the turtle referred in the most disparaging language to a "long drink of water," who used to be seen hanging about the place and whose absence he noted with gratification. Mr. Lamb, fully appreciating the fact that he himself was the long drink of water in question, cursed the turtle roundly and was in turn as roundly cursed.

The fat was in the fire when Mr. Lamb wrote one evening for the benefit of his wife the following disquieting announcement:

TODAY A FISH: TOMORROW A SNAKE

Upon reading this warning Mrs. Lamb realized that it was high time to act. Her husband as a snake would be a far different matter from her husband as a goldfish. She nerved herself for action, endeavoring to absorb into her spirit the murky mood of Lady Macbeth on one of her bad days.

When the household was quiet that night she corded her dressing-gown round her waist and crept downstairs. For a wonder Mr. Lamb was actually asleep and balanced on an even keel in his own private corner. This time Mrs. Lamb's hand was swift and sure. With a sharp intake of breath, she seized her unsuspecting husband and carried him to the kitchen. Here she looked desperately about for something in which to put him—not the garbage can, for his remains might be discovered there and the crime traced to her. Mrs. Lamb wanted a modest but secure sarcophagus for the body of her husband. An empty sardine tin would have done splendidly. A soda box would have been a great help at the moment. She was even considering the possibilities of squeezing him into a small bottle when Mr. Lamb made an energetic flip for liberty and life. The flip was only partially successful. It transferred him from Mrs. Lamb's hand to Mrs. Lamb's stomach where he continued his flipping, the cord round his wife's waist successfully preventing further descent.

Mrs. Lamb was no fit woman. She is not to be blamed. No woman is quite at her best with a wet and determined goldfish flipping clammily against her stomach. It is to be doubted if many men would have retained the stoicism and dignity of the more insensitive male under the same circumstances.

The picture Mrs. Lamb presented was that of an utterly abandoned muscle dancer, one thoroughly interested in her profession. It was an animated picture. Nor was it unaccompanied by sound. Little ecstatic cries, sharp exclamations, gasps of vital anguish fell from the convulsive lady's lips. They made the picture complete. At least so thought Hebe as she stood in the doorway and witnessed her mother's contortions.

Then before the girl's startled eyes an amazing thing took place. She saw Mrs. Lamb suddenly bulge to almost twice her size. She heard the rip of her nightdress, and before she had time to realize exactly what she was witnessing, she saw her flat on her back on the kitchen floor and her father, dripping wet, standing beside her. The little russet man had not deserted him. Mr. Lamb had been saved in very much less than the nick of time.

Mr. Lamb was breathing hard and apparently his wife was not breathing at all. When she did breathe it was to give utterance to a wild cry.

"Murder!" she announced. "Murder! Your father's trying to strangle me."

"You damn near did strangle me," said Mr. Lamb.

He turned and grinned at his daughter.

"Hebe," he continued, "be a good girl and mix me a stiff drink. You may have one for yourself if you feel like it. These lightning changes are not so good for the nerves."

He extended a hand and helped his wife from the floor.

"Sorry, Sapho," he remarked apologetically, "but I could never fit in that bottle now."

Sapho was beyond speech.

Having failed lamentably to emulate the example of

Lady Macbeth, the wife of the ex-fish felt that at least she could follow her advice. She stayed not on the order of her going, but went at once. Mr. Lamb picked up the bottle and considered it with a peculiar feeling.

"This," he said, extending the bottle to Hebe, "was intended to be your father's last resting place. I might have been a bottle baby, but be damned if I'll be a bottled corpse."

"Maybe the next time she'll have to use a cage," suggested Hebe.

"Perhaps," said her father dryly, "but you can use the bottle now."

Hebe did.

CHAPTER XV

Sandy Gets Her Man

MR. LAMB WAS NOT IN THE PINK. HE HAD RETURNED from his office far from well either mentally or physically. His life as a goldfish had not improved his health. He had absorbed too much stale water and overlooped a bit. Furthermore, the requirements of constantly readjusting himself were proving altogether too exacting.

Brother Douglas, fresh from a convention of the Directors of American Youth, handed him a letter. Without comment he received it and began to read. Hebe watched her father. When he had finished the letter he swore more from amazement than anger.

"Listen to this," he said. "It's good."

Then he began to read:

"I can no longer live under the same roof with a murderer. Therefore I fly. I have stood every humiliation, every form of abuse, but I do not feel called upon to sacrifice my life for a man who turns into various things at a moment's notice. My life is in danger, therefore I fly. Do not attempt to find me. Do not attempt to follow. I fly. Pursuit is in vain. This is the end."

A dazzled silence followed the reading of this tragic epistle. It was broken by Mr. Lamb.

"Now, who in hell," he asked almost pleadingly, "does she expect to follow her?"

"I'm glad she remembered to send love and kisses to her unnatural daughter," said Hebe.

Douglas got up and began to whistle, "All Alone on the Telephone."

Mr. Lamb looked at him and grinned.

"Douglas," he asked, "how do you manage to be such a damn fool without ever an intermission?"

Brother Dug looked back at Mr. Lamb and also grinned.

"I was merely trying to keep you from breaking down," he replied. "When face to face with tragedy, sing, whistle or do both. Hebe, play something on the piano, and we'll all have a bit of a song."

Without a word Hebe went to the piano and struck a resounding chord. Had Mrs. Lamb not been so busy flying she would have had the pleasure of hearing floating through the windows of her abandoned home the words and music of the old familiar hymn, "Praise God From Whom All Blessings Flow." The voices of the three singers blended rather well, and the rendition of the hymn was marked by a certain sincerity of feeling not always to be found in church.

"Well, Douglas," asked Mr. Lamb, when the hymn had been brought to a crashing climax, "are you going to desert us now?"

"No," said Douglas, displaying an unexpected streak of embarrassment. "That is, not unless you want me. I'm a little too fat for flying, and I'm sure no one really wants to murder me, although once I was pretty nearly scared to death."

When he made this reply he carefully avoided looking at Mr. Lamb.

"Such loyalty, not to mention heroism, calls for one drink at the very least," said Hebe. "Perhaps more."

They had more.

When dinner was served Mr. Lamb looked beamingly upon Thomas.

"Thomas," he said, "Mrs. Lamb may not be with us for some time to come. Her presence is indefinitely postponed."

For once Thomas was taken off his guard. With eager hands he hastened to the table and started to remove the absent lady's plate as if to make sure of his master's statement. His face was alight with pleasure. Mr. Lamb's voice interrupted his activities.

"Not so ruthless, Thomas," he admonished. "You needn't do it now. Just remember it in the future. And Thomas," he added, "is there any of the old stock left, the wine you drank in the days of my youth?"

"I didn't think you remembered, sir," replied the old man.

"Unfortunately for you I did," said Mr. Lamb.

"There are some bottles," said Thomas. "A few, sir."

"One," his master ordered.

Thomas departed under full sail. As Nora hurried past him in the pantry she felt herself unexpectedly pinched and heard him humming a song he had unearthed from some dim recess of his memory.

"I'll get the evening out for that," this highly competent maid confidently promised herself.

As Mr. Lamb sat at dinner his eyes kept constantly straying to the aquarium where the three goldfish he had come to know so well were drifting drowsily about as if in languid expectation of a lost leader. It gave him a feeling of satisfaction to know that his old enemy, the turtle, was once again forced to peer out at the "long drink of water" he had spoken of so disparagingly. Impulsively Lamb rose from the table and with his knife budged the old fellow across the bottom of the tank.

"How indignant he must be," thought Mr. Lamb. "I only wish he could appreciate the full flavor of the situation."

Then he singled out the lady goldfish and considered her for a moment.

"I might have been the father of her children," he mused as he returned to the table. "That would have been a pretty state of affairs."

Throughout the remainder of the dinner he could not shake off the weird knowledge that only a short time ago he had been swimming about in that tank and looking out at his wife and daughter and the ubiquitous Mr. Gray. It would be difficult, he decided, for the little russet man to provide for him a more novel experience. Lamb heartily hoped it would be the last. He was more than willing now to remain a normal human being for the rest of his life. His desire to remain himself was greatly intensified now that his wife was absent, permanently absent, he hoped. This line of thought automatically brought him round to Sandra Rush, and a dark, brooding look came into his eyes.

He recalled her faraway expression when she had watched the scenery that morning on the train, and the story she had told him about the two little ponds. She was not always depraved. Sometimes she could be quite decent. Very seldom though. Mostly mad and wild and reckless.

"Too old," he said, unconsciously speaking aloud. "Too damn old."

"Beg your pardon, sir," said Thomas. "Is the chicken too tough for you?"

"Chicken's fine," replied Mr. Lamb. "Why?"

"I thought I heard you say it was too old, sir," said Thomas. "I felt sure it was about the suitable age, sir."

"But I'm not, Thomas," Mr. Lamb replied. "I'm too damn old. Don't you think so?"

"That depends," answered Thomas consideringly. "Too old for what, if I may ask, sir?"

"Oh, go to the devil, you fossilized lump of sin," said Mr. Lamb. "I didn't mean six-day bicycle racing."

"Well you might be a few years over for that," was the imperturbable decision of Thomas, "but you're still good for your share of—er—sport, if I make myself clear, sir."

"Most delicately so, Thomas," put in Hebe. "I quite agree with you. It pleases our major to believe that he is of ancient vintage. By cultivating that frame of mind he hopes to escape adventure."

"I've had adventures enough, God knows," said Mr. Lamb.

"But not of the nature I mean," responded his daughter. "Those still lie ahead."

"There's not much good in either of you," declared Mr. Lamb, putting down his coffee cup. "You'll excuse me now if I retire to my study. Douglas, I hope you'll remain uncorrupted now that your sister is no longer here to protect you."

"I have nothing to fear in that line," observed Douglas. "My adventures lie neither behind me nor before. That's one of the tragedies of a fat man."

"He throbs out his sex in song," said Hebe, as Mr. Lamb left the room.

Retrieving the much interrupted Kai Lung, Mr.

Lamb elaborately arranged himself in his chair and prayed to God that he should be allowed to proceed at least a few pages in the book before he was transformed into another animal, bird, reptile, or fish. He had read exactly two paragraphs when the door flew open and Sandra burst into the room.

"I thought you'd be glad to see me," she cried, standing radiantly before him.

"What led you to form that totally erroneous impression?" asked Mr. Lamb, looking at the girl over the top of his book.

"Why, Sapho's decamped," she went on happily. "And now everything's going to be all right."

"All right for what?" Mr. Lamb demanded unbendingly.

"For us," said Sandy breathlessly. "The coast is clear."

"It isn't at all clear to me," Mr. Lamb replied. "What form of depravity are you now suggesting?"

"Any and all," said Sandra. "You're my man now."

In spite of himself Mr. Lamb could not repress a grin.

"Get the hell out of here," was all he said.

"Put me out," she challenged.

"Go on," warned Mr. Lamb. "Get the hell out."

"Get the hell me out if you can," she answered.

Mr. Lamb rose slowly and stood over the girl. Quite deliberately, quite effortlessly, he picked her up in his arms and held her suspended.

"I don't know whether to spank or to kiss you," he remarked, looking unsmilingly down into her deep and disturbingly provocative eyes.

"I'm all set for a little of both," said Sandy.

Lamb did the latter. He did it extremely well, so well, in fact, that Thomas, entering with a decanter of whisky, remained unnoticed in the doorway. Quietly the old fellow closed the door and seated himself on one of the dining-room chairs, a liberty he had never taken. Then he raised the decanter to his lips and drank a silent toast. Things were indeed looking up in the house of Lamb.

Somewhat subdued, Sandra and Mr. Lamb were sitting a little later on the private veranda adjoining his study.

"I hope you don't turn into a bear," said Sandra.

"I hope I've done my last turn," said Mr. Lamb.

"So do I," she answered. "I'd hate to lose you now."

Mr. Lamb turned in his chair and found her eyes in the darkness.

"You're sure you're not kidding me?" he asked. "You know you're such an exaggerated person. I'm never sure whether you're making fun of me or not. You see, I'm not used to young girls. I've always been sort of out of it and faithful—not to her so much as to myself. This thing sort of puzzles me. I don't see where I get off with a fine-looking girl like you. Old enough to be your father."

There was something so utterly helpless and fumbling in this speech of Mr. Lamb's, something so amazingly innocent and sincere that Sandra for no reason that she could fathom felt very much like crying. Dimly she sensed the repressed youth and longing behind the unappetizing years through which this long, sardonic, quietly observant man by her side had lived. While his wife had been mouthing about beauty and living quite an unbeautiful life, he had just grinned his slow, irritating grin and silently kept on wanting. And being decent and rather commonplace. Yes, Sandra was more than sure that she was not kidding. But she did not reply to his question. She did not want to hear her own voice. She merely reached out and taking his long, lean hand, held it against her breast.

Way down below them in the darkness the lights of the town lay against the other side of the valley. Even the blot contributed its share to the general illumination.

Mr. Lamb was not unhappy. Neither was the girl. Both were silent. It seemed better so.

Some hours later when Thomas was pouring Mr. Lamb his invariable nightcap, the old servant paused with the decanter half raised and regarded this man whose toys he had once mended.

"You're fit as a fiddle, Mr. Lawrence," he offered.

"Even for bicycle racing, or I am very much mistaken, sir."

"What leads you to believe that, Thomas?" Mr. Lamb asked suspiciously.

"General observations, sir," said Thomas. "General observation. Nothing more, sir. Good night."

Leaving Mr. Lamb slightly puzzled, Thomas with an annoyingly self-satisfied expression, quietly withdrew.

"Now, I'm in a devil of a mess," thought Mr. Lamb, as he pondered cheerfully over his glass.

Even Kai Lung lay forgotten upon his knee.

CHAPTER XVI

Less Than the Dust

WHEN MR. LAMB WOKE UP NEXT MORNING HE WAS AS sick as a dog. And he was a dog. Weakly he flopped himself out of bed and crawled across the room to his mirror. He had not the vaguest idea of what he was. He knew he was something. He knew he was not himself. He was some sort of four-footed animal with fur, and from the looks of his feet Mr. Lamb felt convinced that he could not be much of an animal.

"That looking-glass," he thought to himself, "has reflected many weird and startling images, but this time I think it's going to get the shock of its life. So, perhaps, am I."

Lamb was right. The most woebegone, flop-eared, putty-footed, miscellaneous assortment of canine maladjustments leered out at him from the mirror.

On previous occasions the little russet man had always done well by Mr. Lamb. He had been the best of everything, no matter what it was. He had been an imposing stallion, a bang-up seagull, a two-fisted kangaroo, and a goldfish of note. Now, however, he was the worst dog he had ever seen, obviously the son of a mother who had possessed an unlimited capacity for experimentation, relieved by a certain jocular capriciousness.

Of this dog confronting him, Lamb recognized little of himself save perhaps a broodingly speculative cast of the eye. His ears were long, spiritless, and yellow, seemingly sewed onto his head as an afterthought. His hair grew over his black and tan body in unbecoming fits and starts, first here and then there. He was a tufted dog. His feet were large and woolly. They splayed out in front, giving him the appearance of

149

wearing old turned-up carpet-slippers. He was a long, low, ribby dog. One side of his face was black, the other side yellow. Along his body this color scheme had been reversed. He would have made a striking model for a woman's bathing costume, his haunches being black and yellow and his chest yellow and black. Taking him all in all he was a dog to give one pause, a dog to walk around and speculate upon, one to examine in detail at close range and then to view from afar for a full effect.

Mr. Lamb did not regard himself in this light. Sick as he felt, his heart was filled with shame. He had a desire to crawl away to some quiet place and there to make an end of it all. Life which last night had tasted so sweet now lay sour in his mouth. His long, thin, spineless tail drooped despondently on the floor.

"I can't possibly let myself be seen in this appalling condition," he decided, as he placed a mop of a paw against his swimming head.

When he had retired the previous evening he had known he was going to be ill, but he had not taken into consideration the fact that he was also going to be a dog—and such a dog as he had turned out to be.

Because of the absence of his wife he had allowed the door between the two rooms to remain open. With a loose, uncoordinated motion he shuffled through and by a little clever, but exhausting manipulation got himself out into the hall. Downstairs he found an open window through which he made a furtive and inglorious exit, landing with a thud on the grass. For a moment he lay there painfully recovering his breath and strength, then he shambled weakly off across the lawn, his body aching and tongue lolling out.

Hebe from her window witnessed the departure of this unfortunate-looking animal, little realizing that it was her father she saw, fleeing to escape the eyes of those who knew him.

Mr. Lamb has only the haziest memory of what occurred to him after leaving his home. Certain episodes stand out in his mind like flashes caught from a fast-fading dream.

He recalled, for instance, slinking along the shadowy

side of the road until he came to a rustic bridge where
two men were holding a heated debate upon religion,
the day being Sunday and their flasks potent with applejack. Here in an unneeded little patch of sunlight
Mr. Lamb lay down to rest and to warm himself a bit.

"Believe in your miracles if you will," one of the re-
ligious fanatics was saying, "but as for me I think
they're a lot of apple-sauce invented by a gang of graft-
ing old prophets who couldn't even predict the next
day's weather."

"Sure they could," said the other. "Didn't they call
the turn on many a blight and famine? You should
read about all the things they figgered out—floods, pes-
tilence, the destruction of towns, battles and alarms
and—and—all sorts of calamities."

"They must have been a cheerful little bunch of pre-
dicters," observed the unbeliever ironically. "Didn't
they ever say something pleasant?"

The other paused to consider this difficult question.
It was a bit of a poser for him, yet he felt duty-bound
to stand up for the prophets. Suddenly his face cleared.
Light had been given him.

"Sure they did," he answered. "Judgment Day."

"A very pleasant day that'll be," said the other. "Especially for you. And if they did, it was guesswork,
pure guesswork."

He took a swig at his flask and looked triumphantly
at his friend, then let his gaze drift to the dog lying
huddled up in the grass and leaves.

"Well, if all them things weren't miracles," the de-
fender of the faith demanded, "just what would you
call a miracle?"

"This is what I'd call a miracle," was the other
man's ready relpy. "If that there mut should get up
right now and, putting his nose in the center of this
bridge, make a complete circle with his awful-looking
body that would be some miracle."

Sick as he was, Mr. Lamb could not resist the temptation. He got up and walked to the center of the
bridge. Then placing his nose down in the dust he held
it firmly in position and described a complete circle
with his body. With his nose still in place he rolled up

his eyes to see if he had produced the desired effect or if he should continue on. The men were stunned. They returned the dog's inquiring gaze with eyes full of applejack, wonder, and trepidation. The unbeliever was actually frightened. He took another pull at his flask and timidly fixed his eyes on the dog. Mr. Lamb once more deliberately described a circle and sat down in the middle of it, holding up one paw as if in benediction.

"God Almighty, it's a miracle," breathed the unbeliever. "Do you think we should kneel down and pray?"

"Let's get rid of these flasks," suggested his friend. "It doesn't look quite right."

The two men tossed their flasks in the bushes, then looked at Mr. Lamb for some sign of approval. Mr. Lamb nodded his head three times, rose and shambled weakly down the road. The men gazed after the retreating dog until a turn in the road hid him from view. For a moment they looked silently at each other, then like the vast majority of converts, they backslid completely and, diving into the bushes, returned with their flasks, which they drained with great speed and dexterity. By nightfall they were telling their friends about a dog that sang hymns and preached sermons.

Mr. Lamb's next memory is not so pleasant. It was night and he was standing on the lawn of a low, rambling, brightly lighted house. Shouts and laughter came through the windows. Someone was singing, or trying to sing, "Frankie and Johnny." Behind the house was a background of high black trees. They were silent as if listening.

Lamb dragged himself to the porch and peered through the open door. He saw three women and four men sprawled about the place in attitudes of drunken abandon. One of the men was propped up in a narrow, lounge bed. Although the night was warm, a bathrobe was thrown round his shoulders. He was coughing and smoking and drinking. From time to time he would call to one of the women, apparently his wife, and ask her to replenish his glass. Apart from this tender attention the woman gave scant care to the sick man. She was completely wrapped up in a tall, languid-looking person, and she was drunk enough to show it. Her form of love-making consisted in displaying her legs and contradicting everything said by the object of her affection. Gin and whisky bottles and overturned glasses were everywhere in evidence. From time to time violent quarrels would break out between one of the couples, and then the air was filled with abuse and recrimination.

"Lower away," called the sick man at last to his wife, pointing to her bare thighs.

"Aw, don't be an old woman," she answered across the room, as she lolled back on a couch with her evening's selection. "Everybody knows I got legs. What's wrong in taking things easy?"

Then she proceeded to tell the entire room just how jealous her husband was, and quoted some remarks he had made about one of the men present.

Mr. Lamb crept across the floor and seated himself by the sick man's couch. The sick man reached down and fondled one of the dog's long, aimless ears. No one else seemed to pay any attention to Mr. Lamb. They were all too busy with their own affairs. When the sick man's eyes looked down into his, Mr. Lamb read nothing in them but drunken despair.

"This is not going to be so good," said Mr. Lamb to himself. "This man is not only sick and drunk but also nearly out of his mind with jealousy. Can't say that I blame him. Something is going to happen."

For a moment he saw the dark, brooding trees waiting and listening behind the house.

Presently the sick man called to another girl. He whispered something in her ear, and she brought him a bottle of gin which he kept by his side, drinking the stuff raw from time to time. He was very drunk now, hardly able to see. Opposite him on another couch his wife was openly kissing her companion. The room had grown quiet. Some of the lights had been turned out.

In the stillness could be heard the broken voice of the sick man trying to sing a nursery song:

"'To bed. To bed,' said Sleepy Head
'Let's tarry a while,' said Slow."

The song seemed plaintively incongruous in that unhealthy setting. The girl who had brought him the bottle of gin was kissing her partner and crying at the same time.

Mr. Lamb was beginning to feel decidedly uncomfortable, but some instinct kept him by the side of his companion. Coughing violently, the man reached down for the bottle, groped about until he had found it, then raised it to his lips. When he took it away the bottle was empty and the man's face was bathed in sweat. A broken sound came from his chest.

" 'To bed. To bed,' said Sleepy Head." The voice stopped and the man slumped forward. He stopped coughing.

His wife looked at him for some minutes, then turned to her friend and nodded. They rose and quickly passed through a door leading to a dark room. Half an hour passed, and still the drunken man did not stir. One hand hung limply over the side of his couch. Mr. Lamb sniffed it and suddenly crouched back. He knew that the man was dead.

When the wife returned with her partner, her eyes dark, heavy, and drunken, his sleepily triumphant, she went over and shook her husband by the shoulders.

"Wake up, old woman!" she cried. "You're missing all the fun."

Mr. Lamb crouched cold with the horror of the situation.

"Why, the old woman's dead-drunk," his wife announced, as the dead man slid over on the couch. "Come on everybody, let's have some fun. The killjoy's through for the night."

With this she took a drink of gin, and pulling up her already short skirts, threw her arms round her lover's neck and danced madly about the room. The others followed her example.

More drinks and more dancing. A girl went over to the still figure on the couch and took its hand. She gave a start, and bent over to examine its face, feeling the cold skin with trembling fingers. Then she hurriedly called one of the men to her and together they examined the crumpled form. The man placed a hand over the stopped heart. When he rose his face was white.

"You tell her," was all he said.

"Come here," called the girl to the wife.

"Like hell," she replied. "I'm comfortable here on the couch. He'll sleep all night. Let him alone."

She took a drink from a bottle and swayed back on the couch. She was head down in gin. The other girl approached and stood looking down at the two locked figures.

"Your husband is quite dead," she said quietly.

"Come again," replied the other, sitting up and holding her head in her hands. "Dead, you say?"

Then she began to laugh.

"Dead, you say? God, that's funny! He would do a thing like that. Always spoiling a party."

Day was breaking, and as Mr. Lamb slipped through it he kept hearing the dead man singing, " 'To bed. To bed,' said Sleepy Head."

Mr. Lamb next remembers himself lying weak from exhaustion and nausea in the sunlight before a small cottage. Through the door he could see a man and his wife facing each other across the breakfast table. A good-looking couple, but hostile. Their eyes met with studied indifference. No words were exchanged between them. When the man rose to get his hat a new expression came into the woman's eyes as she furtively followed his movements. There was in them something soft, a sort of silent cry. Without uttering a word of farewell, the man went to the door of the cottage, then stopped when he saw the sick dog. With a low murmur of friendship he bent over Mr. Lamb and lifted the weary head. Then the man brought the dog into the cottage.

With a bitter expression about her lips, the woman stood by the stove and watched her husband patting and fondling the dog. In one hand she held a pan of hot water. When the man asked her for some hot milk she shrugged her shoulders and turned away.

"Damn you," said the man in a low voice. "Get me some hot milk for the poor, sick creature."

Lamb hated hot milk, but appreciated the man's good intentions.

"Will you get that milk?" the man demanded, his voice still low and impersonal.

Suddenly the woman flared up and turned on her husband. Her face was white with something deeper than anger.

"No!" she cried, dashing the hot water over Mr. Lamb. "No! No! No!"

Mr. Lamb gave a low moan of pain, but made no move. His eyes were on the woman. She was trembling with the little shudders of revulsion. He saw the man spring forward and slap the woman sharply across the face. The woman swayed slightly, then stood quite still looking straight ahead of her, the same bitter smile fixed on her lips.

Then Mr. Lamb saw the man slowly turn his back upon the woman. His head dropped, and two tears trickled down his cheeks. His hands were clenched by his sides. Gradually the bitter smile melted from the woman's lips and in its place came a certain tenderness.

"Come here," she said at last, holding out her arms to the man. "Come here, come here to me."

And the man went to his wife's arms. She held him fiercely, and Lamb beheld her face with pleasure. A pretty woman she was, he thought, and well set up. Just a trifle too impulsive.

He stayed only long enough to show that there was no hard feeling, then quietly slipped away, leaving the man and his wife with their tongues at last unloosed. Once more he took to the road, feeling somewhat Boy Scoutish, having just performed his daily good deed.

Exactly when it was Lamb never rightly remembered. All he can recall is seeing a large, handsome hall with the open doors of a library at one end. He also recalls a wide stairway mounting up majestically to a balcony. A fine, lean, white-haired old gentleman was having a row with an equally fine and lean-looking son. Both were saying things they would regret the moment they were uttered.

"Your political ideas, like all your ideas, are

fallacious right through," the old man said. "Those
radical friends you are now cultivating should be taken
out and shot. Yes, sir! Shoot 'em down. They're Reds
. . . the scum. And furthermore they are not welcome
here. I forbid them the house."

"So I can't bring my friends into my own home," replied the young man, rising excitedly and facing his father. "Then it isn't a home of mine. I forbid myself the
house where my friends are not welcome."

The old gentleman stiffened. There was a cold smile
on his lips.

"Forbid and be damned," he said distinctly. "Go live
with the friends of your choice."

Without another word the young man raced up the
stairs. Mr. Lamb remembers watching from his place
of concealment the old gentleman's eyes as his son
rushed away. They were filled with anxiety and loneliness now that the mask of pride had been momentarily dropped. He paced up and down the heavy carpet,
opening and closing his hands helplessly. Now he
looked old indeed to Mr. Lamb—old and somewhat
smaller.

In a short time the boy returned with two suitcases,
and once more the old gentleman stiffened, forcing the
years and the loneliness back by an effort of his stub-
born old will, his pride of race and breeding, his belief
in lost traditions.

"You will not be inconvenienced any more," said the
young man. "Good-by, sir."

"Your consideration is appreciated," replied his father. "Good-by."

The young man looked back once, hesitated, but
seeing his father standing with his back to him, he
turned away and disappeared through a door in the
hall. The moment the door closed the old gentleman
altered his rodlike attitude and stood as if listening.
Presently he heard the hum of a motor, and something
like a sigh escaped his lips. He fumbled in a cigar box
and automatically selected a breva, then he sank to a
chair and looked dully at the unlighted cigar.

It was at this point that Mr. Lamb slipped out of his
corner and lurched to the gravel driveway. He did not

know what he was going to do, but he fully intended to do something. This silly impasse between the old fool and the young fool must be broken. He saw the glare of the headlights sweeping round the curve from behind the house, and he began to bark and howl the best he knew how. Dragging himself to the middle of the driveway, he pranced on his hind legs and waved his foolish-looking paws commandingly.

Too late. The lights swerved sharply. Mr. Lamb felt himself smashed and hurtled through the night. Then he heard the crash of the automobile as it collided with one of the trees on the lawn. Still Mr. Lamb retained consciousness.

He saw the old gentleman, followed by several servants, hurrying down the driveway.

"My boy," the old gentleman called through the darkness. "Are you hurt?"

"It's all right, dad," came the relieving response. "I'm looking for a poor mut I hit. Bear a hand and help me find him."

"It's a wonder your damn fool neck isn't broken," said the old gentleman, coming into the flood of the lights.

He put his arm round his son's shoulder.

"Sure?" he asked.

"Sure, sir," said his son. "But the mut is, I'm afraid. Odd acting dog. He seemed to be deliberately trying to stop the car."

"A good sort," said the old gentleman. "Hope we can patch him up."

With the aid of a flashlight, Mr. Lamb was eventually plucked from a bush. The old gentleman himself carried him into the house. A man was dispatched in another car for a doctor. Just before Mr. Lamb lost control of the situation, he had the pleasure of seeing two suitcases being carried up the broad stairs. Then Lamb for the nonce let the world go hang. It was too full of trouble for him. He could not be expected to arrange and settle everything.

When he once more favored the world with his presence, Mr. Lamb found himself on the clean, warm earth. He was in a sort of wired runway at the end of which was something that appeared to be a dog-house de luxe. A soft pillow was beneath his head, and a broken bandage trailed from his left foot. But what was more disconcerting still was the large, red face of a man in proximity to his.

"What did you want to get in here for," the face inquired reproachfully.

Mr. Lamb looked down at himself and realized with a start that he was no longer a dog. Once more he was Mr. T. Lawrence Lamb, a conservative investment banker in an extremely embarrassing position.

"I didn't want to get in here," was all he could think of replying. "Where in the deuce am I?"

"You're in one of the finest dog hospitals in the country," replied the face with pardonable pride. "One of the smartest and the swellest."

"That," said Mr. Lamb, "might make a profound impression on a dog, but it leaves me quite unelated. I don't want to be in a dog hospital no matter how swagger it may be."

"Then why did you get up out of bed and deliberately sneak over the wire in your pajamas?" asked the face.

It was true. Mr. Lamb was clad only in his sleeping togs. He had to admit that undeniable fact. But he very much disliked to be lying down on the flat of his back and talking up to that red face suspended above him like the sun.

"Listen," said Mr. Lamb, after a moment of swift considering. "If you'll only remove that face of yours I'll try to get up and talk to you on my feet."

The face was slowly and reluctantly withdrawn, and Mr. Lamb felt less like a bug under microscopic examination.

"Well?" said the wearer of the face, when Mr. Lamb stood confronting him.

"Ah yes," replied Mr. Lamb easily. "I was thrown in here."

The man looked more hurt than surprised.

"Come again," he remarked brutally.

"Very well," said Mr. Lamb. "I'm a somnambulist."

"That kind of talk ain't going to get you anywhere," replied the man.

"I'm a sleep-walker," explained Mr. Lamb.

"You're a damn poor liar," said the man.

"I'm doing the best I can," said Mr. Lamb. "Help me out, won't you?"

"What did you do with the dog?" the man demanded inflexibly.

"The dog must have gone out as I came in," said Mr. Lamb. "I never saw a dog. I was sound asleep."

"And snoring," supplied the man with heavy sarcasm.

"Now you're kidding me," said Mr. Lamb. "I'm serious."

"I know," replied the man. "That's what makes it so funny."

He looked up and down the runway.

"Well, the mut's gone," he remarked, "and it's good riddance of bad rubbish. Never had such a clown in our kennels before. It mortified me to have to look after him, he was that low-blooded. Some rich gentleman sent him to us."

Mr. Lamb had heard quite enough about the dog. He looked at himself in perplexity, then turned once more to the man.

"Listen here," he said, "we're getting nowhere this way. Lend me an overcoat and get me a taxi, and I'll write you a letter all about it . . . and the letter will have something in it much more interesting than news. Get me?"

The man got him. Also he got him an overcoat, something in the line of slippers, and a taxicab.

And, with the help of these, Mr. Lamb got home . . . gratefully, wearily and with the utmost discretion.

CHAPTER XVII

In Sandra's Bed

BEEN OUT FOR A BIT OF A WALK," MR. LAMB WHISpered, suddenly meeting Thomas face to face as he, Lamb, was tiptoeing through the hall. "A bright, fresh morning."

"It is, sir," replied Thomas blandly. "Just come back from a nice, long swim myself."

Mr. Lamb appeared not to have caught this surprising announcement of the old servant. He was about to hurry to his room when he suddenly remembered something.

"By the way," he called back. "There's a taxi man outside. Slip him a good tip. I got tired, and he brought me home."

Thomas, making some innocent observation about the convenience of finding taxicabs in the early morning on deserted country roads, departed on his mission, and Mr. Lamb sought the seclusion of his room. Here he bathed, shaved, and dressed, and once more faced the world as a respectable member of society. Then he sat down and thought.

His experiences as a dog had given him enough to think about. He had never realized before that so many melodramas were taking place about him—so many tragic, stupid, and sordid ones, so many touchingly human. During the time that had elapsed since he had been a terribly sick dog Lamb had unconsciously grown. Always tolerant, his tolerance now was vouchsafed a deeper understanding. He could not keep himself from wondering how that drunken girl had felt when she finally came to her senses and fully appreciated all that had happened. Would her open betrayal and the death of her husband trouble her mind greatly?

161

Mr. Lamb doubted it. She would probably get drunk again and continue on with her furtively vicious life. He wondered, too, how such women acted when they grew old, what memories they dodged, what thoughts haunted the shallow reaches of their brains. Her husband could hardly have been an admirable person, yet for some reason Lamb had taken rather a fancy to the chap, drunk as he had been. Boredom and bad gin were responsible for so much.

Mr. Lamb looked at his calendar and found that he had been a dog for a little more than a week. Where he had lain and strayed during that time, how long he had remained at the kennels under the care of the moon-faced man, he had not the remotest idea. He went to his desk and wrote a letter to this individual. This letter bore no signature, but contained a ten-dollar bill. When Thomas entered with a pot of coffee and some eggs and toast, Mr. Lamb gave him the letter and, indicating the overcoat and slippers, told him what to do with them. Thomas needed no instructions having had a brief but illuminating conversation with the taxi-driver.

Although the thought of the office was distasteful to him, Lamb went in by a late train. He would have liked to have seen his daughter, but learned that she had spent the night with Miss Rush, the house being rather lonesome on account of the absence of her father.

He found that his office was still doing business, although much remained to be done. This he proceeded to do as well as he could during the hours at his disposal, then, after reassuring Billings as to the state of his health and mind, Mr. Lamb hurried home. The sanity of the office had helped somewhat to restore his mental balance and to dispel the morbid speculations that were disturbing him. The nursery song of the dying man kept floating across his thoughts. Lamb could not fight down the growing impression that he was a man apart, that somehow the lines of communication between himself and the rest of the world had been severed, perhaps for all time. He was seriously worried now by the situation in which he found himself. If the little russet man set his mind on it, he could take him clean through the animal kingdom, not to mention birds, fish, and reptiles—insects even. Mr. Lamb was appalled by the thought. Any sort of arrangement with Sandra was entirely out of the question so long as he kept on changing. Even Hebe would eventually grow tired of a father who possessed within him the makings of a complete jungle.

It was in no cheerful frame of mind that Mr. Lamb sat down to dinner that night. Nor was his hilarity heightened by what Hebe had to report.

It seemed that during his absence Mrs. Lamb had returned to the house, packed most of her possessions and, with the aid of two taxicabs, departed mysteriously to parts unknown. She had been accompanied by her maid. This news was not in itself disagreeable to Mr. Lamb, but what went with it was not so reassuring. Hebe gave her father to understand that in the course of a little chat with her mother the good lady had shown she possessed some very accurate knowledge of the recent activities of her husband. It appeared that she was quietly collecting stray but alarming scraps of evidence as well as interviewing certain parties. Just how she intended to use this evidence and what her ultimate intentions were Hebe was unable to say. However, it was agreed between father and daughter that Sapho's intentions so far as they were concerned could hardly be of a rosy hue.

"Would you object very much to being divorced?" asked Hebe.

"No," answered Mr. Lamb readily enough, "but I would object very much to being displayed. I have no desire to furnish material for the Sunday supplements and medical journals. Nor do I want to be interviewed by reporters on how it feels to be a goldfish or a kangaroo's opinion of New York's night clubs. Your mother, my child, is not only after her freedom, but also her revenge. You see, Hebe, we've really kidded her unmercifully even though she did try to cram me into a bottle. Have you no sympathy at all for her? My indifference is of course natural, but you're a sort of blood relation. I don't quite understand—"

"Mother never had much time for me," Hebe broke in upon her father. "That's one of the reasons I'm such a hard-boiled egg. When I was a kid I thought I was fond of her, tried to make myself believe I had a regular mother, but that hopeful phase didn't last long. Sapho didn't really ever care except in front of company. Then another thing, major: I'm in the way of being a woman creature and I get some purely feminine slants on the workings of her mind. She's her own woman, major, first, last and all time. If she can't be the bell cow she's not going to trail along. That's all there is to it. When I think of that worm Leonard Gray, I can find no sympathy in my system for Sapho. She isn't breaking her heart about us and hasn't been for years. The thing that surprises me is that she ever let me be born. I know for a fact that since I've been a so-called young lady, she's resented my existence. Sapho brooks no competition. She wants no reminder of the advancing years. Hope you don't mind me speaking like this of my own mother, but I've known for some time past I should give tongue. One can't be loyal to two warring factions without getting shot full of emotional holes. When you happen to be with us I prefer to be loyal to you."

It was a tremendous speech for Hebe. Her father gazed at the girl in surprise. He had never before heard her speak so earnestly or at such length. She was indeed a young lady with a head as level as her tongue was light.

"Well," he said, rising from the table and stretching his long arms, "I do wish things would settle down a bit—myself especially. Ever since we gave that little old chap a lift my life has been just one long atavistic orgy."

That evening he was given ample opportunity to peruse his book without interruption. As a matter of fact he had a little more privacy than he needed. For an hour or so he waited impatiently in his study for Sandra to put in an appearance, then abandoning hope he turned to his book and soon became absorbed. About midnight Thomas came in to arrange a drink for his master and to see if he wanted anything. It was a ceremony with Thomas, one he loved to perform, and Mr. Lamb, realizing this, permitted his old friend to go through with it.

"You're feeling quite yourself, sir?" inquired Thomas as he was about to withdraw.

"Yes," answered Mr. Lamb dryly. "For a change."

"Glad to hear it, sir," said Thomas. "Good night."

"Good night," replied Mr. Lamb. "And, Thomas, don't forget to leave a window open in the library. This house needs a little downstairs ventilation."

Thomas understood. Ever since these strange disappearances of Mr. Lamb the old man had been taking this precaution. It had been Hebe who had first suggested the idea to him.

After Thomas had quietly closed the door Mr. Lamb returned to his book and his drink. Presently his head began to grow heavy, and at last he fell asleep.

Some hours later he awoke with the impression that all was not as it should be. His drowsy eyes focused themselves on a long tail conscientiously striped with gray and black bands.

"Either that tail belongs to me," he thought dreamily, "or else a cat is sitting on my lap."

After some minutes of gloomy speculation he worked up enough enterprise to settle the question. If the tail moved when he bade it move then the tail belonged to him, or rather he belonged to the tail; and if he belonged to the tail, then it followed that he was a cat. He thought the tail into action, and it moved with graceful majesty. "It's mine," he said to himself regretfully. "I'm it again."

He remained as he was in the chair, all curled up and considering. If he were half as fearful a cat as he had been a dog, he decided he would remain in that chair without budging until the little russet man, in the fulness of time, saw fit to turn him into something else. He held out one paw and studied it critically. It was a sizable, efficient-looking paw and appeared to be well equipped with claws especially designed for back-yard combats. So far so good, he decided. Then he turned his attention to his tail. The tail, too, was not to be despised. It was a long, lashable tail, sleek and artistically groomed. Mr. Lamb took heart. Nevertheless he was loath to take a full view of himself in the mirror. The last shock had been too great. He dared not run the risk of another. Then his eyes fell on the decanter.

Now, it is a strange example of perverseness that, as a man, Mr. Lamb drank consistently but, except on rare occasions, always with moderation, whereas, whenever he became an animal, his first desire was to get himself well-potted and to go about in search of trouble. Only extreme nausea had prevented him from being a drunken, roistering dog, ill-favored by nature and disorderly through inclination. He now began to scheme and plan how he could best extract a drink from the decanter. It would require no little doing—that he fully realized—but the difficulty of the undertaking made him concentrate upon its accomplishment the more earnestly.

Finally he rose and, taking his empty glass from the table with his two paws, he managed to place it on the arm of his chair which was next to the table and a little below its level. Then he inserted a paw into the mouth of the decanter and dragged it to the desired position. Judging the distance to a nicety, Lamb slowly tilted the decanter until a satisfactory stream curved out and fell into the glass. It was a neat, clean-cut achievement, and Mr. Lamb could not refrain from admiring his own dexterity.

"Gad!" he exclaimed to himself. "Didn't even spill a drop. Not one. I really deserve this drink."

Whether he deserved the drink or not he proceeded to take it with avidity, lapping up the fiery liquor with a long, red, ladle-shaped tongue.

"I would have saved you the trouble, major," came a level voice from the doorway.

Mr. Lamb interrupted his lapping just long enough to nod busily at his daughter, then continued to polish off his drink to the limit of his tongue's effectiveness, after which he sat down in his chair and turned two glittering eyes on Hebe. The girl came into the room and closed the door.

"I discovered you weren't in your bed," she remarked, "so I naturally suspected the worst. Well, you're not a bad-looking cat," she went on. "As a matter of fact you're about the swellest thing in the line of a cat I've ever seen—and one of the largest."

This gave Mr. Lamb an idea. He had long entertained a grudge against the unmannerly back-yard despot that had attempted to make the bowl of puffed rice his own, when Lamb had been a seagull. He would settle this grudge without further procrastination. It should be done.

Leaping from his chair he raced to the open window in the library and literally hurled himself into the darkness. The huge drink of whisky he had consumed was hot in his veins. He was ready and willing to do battle to any gang of cats in the town. Within a very few minutes Hebe's ears were pierced by the most blood-curdling assortment of feline imprecations and screams of anguish she had ever had the misfortune to hear. Shortly after this outbreak Mr. Lamb, redolent with whisky and with every hair in place, swaggered into the room and resumed his seat with a triumphant flourish of his long, sweeping tail. He looked significantly from his glass to the decanter, then fixed his eyes on Hebe.

"A cup of warm milk would do you a lot more good," his daughter told him.

Mr. Lamb shrank back in his chair and shivered. At the moment he thought it was the worst suggestion he had ever heard. Hebe laughed in spite of herself, so eloquent was her father's disgust. She went to the pantry and returned with a bowl into which she poured a drink appropriate to an occasion of victory.

"Not so loud, major, not so loud," admonished Hebe, as Mr. Lamb once more began his fast and furious lapping. "See if you can't run through the gears without grating."

Mr. Lamb paused a moment to get his breath, looked at his daughter with owlish eyes, then again fell to and did not raise his head until the bowl was dry. Then he staggered into the dining-room and thrusting his face close against the side of the goldfish aquarium, glared in at the turtle. It was an edifying example of drunken futility. The turtle was fast asleep, conse-

quently entirely indifferent to this display of frightful-
ness. Even had the old fellow been up and stirring he
probably would have mistaken Mr. Lamb's terrible
face for some new kind of rug or dining-room decoration. Apparently maddened beyond endurance by his
recent enemy's unresponsiveness, Mr. Lamb thrust a
paw into the tank and roughly mauled the turtle about.
Consternation broke out among the goldfish. They
darted through the water in wild confusion. This gave
Mr. Lamb some slight satisfaction. He would have continued to torment the poor creatures until they were utterly exhausted had not Hebe lured him away with the
promise of a drink.

"The mistake you're making," she told him as he
was rapidly tucking his grog away, "is that you're trying to drink like a horse when you've only the capacity
of a cat."

Mr. Lamb elevated one side of his dripping mouth
and mewed scornfully. This, however, was his last
demonstration of defiance. When he attempted to
mount the stairs he fell asleep on the fifth step, but
when Hebe tried to carry him to his room he kicked
and wriggled so indignantly that she was forced to put
him down. Laboriously, yet with a certain dignity, Mr.
Lamb navigated the stairs under his own steam, his
daughter helping him occasionally to regain his balance. At the door of his room he paused and leaning
against the jamb, nodded gravely at Hebe in token of
dismissal. The girl nodded back as gravely, and thus father and daughter parted for the night.

Mr. Lamb achieved the summit of his bed in four
desperate leaps, the first three landing him all sprawled
out on the floor, but once in bed he was there for good.
When Hebe came in to turn out the light he was snoring gently on his pillow.

The next morning he appeared at breakfast with a
slight hang-over. Either forgetting he was a cat or not
caring whether he was a cat or not, he took his place at
the head of the table and looked with favor upon his
daughter.

"You're not a very respectable cat," she observed,

returning his look rebukingly, "even if you are my father."

For answer he opened his mouth to its fullest extent and protruded his long red tongue, curling the tip ever so slighty, then making it quiver like a leaf. It was a remarkable, but not picturesque spectacle, and Thomas, coming into the dining-room, bent almost double the better to view it.

After breakfast Mr. Lamb was seen dragging the morning paper across the floor to his study where he remained all day alternately reading and sleeping. While he was engaged in the latter Hebe quietly entered and removed the decanter.

"I'll not have a drunken cat raising hell all over the place," she said to herself. "He might get himself all banged up."

At nightfall Mr. Lamb, having wheedled a drink from a not unsympathetic Hebe, made his escape from the house and betook himself to town. The first person who attracted his attention was Simonds, walking peacefully down the street with his family. Once more the imp of malice ignited Mr. Lamb's imagination. Suppose he should startle Simonds. The idea was no sooner conceived than it was put into execution. Getting a flying start he raced after the unsuspecting Simonds and, leaving the ground with a wild shriek, landed heavily between the man's shoulders, clawing and nuzzling him harmlessly but frantically. The Simondses parted in disorder like pool balls on a table. The purveyor of choice lots pitched headlong to the pavement where he remained in a half-swoon. By the time the crowd had collected Mr. Lamb was well out of it all and gliding snakishly along in the direction of Sandra's dwelling. On the way he encountered a large dog whose heart and soul were wrapped up in the business of regaining some much needed sleep. Mr. Lamb approached the dog and deliberately cuffed him on the side of the head.

Now this was where Mr. Lamb made an error of judgment if not of good taste, for this dog, this slumbering brute of a beast, made a business of cats. He specialized in their destruction. In his dreams he slew cats. In his waking hours he lived his dreams. But Mr. Lamb was ignorant of all this. He desired to put to the test the theory of the nine lives. His curiosity was well rewarded. No sooner was the cuff received than the dog automatically lunged at Mr. Lamb. His movements were swift and sure, his technique flawless. Lamb was smothered beneath the weight of the mighty dog. The world seemed to have turned into a pair of flashing teeth and snapping jaws.

"This," thought Lamb to himself as he crawled between the dog's hind legs, "is decidedly no go. What a mad dog this one turned out to be."

To make matters worse the dog was not without his followers, and these followers now followed Lamb as he sped along the street.

"Nine lives would not be quite enough," he decided, glancing back over his shoulder at the baying rabble at his tail's end. "I'd be four lives short in the jaws of that mob."

It was no laughing matter now. Mr. Lamb was winded and rapidly losing ground. One of the dogs caught up with him and bowled him over. The pack came thundering down, but Lamb with a desperate wriggle managed to shake off the dog and make a little headway.

From her lawn Sandra was watching with indignation the uneven pursuit of the cat, not knowing it was Mr. Lamb whose life was in peril. She only realized that some poor cat was being unfairly attacked, and her eyes grew bright with anger.

The dogs were upon him now and Lamb, fighting gamely, was borne down beneath their numbers. Then he heard a voice calling and he recognized the voice. Sandra had waded into the seething mass of dogs and was trying to extricate the cat. With his last ounce of energy Mr. Lamb eluded a large red mouth, jumped free from the pack and sprang into the girl's outstretched arms, where he lay panting and completely through. For a few minutes the dogs swirled dangerously round the girl, then gradually and cursingly withdrew before the commanding light in her eyes.

Holding Mr. Lamb close against her breast, she took

him to her room and placed him gently on her bed. Later she brought him a bowl of milk which he drank gratefully. After this she undressed and went to bed, the cat being already asleep.

When she awoke a man was lying in bed with her. The man was Mr. Lamb. This was better than a perfect stranger, but still it was not so good. She saw with relief that he was fully dressed, but quite rumpled. She also realized that as far as clothing was concerned, he had the decided advantage of her. Sandra's sleeping arrangements were always of a sketchily attractive nature. She smiled to herself as a thought tickled her mind.

"Well, here I am at last in bed with the man I love," she mused to herself.

Mr. Lamb opened his eyes and looked at her resentfully.

"Whom are you laughing at?" he demanded.

"Oh, nothing," said Sandra. "But the situation, even you must realize, is highly compromising."

Mr. Lamb was about to drift back to sleep without deigning to reply when she dug him in the ribs.

"Don't do that," she said. "You can't sleep here."

Mr. Lamb gave a startled grunt and again eyed her disapprovingly.

"Get out of this bed," said Sandy.

"Why don't you get out?" Mr. Lamb protested. "I don't have to go to work."

"I can't get out," replied Sandy.

"Don't be silly," said Lamb. "I've seen you in less than nothing before."

"That was in my professional capacity," she explained. "This is entirely different."

"Much better," said Mr. Lamb, "so far as I'm concerned."

"And all this time," the girl replied, "someone is probably listening at the door. Mrs. Cummings doesn't object to Hebe sleeping with me, but I doubt if she'd carry her tolerance to the point of granting you the same privilege. She saw me going to bed last night with a cat in my arms. If she saw me going to bed this morning with a man occupying the same relative position, things would be hard to explain. Her mind is not oriental enough to understand."

"Listen," said Mr. Lamb, as his mind reverted to the events of the previous night. "You damn well saved my life."

"And for thanks you crawl into bed with me and compromise practically all that remains of my rep," she replied.

"You deliberately put me in your bed," he retorted.

"But I little realized you were a lamb in cat's clothing," the girl replied.

"Neat but not altogether new," said Lamb. "Slip me a little good-morning kiss and I'll try to get the hell out of here."

"You're forever getting somebody the hell out of somewhere," replied Sandy, throwing two lovely arms round his neck and kissing him in no undecided manner.

"Now get out," she murmured, pushing him from her. "Go and get yourself to hell out of here."

"We'll call this a trial trip," said Mr. Lamb as he eased himself out of bed.

"Pig," said Sandy with glowing eyes.

"Don't call me that," replied Lamb pleadingly. "I might be one at any minute for all I know."

"You'll have to stop being things," said Sandra, "before we can come to terms."

"I know," replied Mr. Lamb, "and I'm praying to God I do."

He went to the window and peered cautiously through one side of the curtain. A long shed roof sloped down almost to the side of the adjoining yard. If he could cross this roof unobserved he might be able to jump into neutral territory. It seemed about the only thing to do.

"I'll have to try it," he said to Sandra. "Are there many people in the back of this house?"

"Only about six or seven possible pairs of eyes, but they should all be fixed on their plates at this hour," she answered easily.

If the truth must be told Sandra did not in the least object to being compromised officially. She was out to get her attenuated Lamb and the sooner she got him divorced the happier she would be. She was abandoned enough to hope that he would be seen when he made his escape from the house.

Mr. Lamb raised the window to its limit and thrust out an inquiring head.

"Hasn't something slipped your memory?" asked the girl in bed.

Lamb came swiftly across the room and gathering Sandra's yielding body in his arms held her against him for a moment, then dropping her suddenly as if she had been an old sack, he slid his long form through the window. At the edge of the roof he gathered himself together and sprang into the air, landing neatly in the next yard right beside a lady engaged in cutting flowers. Luckily the lady's back had been turned when he had made his desperate leap so that she did not have a chance to see his point of departure from the roof.

"Gur-r-r," said the woman, unable to think of anything else to say as she turned round abruptly. "O-o-o-oh, where did you come from?"

"I was just admiring your roses," replied Lamb with his most charming smile.

This remark did much to restore the lady to her usual state of assured rectitude.

"They're not roses," she said. "They're sweet peas."

"My mistake, madam," apologized Mr. Lamb. "You see I'm rather near-sighted."

The lady regarded Mr. Lamb's eyes for a moment as if they were things of glass. Her expression was entirely unsympathetic.

"Well," she remarked at length, "the next time you want to admire my sweet peas, which you don't seem to be able to tell from roses, don't come creeping up behind me like a thief in the night. You'd get just as much fun staying at home admiring an onion, or a cabbage—it's larger."

Thereupon she walked jaggily off down her garden path, and Mr. Lamb, feeling remarkably well in spite of his strenuous encounter with the dogs, returned to his home.

"I always suspected," he observed to himself, "that an investment banker and a second-story man had a great deal in common."

CHAPTER XVIII

The World's Worst Bootlegger

MELVILLE LONG WAS READY TO PROVE HIMSELF AT last. He was now the proud possessor of much bad whisky and gin. A man in the blot was responsible for its quality. In spite of this damning fact the man continued to enjoy deep and unbroken slumber. Already Mr. Long rejoiced in three customers. His heart was hopeful, and Hebe's was in very much the same condition. But Hebe did not know all of her Melville. She had an inkling, but no real knowledge of the profundity of that engaging youth's ignorance of worldly affairs. Everything was set for the initial delivery.

Melville Long had selected his list of prospective customers more or less at random. He prepared it sketchily, according to the appearance of the homes he chanced to pass in his rather purposeless rambles. One house had especially impressed him, and into this house he had insinuated his ingratiating presence. That this house was the residence of Mr. Brickett, the most important bootlegger within a radius of twenty miles, was unknown to Mr. Long.

Mr. Brickett received his caller with his usual urbanity, believing him to be a new customer. His shock was therefore the greater when Mr. Long offered to sell him an unlimited supply of gin and whisky at a price well below Mr. Brickett's minimum.

Beneath this blow the bootlegger rallied gamely and lent an interested ear to his young competitor's plans. It seemed, according to Mr. Long, that all the bootleggers in the neighborhood were slow and inordinately expensive poisoners. He, Melville Long, was going to put an end to all that. From now on, all other bootleggers would have to reckon with him. He had no doubt that within a month or so they would either move away or give up the game. Now, all of this interested Mr. Brickett a greal deal more than Melville Long realized. And the fateful part of the interview was that both of them placed a certain amount of credence in the words of Mr. Long. In this smooth, well-turned-out young gentleman Mr. Brickett saw the potentialities of a dangerous if not successful rival. In himself Mr. Long saw the possible solution of the liquor question, and the longer he listened to himself talk the clearer and closer grew the solution.

The interview ended on a note of mutual confidence and respect, Mr. Brickett requesting Mr. Long to deliver two cases of gin and one of whisky on the evening now at hand. Upon the departure of the budding young bootlegger, Mr. Brickett got in touch with numerous minions of the law who had reason to love him well, and with these same minions arranged a little surprise party for Mr. Long on the evening of his virgin delivery.

It was to this party that Mr. Lamb in a state of blessed ignorance was being driven. He had been told by Hebe that it was to be a mere pleasure trip, a short spin in the cool of the evening. She wanted her father along to lend an atmosphere of eminent respectability to a rather dubious enterprise. And because she wanted to do well by her father she dropped by and picked up Sandra. Thus they sped with high hopes and hearts aglow to the scene of the treacherous ambush. Mr. Lamb afterward remarked that the spot should be marked by a double cross.

The car drew up before the residence of Mr. Brickett, and on some flimsy pretext Melville Long, who had been driving, made it known that he had to see a man for a minute. He hurried into the house and was affectionately greeted by the double-dealing Mr. Brickett. If Mr. Long would unload the cases, Mr. Brickett would send some servants to carry them into the house. Mr. Long then returned to the automobile and much to Mr. Lamb's surprise extracted a box from the trunk on the rear of the car. Mr. Brickett's servants, it turned out, wore the livery of the police department, and when Mr.

Long hurried forward with the box in his arms he found himself on the point of entrusting its safety to one of these gentlemen.

It can be said for Mr. Long that when light dawned in his mind it dawned with sudden clearness. In a blinding flash he saw and comprehended the situation. With a cry of warning he flung the box into Mr. Lamb's lap—that startled gentleman receiving it with a grunt of pain—and swinging himself to the running board urged Hebe to take the wheel and to drive practically anywhere at the highest attainable speed. The officer of the law dashed forward to lay hands on Melville Long only to be met with that agile youth's foot in the pit of his undefended stomach. As several other officers rushed for the car Hebe got it started and swiftly under way. The chug of a motorcycle apprised them of the fact that they were not to be unaccompanied.

Mr. Lamb removed the box from his lap and carefully placed it on the floor of the speeding car. Then he turned questioning eyes on Sandra.

"Is this to be our habitual method of progress?" he inquired. "Because if it is I'd prefer to alight and to let the merry whirl continue without my superfluous presence."

"Would you leave me here all alone?" demanded Sandra.

"Wthout a moment's hesitation if you were mad enough to remain," Mr. Lamb replied. "Of course, I would much prefer your company."

By this time Melville had climbed into the back of the car and was about to join the busily occupied Hebe in the front seat.

"Melville, my boy," asked Mr. Lamb, "may I ask what is in this box that made that officer so angry?"

"It's just his way," muttered Long, struggling forward to hide his confusion. "They're all that way, Mr. Lamb. Don't mind them."

"I wouldn't mind them in the least," Mr. Lamb replied, "if they didn't display such feverish interest in us."

By this time the telephone in Mr. Brickett's home had been pressed into active service. The key points throughout the country and the state were warned to be on the lookout for Mr. Lamb's automobile, the license number of which was given with a businesslike description of the automobile itself and its occupants.

Hebe had wheeled into a rough dirt road, and for a few minutes they thought they had lost the motorcycle policeman, but as she stopped the car to enable Long to change places with her they heard a faint but persistent throbbing behind them. Looking back they made out the motorcycle and its implacable rider bounding along in the distance. Both were having rough going of it.

Then began a grim chase which Mr. Lamb to this day views with alarm and disapproval. On the rutted dirt road they more than held their own with the motorcycle, but when this road abruptly deposited them on a main thoroughfare, the persevering policeman began to gain. And when the road eventually placed them in the dead center of a thriving village they were indeed in great trouble, because it was here that two state troopers, also equipped with motorcycles, joined the chase. These alert and determined gentlemen were of a different caliber from that of the flying motor's former nemesis. They believed in producing revolvers and pointing them at things. The sound of shooting brought joy to their hearts, and they now began to enjoy themselves to their hearts' content. As the automobile hurriedly cleared the town they yanked out their gats and gave the party ahead what is sometimes known as what for, or a piece of their collective minds. The revolvers spoke eloquently in Mr. Lamb's ears. He heard the whistle of bullets going by at full speed and he knew that those self-same bullets were busily looking for them. This knowledge brought him scant satisfaction.

"Our two new escorts," he observed to his daughter, "seem to have an even greater capacity for anger than that other chap. Do you know why they're trying to murder us all?"

"Well, major," his daughter called back to him, "this automobile happens to be loaded to the scuppers with gin and whisky, and it seems that our guilty secret is known to practically the entire universe."

"I knew nothing about it," replied Mr. Lamb, lurching heavily against Sandra.

"You're the practically part," said Hebe. "Now everybody knows except possibly an old gentleman on the extreme peak of Mount Shasta."

"Does it so happen," continued Mr. Lamb, as the automobile skidded around a corner and the shooting died away, "that a few samples are lying within easy reach?"

Hebe produced a bottle from a side pocket and passed it to her father. Mr. Lamb received the gin with undisguised relief.

"I might as well be poisoned as shot," he remarked, raising the bottle to his lips. "If I must meet death face to face I'd prefer to be wearing a broad, fatuous smile."

"You're not alone in your preference," said Sandy. "My throat is parched with panic."

Mr. Lamb handed her the bottle.

"No foolishness, remember," he warned her. "This is to be serious drinking."

Sandra gulped a few swallows of extremely vile gin, relinquished the bottle to Hebe and turned her deep, passionate eyes on the man at her side.

"I'd love to meet death with you," she murmured. "With your kiss on my lips and our bullet-riddled bodies locked in a last embrace."

"Bleeding profusely from every pore," added Mr. Lamb. "Hebe, pass me that bottle quickly. This woman is turning me numb."

Mr. Lamb drank deeply, clinging with one hand to the swaying car. Sandra relieved him of the bottle and followed his example. Melville Long was too busy to drink. If there was one thing that young man knew it was roads. In his own roadster he had explored the highways and byways of the entire state. He was in the way of being an animated road map. He now called on his knowledge and played a little trick on the state troopers, still hidden from view by a bend in the road.

Turning the car sharply, he drove it at full speed up

what appeared to be a private driveway leading to a farmhouse. The road curved round the house and continued surprisingly on through a field of corn, down a short but steep incline, followed the arc of a meadow, and at last lost itself in the shadows of a forest. It was not a road for a large, heavy automobile, but Mr. Long made it so today. Once in the forest he stopped the car and silently took the bottle from Hebe. When he removed it from his lips it was good only for disposal. Hebe produced another one and passed it back to her father. Melville Long got out and listened. For the moment they seemed safe from pursuit.

"The rear mudguards have been dented by five bullets, and there are two holes in the body," he announced with his usual optimistic smile. "It's lucky they didn't hit the trunk. The thing's full of grog."

"An act of God," breathed Sandra.

Daylight was growing thin, and the late summer night was about to open for business. Mr. Lamb was making inroads in the new bottle. The gin was taking effect. He could hardly have felt better.

"Melville," he asked, "would you mind telling me the name of that near customer of yours? A shade of memory has just passed across my rapidly receding brain."

"Name of Brickett," Long answered a little bitterly. "Seemed to be a pleasant sort of man."

"Oh, he is," Mr. Lamb continued. "He's one of the pleasantest and most progressive bootleggers in the neighborhood. I've done business with him myself."

An expression of infinite pity welled up in Hebe's eyes as she regarded her future husband.

"Darling," she said, "you've proved yourself far beyond any reasonable doubt, and what you've proved is that you're the world's worst bootlegger barring none."

"I'm not even that," the young man answered moodily. "Haven't sold even one bottle yet. Didn't ever get started."

"And what, may I ask, was the reason for all this illicit enterprise?" asked Mr. Lamb.

Melville looked helplessly at Hebe, and she put her hand on his.

"Well, you see, major," she explained. "We were trying to get married and it was all my fault. I suggested the idea to this billiard ball with a view to obtaining quick and ample funds. I thought it would be better than his just doing nothing. He absolutely refused to ruin me."

Mr. Lamb looked at the pair with sad, reproachful eyes.

"He's absolutely ruined me," he said at last. "And between you you have made us all eligible for full membership in the Atlanta Country Club. Your short cut to matrimony leads but to the jug. If you succeed in getting me out of this fix alive I'll carry you both in my arms to the nearest church and not leave the place until you are married to a turn."

"Let's have a drink on that," suggested Sandy. "It sounds like a sporting proposition to me."

The second bottle went the way of the first, and a third was pressed into service. This time they switched to whisky with the aid of a corkscrew attached to a versatile pocket knife in the possession of Melville Long. Merely as a matter of interest Mr. Lamb also sampled this unworthy liquor, then leaned back against the seat.

"Damn the torpedoes," he quoted to his probable son-in-law. "Get me back to my bed, and I'll settle a fortune on Hebe."

He rested his head on Sandra's shoulder and became a very quiet and contented man. As the car sped through the woods slumber claimed him for her own. Sandra, too, for lack of anything better to do, dropped into a light sleep, and failed to notice how heavy the head on her shoulder was growing. Hebe and Long kept their eyes to the front.

Some time later, when the automobile drew up at an innocent-looking roadside garage to replenish the nearly exhausted supply of gasoline, the pair continued sleeping. Nor did either sleeper awake until the sound of coarse, commanding voices penetrated their remoteness.

Sandra sat up with a start only to find that the automobile was completely surrounded by state troopers.

She turned to Mr. Lamb to inform him of this dishear-
tening fact, then stopped with her mouth open.

"Hebe," she said in a low voice, "just turn round
and look at your father."

Hebe stopped insulting the state troopers and obeyed
Sandra's urgent request. Her mouth also hung suspended. Then she closed it and swallowed hard several
times. Mr. Lamb woke up and looked helplessly about
him. He knew he was something else again, but for the
life of him he could not make out what it was.

"Come out of there," an unpleasant voice broke in.
"We want to search the back of this car."

The man thrust in an inquiring head, then immediately abandoned his inquiry. It is to be questioned if
any man ever changed his plans so swiftly and radically. His head was no sooner in than it was out. And
no sooner was it out than his voice made horrid
sounds.

"May God save us all," he announced. "They've got
a live lion in the back of that car"—and leaping on the
nearest motorcycle, he disappeared down the road.

"So that's what I am," thought Mr. Lamb with a
thrill of pride. "Well, here's where I assert myself to
the limit of my capacity."

With an ear-splitting roar of mock rage, he jumped
heavily to the road and scattered disorder among the
troopers. Some of them left on foot, some of them left
on motorcycles, some of them seemed to have dis-
carded both methods of leaving in favor of flying. The
fact remains that where there was once a compact little
gathering of state troopers, there was now not a single
trooper. A few abandoned motorcycles remained behind, but had it not been for these there was no evidence that a state trooper had ever been within miles
of the spot. High up on the top of the gasoline pump
the garage owner looked on the scene of desolation and
felt very lonely indeed. Nor would he come down in
spite of the urgings of Sandra and Hebe and the apparent amiability of the lion. They left the man aloft,
and drove noisily down the road, everyone talking at
once save Mr. Lamb, who was practicing up on his

growls and modestly receiving the congratulations of
his three companions in flight.

Then Melville Long, without much effort, conceived
another bright idea. He drove swiftly and directly to
the seacoast—to a place of sand and pines where a secluded hotel quietly dreamed away a peaceful, fragrant
existence among the trees that forever held in their
arms the far-off throb of the surf. The lights were out
in the hotel when the automobile rolled up the gravel
drive. They had previously decided what they were going to do with Mr. Lamb. The lion was to become a
dog. They had figured out exactly how to do it. Mr.
Lamb alone was skeptical. He failed to see how he
could compress himself into a dog no matter how hard
he squeezed. However, since the party had decided to
make a dog of him, he was perfectly willing to cooper-
ate to the best of his ability. It had taken nearly half a
case of liquor to get him into this pliable frame of
mind. He was now a trifle unsteady on his feet. Instead
of stepping quietly out of the automobile he fell
through the door held open by Sandra, and spread
himself over the drive.

"Come on, major," pleaded Hebe. "This will never
do. Wait till we get our rooms."

The thought of a comfortable bed gave the lion the
strength to rise. Then began the transformation. As if
they had previously rehearsed the scene each member
of the party bore down on Mr. Lamb with an automobile robe. In these they completely muffled him. Even
Melville Long's raincoat was pressed into service.

"Now squeeze yourself together, major," his daughter urged him. "That's the boy. Squeeze hard, hump
your back and walk low to the ground."

The young lady was red with exertion as she tied the
robes about the contorted form of the lion. From time
to time Sandra was forced to retire as her mirth got the
better of her. Low pants and grunts issued from the
lion. Only his nose and eyes were now visible, his tail
having been firmly strapped to his stomach. From the
blankets his eyes peered out wistfully—hopefully—
upon his three companions. Sandy could not meet

those eyes bearing the mute question of, "Do I look much like a dog?"

When she had finished her operations, Hebe stepped back and surveyed her handiwork.

"He doesn't look much like a dog," she admitted, "but then again, he doesn't look much like a lion, and after all that's what we want."

"He doesn't look like anything else on the face of God's world," pronounced Melville Long. "We've got as much right to call him a dog as any other animal."

"Now, major," continued Hebe, "remember this, and for heaven's sake don't laugh. You're a sick dog and an extremely self-effacing one. You're shy and you don't like strangers. Now show us how you can walk. Just think of a beetle and crawl along."

Thinking hard of a beetle, Mr. Lamb crouched to the ground and, hunching up to his utmost, took a few trial steps. The effect was irresistible. It was heightened by the obvious earnestness of the lion. The three witnesses of this odd scene sat down on the running-board of the automobile and clung to their stomachs. Sandra was aching all over. And when the lion peered wanly back at them over his shoulder for some indication of approval, she collapsed into Hebe's arms.

"Come on everybody," said Hebe in a low voice. "I've taken a lot of trouble with that lion, now we've got to get him in. That will do very well, major," she continued, going over to the crouched and muffled object. "Just keep up the harmless deception till we reach our rooms."

Collecting several suitcases containing nothing but gin and whisky, Long rang the hotel night bell and waited on the broad veranda until a light appeared in the reception room. When a sleepy-eyed clerk with bushy hair and a large, smooth, well-fed face appeared at the door, the young man made known his needs and was invited to enter with his party.

"Ah, yes," Long said to the clerk in as nonchalant a voice as he could muster when the robed lion made his mincing entrance. "I'd forgotten our most important member—one sick dog. I take personal charge of him myself."

From behind his counter the clerk looked in astonishment at Mr. Lamb, who cast his eyes down and gazed demurely at the floor.

"Do you say that's a dog?" the clerk demanded.

Melville Long laughed falsely as Hebe bent over her father and gave him a pat of encouragement.

"Of course he's a dog," put in Sandy. "What would you call him if he isn't a dog?"

"Well, miss," replied the clerk thoughtfully, "I don't rightly know just what I'd call him. He's unlike anything I ever saw before, or ever hope to see again. Are you certain he's all right? This is a very quiet hotel, you know. It's a sort of retreat for nervous persons—wrecks."

Everyone, including Mr. Lamb, felt that they had come to the right place. As Melville Long was signing the register in such a way that Hebe became his sister and Sandra Rush her friend, Mr. Lamb suddenly remembered his daughter's admonition about laughing. No sooner had he remembered this than he was seized with an uncontrollable desire to laugh. His legs gave way completely, and, sinking to the floor, his body shook with suppressed mirth as a gasping noise escaped his lips.

With blotter in hand the clerk forgot every other consideration in his interest in the convulsed animal.

"What's wrong with him now?" he asked.

Long, studiously averting his eyes from the great, quivering hulk at his feet, looked impassively at the clerk.

"A bit of a chill, I guess," he replied. "It's the night air. A very delicate dog, that, and an expensive one. Only a few in captivity—I mean, only a few grow to manhood."

"Or attain their majority," put in Hebe sarcastically.

She bent tenderly down over the now hysterical lion and gave him a vicious jab in the ribs, from which the poor creature grunted so explosively that the clerk jumped back.

"There, there, Fifi," she said. "Be a good doggie or you'll get no nice warm medicine to make you sleep."

At the inappropriate appellation of Fifi, Sandra

broke down completely. Throwing her arms on the counter she hid her head in them and rocked her body to and fro in agony. The clerk scratched his mop of a head in perplexity, looked closely at the register, then giving everything up as hopeless, led the way to the rooms.

This entailed the mounting of several flights of stairs, a difficult task for Mr. Lamb in his present strapped and highly compressed condition. To add to his discomfort his robes began to slip off, and Hebe and Sandra were forced to hold them on as he dragged himself up the interminable stairs. Once the clerk looked back, and the sight he caught of the straining lion was enough to keep him from looking back again.

When finally the door had closed behind the mystified man, Mr. Lamb burst his bonds and lay exhausted on the floor. Sandra flung herself on the bed and Hebe sank down in a chair. Melville Long alone retained his composure. Quickly opening a suitcase, he extracted a bottle of whisky which he deftly uncorked and thrust into Mr. Lamb's mouth, holding it there until its contents were half drained. From the bed came a series of muffled gasps. Sandra was still at it. Revived by the whisky, Mr. Lamb, trailing robes behind him, walked to the bed and gently spanked the prostrate form of Sandra. Gentle as it was, the spanking was sufficiently firm to bring her back to sobriety. She sat up on the bed, then suddenly threw her arms round the lion's neck.

"Fifi!" she cried. "Fifi, us girls must stick together."

Mr. Lamb drew back and, looking at his daughter, made it clear by a wave of his paw that he desired to retire. Sandra was all for sleeping with her Fifi, but compromised with tucking him into bed. This he permitted her to do with bad grace.

"I don't quite like sleeping with a drunken lion, even though he is your father," Melville Long told Hebe in a low voice. "He's gentle enough now, but suppose he should dream he was back in the jungle? He might make a meal out of me and never even remember it."

"The major," replied Hebe with dignity, "is very careful about the quality of the food he consumes. One bite out of you, and his jaws would automatically cease to function."

With this little parting speech Hebe led Sandra to their own room. Sandra blew a kiss to her Fifi, who gazed back at her with large, glassy eyes.

In spite of the precautions taken by Hebe the next morning to lock the sleeping lion in before they went down to breakfast, the chambermaid, after repeated knocking, entered the room with no difficulty by means of her master key. It is to be doubted if even God clearly understood her prayer so incoherent were her ideas when she pulled down the rumpled bed clothing and came face to face with a lion. Even then she did not move. The terrible sight had robbed her limbs of volition. It was not until the lion awoke and gave her a lazy cuff on a place usually associated with juvenile chastisement that she thought about going. As she left the room her limbs moved jerkily as if she were walking with snowshoes attached to her feet.

"There's a lion in 46," she informed the clerk. "He's asleep and he has a mouth."

The day clerk smiled indulgently at the maid's terror, the night clerk having omitted to give him an account of the late arrivals of the previous night.

"Yes, I know," he replied soothingly. "There's an elephant in 82. Go up and give him his bath."

The maid liked her job, so she did not stop to argue, but within a surprisingly short time a rumor was circulated about that among its other distinguished guests the hotel also entertained a lion. Support was given to this rumor when at noontime an order was telephoned from 46 to send up half a dozen large steaks. The order was duly delivered and consumed, but the waiter who delivered the steaks had no opportunity to see the consumer. When Sandra, Hebe, and Mr. Long appeared in the dining-room for luncheon the kitchen was thrown into an even more feverish state of speculation. A sick dog, no matter how rapid his recovery, could not possibly eat six large steaks. Therefore it stood to reason that the dog was not a dog at all but a lion.

For the remainder of the afternoon Sandra read the

newspaper to Mr. Lamb, who alternately drank and drowsed. When it was about time for dinner she departed, promising to provide bountifully for him on her return. Not being Hebe, she forgot to lock the door.

It did not take many minutes for Mr. Lamb to become terribly, terribly lonely. He crawled out of his bed and wondered what he could do with himself.

"Can't do much with a lion," he thought discontentedly. "Nobody wants you around. Nobody understands."

Then his eyes, falling on the suitcase, brightened a shade.

"Might as well drink," he continued. "Left here alone. Nothing to do. Don't want to drink, but it seems I must."

He opened the suitcase and pawed out a bottle of gin, the whisky being beyond his powers because of the cork. Then he deftly lipped out the stopper and, taking the bottle well into his mouth, swung his head aloft. A river of raw gin ran down his great throat, not without causing him some keen physical discomfort. Nevertheless he took his punishment with fortitude until the river ceased to flow, after which he sat down to think; this in the case of a none too sober lion is not at all a good thing to do. He had been cooped up in the house all day. A bit of a walk would do him a world of good. It was dark now and almost everybody was dressing for dinner, his party having gone down early in order to tend to his needs. He did not doubt for a minute that he could get himself out of the hotel without being observed by a single human eye.

Mr. Lamb went to the door and tried the knob. It turned easily under the pressure of his paws. He was out of the room in a moment. Now, the hall was a narrow hall, and Mr. Lamb had been perfectly right in assuming that the majority of the guests of the hotel would be in their rooms dressing for dinner. Another thing, Mr. Lamb's tail was long and large. And this long tail thumped imperatively against the doors on either side, as Mr. Lamb made his stately progress down the hall. It was an interesting study of human reactions to the unexpected presence of a lion.

The first summons of the lion's tail was answered by an elderly gentleman wearing horn-rimmed glasses and an undershirt. To this gentleman Mr. Lamb bowed apologetically. For a moment the old fellow did not stir. He peered myopically at the lion as if disbelieving the evidence of his eyes, then closed the door slowly as suspicion grew to certainty. The other guests were more expeditious in their reactions. One lady hurrying out to dinner unfortunately received the lion's tail full in the pit of her stomach and was toppled to the floor. Her terror was heightened by Mr. Lamb's elaborate attempts to show her that the whole incident had been purely accidental. Her screams caused other doors to open, and the lion was discovered in the act of what appeared to be an attack on a prostrate woman, but which in reality was nothing more than a courteous endeavor to make gentlemanly reparations for an unavoidable occurrence.

What had once been a mysterious rumor now became an appalling fact. Few guests appeared at dinner that night. They preferred to remain hungry but safe behind locked and barricaded doors. Not quite satisfied with this precaution some of the more painstaking guests were later unwillingly hauled forth from under beds and the depths of closets.

During this brief period the hotel was decidedly no place for nervous people, although it was occupied by many.

Not altogether unaware of the disturbance he had created, Mr. Lamb made an exit through a side door and was now wandering pensively about in the pines. At last he came to the sea and poised himself on a rock. It was a beautiful night—a night of stars, silence, and beguiling breezes laden with the healing scent of salt and pine.

A man and a maid, new to the place, but obviously not to each other, were walking along the beach.

"What a lovely spot for a statue," exclaimed the maid, pointing to the lion motionless on the rock.

"Funny," said the man, "we haven't seen it on any of the picture post-cards."

They hurried up to the lion and examined it in the darkness.

"Remarkably lifelike," murmured the maid.

"And so are you," said the man, leaning against the lion's flank and taking the maid in his arms.

Mr. Lamb promptly sat down and the couple slid to the rocks.

"Did you push it over?" asked the maid.

"God, no," whispered the man. "The damn thing's alive."

After this they covered their heads and lay perfectly still, each one wondering about how much of the other remained undevoured. When at last they gathered enough courage to look up, the lion was gone. That night they conducted themselves with a certain amount of discretion.

Mr. Lamb found the hotel in a condition of frantic activity. During his absence the state troopers had appeared, this time fortified with a machine-gun. He was just in time to see his automobile bearing Hebe, Sandra, and Long dash madly down the driveway. Troopers were rushing from all directions, and the machine-gun was brought into action. The troopers had no intention of getting too close to the lion they assumed to be in the car.

And Mr. Lamb was equally reluctant to be left alone with a machine-gun and a chorus of state troopers. He longed for the company of his friends. Casting dignity to the winds, he uttered a loud roar of protest and doubling his body under him made the gravel fly.

"Run, lion, run," he urged himself. "Prove yourself now."

Gravel sprayed out behind him. His tail was close to the ground. This did not prevent it from being slightly nicked by a machine-gun bullet.

The car was waiting for him at the end of the drive, and without stopping for the formality of opening the door he lurched over the side. The automobile jumped ahead and continued hurriedly along the road.

"Off again, major," said Sandra resignedly. "How's your head?"

Mr. Lamb was not worrying about his head. His thoughts lay with his tail.

"Not a scrap of evidence left behind," Mr. Long optimistically informed the party. "I lugged both suitcases out. Open a bottle, Hebe."

CHAPTER XIX

Above the Battle

SANDRA LOOKED UP FROM HER DRUM.

"It's a shame we haven't a camera," she observed.

It was.

Mr. Lamb was lying majestically beside an uprooted tree. Its reaching branches still drew vital sap that nourished fresh green leaves. The tawny coat of the lion was splashed with pointed shadows. They shifted over the great, still body as small, inquisitive breezes searched through the arms of the fallen tree.

Round the tip of the lion's tail was bound a once dainty but now bedraggled brassière. Undoubtedly it had once been becoming to its wearer. Despite this fact it failed to add to the dignity of the lion. Sandra had insisted on sacrificing this restraining influence for the protection of the bullet-chipped tail.

The silence of the forest was unbroken save by the sporadic throbbing of the drum upon which Sandra practiced when the spirit moved her. The sound of the drum lent a barbaric note to this already sufficiently fantastic woodland scene.

Through a rift in the trees a green world unrolled far below them. The slanting sun sent a flood of gold along the path of a winding river. There were farmhouses down there, pasturelands and meadows. The quiet of evening seemed to have fallen over forest, field, and farm. From where they were sitting they looked the clouds in the face. Caught in the rays of the setting sun they fell burning down the sky.

Mr. Long was wandering leggily about in his drawers. Sandra and Hebe, from half to two-thirds naked themselves, were sitting cross-legged on the ground and endeavoring to make up for their lack of raiment by fashioning garlands of wild flowers for their hair. Sandra had promised the lion one for himself, but the lion without troubling to move his massive head merely rolled his large, disapproving eyes in her direction, then returned to the contemplation of the gold and green world in which he found himself.

All had been well rained upon. A heavy shower had wet them to the skin. Garments both dainty and ludicrous were decorating the limbs of neighboring trees.

"I find it fresh as the deuce," complained Melville Long, shivering convincingly in his drawers.

"Break out the last case," suggested Hebe. "Your clothes will soon be dry."

At this suggestion the lion moved his head. Turning it to his daughter he nodded gravely several times, as an indication of his unqualified agreement. Sandra laid aside her garland and, picking up her drumsticks, made an enthusiastic noise.

The beating of the drum throbbed weirdly through the silence of the forest. From afar a wandering naturalist heard the broken rhythm and pictured again in his mind's eye a certain clearing in a jungle on a distant tropic isle.

"Strange sound to hear in this part of the world," he thought aloud, as he put some utterly useless-looking stones into his pack and resumed his way.

Back on the mountain top Hebe was asking questions.

"What becomes of the major's clothes when he turns into things?" she demanded.

The lion looked interested. This subject touched him vitally.

"What becomes of all of him?" asked Sandra. "His clothes must go the way of all flesh."

"No," said Hebe. "His arms and legs and things turn into the corresponding parts of the animal he's exploiting at the moment, but it's different with his clothes. They have to go somewhere because they always come back."

Sandra puzzled over this problem a few minutes, then her face brightened.

"I know what becomes of his clothes," she announced. "They naturally turn into fur, feathers, or scales as the case may be."

"But there's his skin to be considered," replied Hebe.

Mr. Lamb did not entirely approve of the drift of the conversation. To him it seemed hardly proper that these two young ladies should sit there as if he were not present, and dispassionately consider his skin and the various parts of his body. He gave a low cough of protest, but the girls continued.

"His skin remains his skin," Sandra explained. "Sometimes stretched, at others shrunken. His clothes merely form the decoration."

"Well, I wish to God I could get my hand in the pockets of his trousers right now," Melville Long put in earnestly.

His wish was fathered by the realization that the money in his own trousers pockets was running low. Only an emergency fund remained, a small one.

To obtain food and supplies they had been forced to resort to rather high-handed methods. These methods had been as simple as they were successful. Mr. Lamb had merely presented himself at the local country store in the little village at the base of the mountain. He did not have long to wait. Everybody went away just as soon as they could and stayed away. Sandra then appeared with a list prepared by the efficient Hebe, and with this list before her deliberately selected the articles desired.

The drum had not been among the items on the slip of paper. The drum had been left behind by a member of the local band. Its existence had completely slipped his memory in the press of departure. One of Sandra's many suppressed desires had always been the mastery of the drum, so seeing one conveniently at hand she made it her own. Some day she promised herself, she would also take up the fife. One thing at a time. Beating the drum very badly indeed, but with great contentment she had preceded the lion through the village and up the mountainside. The lion had carried the bundle of provisions. Through the slits in their blinds the village's entire population had reviewed this incredible procession with bewitched eyes and prayed quite fundamentally to their variously conceived God. Needless to say both the lion and the lady were slightly drunk—not much, but just enough to make them believe they were convulsingly amusing.

For five days now they had been, as it were, on location. Having found the seacoast inhospitable they had gone to the other extreme and taken to the mountains. Through the uncanny driving of Mr. Long and the presence of Mr. Lamb they had eluded the state troopers, but not entirely escaped their memory. The automobile had been left concealed at the base of the mountain, but already, unknown to its owners, it had been discovered and reported. Several intrepid troopers had reconnoitered the position of the fugitives, and certain plans were at this moment well under way.

All these developments would have been highly disturbing to the lion and his three companions, happy as they were in their false security, had they but been aware of them.

That night they finished the last bottle of whisky and ingeniously hid the remaining case of gin in a hollow tree. Mr. Long was now taking no chances. He had agreed to get them alive out of the mess into which he had plunged them. No less than the sun-tanned hand of Hebe depended upon the success of his endeavors.

The lion placed his head on the fallen tree and stretched his massive limbs. A whistling sigh escaped his lips. Sandra, trailing an automobile robe, crept close to him and rested her head on a soft spot just back of his left foreleg. From within the body of the lion came the strong, steady beat of his great heart. The sound of it gave the girl a feeling of confidence and safety. Once she tickled his ribs, and the lion, raising his head from the leaves, gently but firmly nipped the ear that had been the cause of so much trouble. Sandra gave a little scream and draped her arms round the lion's neck.

On the other side of the embers Hebe vainly attempted to interest Mr. Long in her plans. Mr. Long strove manfully to listen to the prattling girl, but sleep was among those things that he held most sacred. The last thing he remembered was a long string of unpleasant names that Hebe was muttering monotonously in his ear. The sound of her voice helped to lull him off to sleep.

In the darkness of the forest, one of the lion's large yellow eyes shone brightly as if it were reflecting the beams from a sharply chiseled star, hanging directly overhead above the trees. Silence . . . only the voice of Sandra singing softly to the lion.

"Hebe," she whispered suddenly. "How's this: the lion and the lamb lie down together—actually in one."

"A little too pat to be funny," replied Hebe. "Tell that great hulk of an animal good night for me. My little prize package has gone by-by."

"So has mine," said Sandra, and presently she emulated his example.

According to his custom Mr. Lamb arose at dawn next morning and took a stroll through the forest. He knew of a certain mountain stream in which he could partially submerge his body. It was a refreshing thing to do in the quiet of the morning. He would lie there and listen to the birds and allow an old squirrel to examine him from a safe distance. Each morning the distance had decreased. Today the old fellow was almost familiar.

Mr. Lamb lay quite still and let the water swirl and chuckle about his haunches. No trains to catch. No bonds to sell. No orderly rows of houses. No meaningless words to say. Not even the sound of a motorcar or the smell of gasoline. Lamb's nerves were resting, taking on a protective coating of fat. He realized now that his life with Sapho had never been restful. There had always been a debilitating undercurrent of irritation. No room for laughter and heedless relaxation. No delirious unleashing of passion. No companionship in sleep. Like so many secretively immoral women, she had hidden her true nature behind a screen of diffidence and niceness. With her one could never be vulgarly natural any more than one could be self-forgetfully passionate. She was bad without knowing how to be bad. Life had entered her only a little way. It had never really settled in her body nor given animation to her brain. He himself had been only half alive. He had accepted things altogether too easily, and too consistently avoided trouble. Perhaps if he had been different Sapho would have been different. However, he knew for certain that he never could have brought himself to mingle with the Woodbine Players or to talk symbolically about sex as if he were actually feeling it with his hands. The thought of sex brought Sandra to his mind. There was a woman—sex with lightness and laughter and with other skylights of interest to let the sunshine through.

Thinking of this beautiful, bare-armed young sinner, the lion rose so abruptly that he startled the squirrel into a frenzy of precautionary measures. It was high time the camp awoke. Shaking the glinting beads of water from his flanks he passed with a consciousness of nobility and power between the trees.

The camp was empty—deserted. No clothing hung from the limbs of the trees. Even the automobile robes were gone. With growing suspicion and alarm the lion nosed about the place. The world which had been so cheerfully ordered only a few minutes ago was now a wilderness of vast discontent. Then his eyes fell on a note pinned to a tree. It had been scrawled hastily and was signed by Hebe. Mr. Lamb read:

> Surprised and captured. The big stiffs are taking us to Brookford to visit the judge. Rescue suggested. They have no evidence, the crooks! . . . Curses.
>
> HEBE.

Then the lion descended from the mountain. As he crashed through the trees and sprang to the road he was a sight to inspire terror in the hardiest of souls. An automobile passing casually by stalled within a foot of the lion, then started again and went into reverse. Mr. Lamb did not even notice the car. Hebe had suggested rescue, and he fully intended to act on her suggestion. Was he not the monarch of all he surveyed? Or was that title a mere piece of flattery? He would soon find out. With powerful strides he disappeared down the road to Brookford, some five miles distant.

A lion is seldom crowded, that is, a lion on the loose. Round him one usually finds a considerable quantity of unoccupied territory. As Mr. Lamb passed down the main street of Brookford no one got in his way. What traffic there was withdrew to the pavements or turned into side streets. An earnest gentleman drove his car clear through the front window of a furniture store, where he partially concealed himself beneath the ruins of a completely demolished bed. A horse harnessed to a farm wagon was found later in the wagon itself, and had to be driven home by a more courageous steed.

Utterly ignoring the small furor he was occasioning, Mr. Lamb padded down the street and entered the court-house ˙ front of which he recognized his parked automobile. Behind his ponderous desk the judge was having a hard time establishing a case against the youthful prisoners. He was rapidly losing heart. No liquor had been found in the car or at the camp, no liquor had ever been delivered or actually seen. On a charge of bootlegging he could find no plausible grounds for holding them for general sessions. He was beginning to dislike the state troopers as heartily as those they had captured and dragged to court without a scrap of evidence. For the twentieth time the judge was trying to discover what had become of the liquor.

"Now, miss," he was saying, "what did you say your name was?"

"Doon," replied Hebe promptly, "Lorna Doon."

"Well, Miss Doon," continued the judge—who officially was not a judge at all but merely a recorder and not as *au courant* as he might have been—"your face looks honest enough. Why don't you help us out and tell us what you did with the liquor?"

"Why should I help you out to help us in?" asked Hebe with her sweetest smile.

The judge looked annoyed and shifted his discouraged eyes to Sandra.

"Will you make a clean breast of it?" he demanded.

"Why, your honor," said Sandra, dropping her eyes. "What a thing to ask!"

"What do you mean?" asked the judge uneasily.

"I wouldn't like to say," the girl replied.

"Do you know what you did with the liquor?" repeated the judge, his face growing gradually red as he gazed into Sandra's eyes now alarmingly raised to his.

"In view of the fact that we drank the liquor, your honor, your question seems rather indelicate," the modest young lady replied.

At this moment a deep growl sounded in the rear of the courtroom. This growl was followed by a general and concentrated drive on the windows on the part of every single spectator present. The judge was about to rap for order when he stopped with gavel poised in mid-air as he found himself gazing into the open mouth of an enraged lion. Never had he seen such a furious animal, and never had he felt less like seeing one. Abandoning his prisoners to the lion and the mercy of God, he withdrew with his attendants to his chambers where he speedily produced a bottle of his own and did what any sensible man would have done under the circumstances.

The lion and his grateful companions wandered round the deserted courtroom for a few minutes, then emerged from the building into the equally deserted street. Leisurely climbing into the automobile, they drove off unmolested. Nor were they molested throughout the remainder of their journey back to their original point of departure, the Lamb residence—a place which its owner had come to fear he might never see again.

"Pardon our lion, Thomas," said Hebe breezily, as the aged servant hurried to meet them. "He's not a bad sort at all if you like lions."

"Never had much of a chance to get acquainted," replied Thomas. "Is there anything I can do for this one, Miss Hebe?"

"Yes," said Hebe. "Give the poor creature all the meat you can find either alive or dead in the kitchen. He's been eating beans for the last five days, and he might start in on us if we don't do something about it."

Thomas hurried away, and Mr. Lamb went to show himself to the turtle, who as usual was not impressed.

CHAPTER XX

A Decidedly Different Something

FOR SOME WEEKS NOW MR. LAMB HAD BEEN QUITE himself. This morning he wished he was not, for he was presently due at court to defend himself in a divorce suit brought against him by the revengeful Sapho. That gracious lady was at last striking for freedom. And she was striking in the worst possible way so far as Mr. Lamb was concerned. The summons had informed him that he should be both ready and willing to defend himself against charges of aggravated adultery, witchcraft, animalism, mental anguish, attempted murder, torture, and non-support. When Lamb read the official wording of the disagreeable document his brain swam. He had never before realized he had been such a versatile blackguard. How that woman must have suffered! And how she was going to let the world know about it!

Sandra Rush had been named as the other half of the adultery charge, and although she was most uninterestingly innocent she was highly satisfied with the trend of events. Her conduct greatly added to Mr. Lamb's uneasiness. She assumed that she was an adulteress and acted the part so well that the poor man began to believe it must be true. Frequently she spoke of their guilty love with downcast eyes and generously declared that she fully intended to share at least half of the blame. When Mr. Lamb appealed to her better nature she accused him of trying to cast her aside like a broken reed and swore violently to God that she would sue him for chronic assault, seduction, and breach of promise. As his own daughter stoutly supported Sandra's charges he held his peace and relapsed into sweating silence. It was all terribly upsetting.

Mr. Lamb had received notice of the divorce on the morning after his return from the mountains. He had awakened that morning quite himself and fully clad. His clothes were in a state of great disorder, and a week's growth of whiskers decorated his face. When he had finished reading the document he somehow wished himself back on the quiet, wind-fanned summit of that mountain retreat where life had been so pleasantly natural and simplified. Already the newspapers were beginning to discuss the amazing charges brought by the wife of a prominent financier against her husband. Apparently this much-sinned-against woman was willing to take the reporters into her confidence at any hour of the day or night. Almost overnight Mr. Lamb had become a national figure. His picture appeared in various papers, but not so large as Mrs. Lamb's.

Only one ray of light penetrated the encircling gloom. Nothing had developed from the bootlegging charge. It seemed that the recorder's report must have been of a nature to discourage further investigation. Flarebacks of this episode also appeared in print. Mr. Lamb's name and that of Sandra Rush were still more firmly linked. The fact that the woman in the case was an underwear model was not neglected. News was scarce at that time, and Mr. Lamb and his affairs were received with thanks by the press.

Hebe and Melville Long accompanied Mr. Lamb to the court. Sandra refused to appear, feeling that her absence would give the impression of an admission of guilt. Looking insinuatingly at Mr. Lamb she assured him that she could never face the world after all that had taken place between them. An expression of indignant protest escaped Mr. Lamb's lips.

"That night you escaped from my window," whispered Sandy. "Wow!"

"Ah!" said Hebe with a deep intake of breath.

"For God's sake, Hebe," her father pleaded. "Don't you see that this girl, this female snake in the grass, intends deliberately to ruin me?"

"She'll be the making of you, major," said Hebe calmly.

"And I wouldn't call people snakes and things," put

in Sandra. "It doesn't sound well coming from you, and besides, you're not out of the woods yet."

"I wish to heaven I was back in them," fervently replied the much beset man.

Now the judge was regarding Mr. Lamb with amused interest. Mr. Lamb was aware that the judge was not alone in his scrutiny. Mrs. Lamb at her lawyers' table alone refused to look upon her husband. She was artistically dressed for the occasion. Her lawyer was addressing the court.

"Your honor," he said a little self-consciously because of the ridiculous nature of the charges he had to press, "I shall prove that my client's husband not only turned into a horse, a seagull, a kangaroo, a goldfish, a dog, a cat, in order named, but also that he actually had the temerity to assume the form of a lion—a dangerous and destructive animal."

The judge's smile of amusement deepened.

"Sounds like a lot of bedtime stories to me," he observed. "Why don't you establish adultery and call it a day?"

"My client insists on justice," replied the lawyer. "We have made no charge in our brief that we are not able to prove."

"If she insists on proving all her charges this case will become a permanent institution I'm afraid," said the judge. "Hurry on with the animal business, and don't make me feel too silly. I'm a serious-minded man in spite of the things to which I occasionally have to listen."

To Mr. Lamb's horror and surprise his daughter was asked if she would voluntarily take the stand. In his desperation he clung to her skirt as the young lady rose eagerly to go to the chair.

"Steady, major," she whispered, "or you'll be having your daughter testifying in the flimsiest excuse for a breech-clout."

Mr. Lamb released her, and the girl swinging herself into the chair sat smiling innocently upon the judge, after she had taken an oath she had no intention of keeping. The lawyer for Mrs. Lamb addressed her.

"Miss Lamb," he asked with the utmost politeness,

"what did you first think when you discovered a horse in your father's bed?"

"Why I naturally drew the conclusion that Sapho had invited him in," she replied with compelling candor.

The judge coughed discreetly behind his hand and looked at the astounded lawyer with eyebrows slightly elevated. The lawyer was in a state of painful confusion. He would willingly have asked the witness to step down, but was afraid of the impression such a move would make. Mrs. Lamb had half arisen in her chair and was staring at her daughter with murder in her eyes.

"I'm a little astray," remarked the judge. "You mentioned someone by the name of Sapho. I thought your mother's name was Tilly, Miss Lamb?"

"It really is Mary," Hebe explained with painstaking patience, "but mother never liked that name. So father always called her Tilly. She thought Tilly wasn't romantic enough, so to humor her whim I called her Sapho because she was always play-acting in father's best pajamas, and lying on the floor with——"

The hands of the plaintiff's lawyer were churning wildly about in the air. His client sat white and trembling at her table. Behind her she could hear the sound of suppressed laughter.

"I protest," the lawyer spluttered. "The witness is introducing a lot of irrelevant evidence. Whether Mrs. Lamb's pajamas——"

"They weren't Mrs. Lamb's pajamas," broke in Hebe. "I distinctly told you she sneaked them on my father."

Then the lawyer lost all control.

"Why quibble about it?" he demanded furiously of Hebe. "What earthly difference does it make whether the pajamas belong to your father or your mother?"

"All the difference in the world," replied Hebe, looking pityingly upon the lawyer. "You see, a woman's pajamas are built according to an altogether different method of construction than a man's. For one thing a woman's pajamas——"

Laughter in the courtroom was now quite general,

and, so far as the judge was concerned, uninterrupted.

"Your honor," said Mr. Wilson with a hopeless droop to his shoulders, "if I hear any more about those pajamas I'll have to withdraw from the case."

"Very well," replied the judge agreeably. "Let's talk about something else."

Mr. Wilson revived a little and turned once more to the willing and anxious Hebe. For a certain reason he wanted to establish a date.

"Miss Lamb," he asked, "please answer this question as briefly as possible: after the appearance of the horse do you remember the exact date when you next found your father in bed?"

"On the morning of the twenty-fourth," the young girl answered without a moment's hesitation. "I remember because Leonard Gray was visiting mother over the week-end, and although she didn't know that I knew it and—"

"You may step down, Miss Lamb," interrupted the lawyer in a dead voice, "unless the defense wishes to question you."

The defense did.

"Miss Lamb," asked the legal representative of Hebe's father, "you can't possibly think of any reason for the viciously conceived rumor of some innocent intimacy existing between your father and the woman, Sandra Rush?"

"Hold on," exclaimed the judge momentarily interrupting work on a picture he was drawing. "I never heard such a perniciously worded question in all my born days. Ask it all over again, Mr. Hedges, and this time don't try to be so subtly leading, or rather, misleading."

"Gladly, your honor," said Mr. Hedges smoothly. "Miss Lamb, there is of course no foundation in fact in the childish gossip that your father and Miss Rush were ever anything more than nodding acquaintances—almost hostile?"

"Hold on again," interrupted the judge. "You might be trying to spare our feelings, Mr. Hedges, but you're not improving a bit. I'm afraid you'll have to ask that question as if you desired information rather than confirmation."

"All right," said Mr. Hedges with ill humor. "Did this Rush woman and your father ever misconduct themselves?"

"Jointly or individually?" asked the literal-minded Hebe.

"Jointly," replied the lawyer. "In each other's company and at the same time and place."

"Well, I wouldn't be surprised," the girl admitted. "Now that you've made yourself clear I'll have to say that I wouldn't be a bit surprised. Not before me, of course, but my father is only human and the Rush woman is so *laissez-faire*. Then again, mother was always so busy. Can't sit up all night and twirl your thumbs, you know."

"She can step down so far as I'm concerned," said Mr. Hedges, turning his back on the young lady.

The judge removed a handkerchief from his face and looked at Hebe with brimming eyes.

"They don't seem to want to play with you any more, Miss Lamb," he told her. "You may step down with the satisfaction of knowing that you have been perfectly disastrous to both sides."

Hebe was popular with neither Mrs. nor Mr. Lamb when she returned to her chair beside the latter.

"What did you want to go and tell lies for?" her father demanded, his whispered words laden with indignation.

"Wasn't telling lies," replied Hebe. "How do I know what you and Sandy do with your spare time? I didn't say you did and I didn't say you didn't."

"No," muttered Mr. Lamb sarcastically. "You did everything but draw a diagram. And why did you call her that Rush woman?"

"Sounded more desperate," said Hebe. "Anyway, Sandy told me not to spare her feelings. She wanted to shoulder half the blame for everything."

Mr. Lamb choked down his wrath. He would have preferred to choke his imp of a daughter. He turned his eyes on the next witness and started. The witness was the man who had bought him at the horse show.

"Mr. Rudd," the opposing lawyer was asking, "did you purchase a horse at a horse show on the twenty-fourth of last month?"

"I thought I did at the time," replied Mr. Rudd.

"Did you notice anything peculiar about the horse when you purchased him?" continued the lawyer.

"I did, sir," said the witness. "That horse was drunk, dead-drunk and snoring."

"And where is that horse now, Mr. Rudd?"

Mr. Rudd looked long and searchingly at Mr. Lamb, while that gentleman returned the look with an ironical eye. Then the farmer pointed an earthy-looking finger at him.

"Wouldn't be surprised if he wasn't the horse I bought," said Mr. Rudd.

At this the judge slapped his leg and leaned over his desk.

"Pardon me," he remarked, "but did I understand you to say the horse was dead-drunk?"

"He was, your honor."

"And how about yourself, Mr. Rudd?"

"Sober as a judge, your honor."

"Thanks for the compliment, Mr. Rudd, but do you mean to tell me you didn't know the difference between that gentleman and a horse?"

"Well, I found him between the shafts, your honor, and the thing I'd bought for a horse had clean disappeared. Ain't never seen it since."

Mr. Wilson intervened at this point.

"How did the gentleman explain his presence between the shafts of your cart, Mr. Rudd?" the lawyer asked.

"Said he was playing horse," replied Mr. Rudd. "Told me a long cock-and-bull story about how he couldn't break himself of the habit of playing horse."

Mr. Wilson laughed scornfully and turned to the judge.

"You can see for yourself, your honor," he said, "what a lame excuse that was under the circumstances."

"There's nothing wrong under the law in playing horse," observed the judge mildly. "It's rather an odd

sort of amusement for a great, tall man like Mr. Lamb.
Still if he wants to ride a broom or even to pull a cart
he has a perfect right to do so."

He paused for a moment and looked curiously at
Mr. Wilson. "Do you actually believe in this man's
story?" asked the judge.

"Certainly, your honor," Mr. Wilson replied. "The
witness is on his oath."

"I know all about that," replied the judge impatiently. "I'm not suggesting perjury, but I've known
men who would have taken an oath that they were
seeing snakes and pink elephants and green devils that
existed only in their feverish imaginations. The judge
that Mr. Rudd said he was as sober as, must have been
a judge of whisky. That's the only way to justify his
obviously impossible statements. Now, Mr. Wilson, let's
get down to cases. If you can't prove that the defendant
was a horse, you're going to have a great deal harder
time trying to prove that he was a goldfish or a lion.
And so far as I'm concerned it's going to be practically
impossible for you to convince me that that gentleman
sitting there with his sweet, innocent young daughter
was ever a kangaroo. This is the silliest divorce case so
far that I've ever tried. It has its amusing side, but I'm
not here to be amused. Why don't you drop all this animal business and press a charge that you can get your
teeth into—something more homelike and understand-
able—adultery for instance?"

"One moment, your honor," said Mr. Wilson hastily.
"Listen to this."

The lawyer drew near the rail and spoke in a low
voice to the judge. Both of them looked with interest at
Mr. Lamb, who under the combined gaze of the two
legal minds began to grow decidedly uncomfortable.

Suddenly the judge broke down and buried his face
in his hands, his shoulders shook and strangling noises
came from between his fingers. Presently he mopped
his face with his handkerchief and fixed his tearful eyes
on the lawyer.

"You're only guessing, Mr. Wilson," said the judge.
"And besides you haven't even established the fact that

he was a horse. You'll have to do better than that or I'll throw this case out of court."

Mr. Lamb's face was flaming. Strange things were going on inside him. If his wife had wished to humiliate him her wish was amply gratified. Through hot eyes he saw that Mr. Rudd's place in the witness box had been taken by the woman in charge of Sandra's underwear shop. His heart sank. Was that scene to be repeated for the benefit of the public? Mr. Lamb wanted very badly to be somewhere else. He would gladly have turned to a stone or to any other inanimate object for a change. Madam was gorgeously arrayed. She seemed to regard the occasion in the light of a pleasant diversion.

"It was an assault partial," she was saying in answer to some question the opposing lawyer had put to her. "Not an assault complete. A moment more and it might have been utter."

"How was the victim of this brutal attack clad?" continued Mr. Wilson.

"The assaulted one was clad in a costume most revealing," explained madam. "An irresistible creation of my own. Should you remove all of your outer garments, m'sieur, and cut the little that remained into ribbons, retaining only the smallest possible protection, you would arrive at something of the same effect."

"Don't try it, Mr. Wilson," put in the judge. "I've stood about enough for one day."

"What was Mr. Lamb doing?" continued Mr. Wilson, striving to maintain his dignity in the face of the quietly mirthful courtroom.

Madam seemed completely surprised by this question. She elevated her shoulders eloquently and seemed to be taking the courtroom into her confidence.

"Why, m'sieur," she protested. "What would you do? What would the judge do? What would any man do under the circumstances?"

"I hate the way that woman talks," observed the judge. "The situation is sufficiently clear, don't you think, Mr. Wilson?"

But madam was well launched on her description and would not be denied. "When I reentered the room—"

At this point the human elements contained in Mr. Lamb seemed to crash and to fall into disorder. The little russet man had at last surpassed all his previous efforts. Either out of pity for Mr. Lamb or through some caprice of his own, he had changed him into what might be roughly termed, a combination animal. Lamb had the feathered head of a large rooster, the body of some strangely designed prehistoric animal and the tail of a lizard. Not knowing what a sight he presented, he was able to gain some slight conception from the fact that even his own daughter shrank from him. The opposing lawyers leaped the rail at the same instant and took refuge with the judge behind his desk. Their bulging eyes slanted across its surface as if the three gentlemen were being strangled. Mrs. Lamb appeared to have swooned. The courtroom was in an uproar. With a strange, whistling gasp Mr. Lamb looked uneasily about him, then turned and shuffled awkwardly down the aisle. No one raised a finger to stay his progress.

"I take everything back," said the judge when order had been restored. "It seems I was all wrong. Do you know what that thing was, Mr. Wilson?"

"I doubt if anyone does," replied the gentleman.

"Well, whatever it was," continued the judge, "I'm sure your client cannot be expected to live with it. I wouldn't do so myself for the world. The papers will be drawn up immediately. This court is officially adjourned, but those who care to remain until they have collected their scattered wits are at liberty to do so."

With dignity befitting his exalted office, the judge gathered his robe about him and withdrew.

CHAPTER XXI

Exit the Little Russet Man

WHEN MR. LAMB CAUGHT SIGHT OF HIMSELF IN A store window he jumped three feet in the air so great was the shock he received. Once more the strange, whistling sound came from between his beak as he hopped and shuffled along the street. More than ever now he felt cut off from humanity. Even the automobiles seemed to shrink from him. What would Sandra think of him? Would she, too, be revolted like Hebe? He was going to find out.

Sandra, having withdrawn from the swollen ranks of the employed, was sitting on her front veranda. No one else seemed to be in sight as Mr. Lamb hopped up the steps and squatted down beside her. He was breathing wheezily from exertion—wheezing and whistling distractedly. His lonely, frightened eyes peered questioningly into Sandra's, then he looked away as if ashamed to meet her gaze. Now that he was there he wished he had not come.

"Sit down and rest," said Sandra quietly. "Don't you think you're laying it on a little strong? I stood you as a lion and a kangaroo without turning a hair. When you were a seagull and a goldfish I did what little I could to protect your interests. When you were a cat I actually took you to bed with me. Not satisfied with your past achievements it now seems that you've begun to make up animals, combining them, trying to be three animals at once. It's a trifle more than a potential wife or mistress can stand. I think its very silly to make up animals. Have you seen yourself yet? Look."

She took a small mirror from her vanity case and held it up before Mr. Lamb. With a strangled, gasping squawk he flopped down the steps and shuffled away as fast as his queer, ill-fashioned legs could carry him. A thin film seemed to have settled over his eyes. He could see only dimly. He was totally unfitted for the world in which he found himself. His heart was heavy, however, with human despair.

Sandra rose quickly from her chair and looked after the retreating animal. Once she called to him, but Mr. Lamb did not appear to have heard her. Filled with misgiving for the safety of this defenseless creature she hurried to Mr. Lamb's home, but he was not there. Hebe greeted her at the door and gave her an account of what had taken place at court, after which they sat down and wondered what had become of Mr. Lamb.

The subject of their speculations knew neither what to do or where to go. News of a strange animal being at large spread rapidly through the countryside. Parties were organized to capture or to kill this animal. Big, quick-tempered, hard-biting dogs were pressed into service. The animal was different, therefore it did not belong. It was the invariable attitude of humanity— destroy what you cannot understand. Mr. Lamb became a hunted thing.

His trail was picked up on the outskirts of the town. Soon he heard the hue and cry behind him. Sheer panic weakened his efforts as he hopped laboriously along. He was about to enter a wood when he spied a small hut before which a man was sitting, a man with vague, troubled eyes and a head of matted hair. Mr. Lamb recognized the man. He was the local half-wit, almost as far removed from his fellow men as was Mr. Lamb himself.

When the half-wit saw the winded and hard-pressed creature he showed neither surprise nor alarm. He rose from the ground and approaching Mr. Lamb, looked sympathetically into his dim eyes. "Tired," he said as if to himself, "and thirsty. Scared near to death."

The sound of pursuit was growing steadily nearer. Three dogs, nose to the ground, were streaming across the field. Behind them came the rabble of the town. The half-wit frowned and looked at Mr. Lamb.

"They're after you," he said quietly. "They've been after me for years. Come along."

Mr. Lamb hopped after him to the hut and drank thirstily when the man gave him a cup of water. Then the man went out and stood before the door. In his hand was a heavy stick.

Within a few minutes Mr. Lamb heard the voices of his pursuers and the snarls of the dogs. The house was surrounded and shouts rang out.

"Leave the poor creature alone," he heard the half-wit saying. "He's not hurting anybody, and I won't let you at him."

The dogs were urged forward, and the crowd fell upon the struggling half-wit. In spite of his terror Mr. Lamb tried to come to his aid.

"There it is!" a voice shouted. "Get him."

A large rock crashed against the side of Mr. Lamb's head and the strange animal sank down, a crumpled, uncouth mass. A dog worried his tail, and by his side the half-wit was feebly trying to rise. Through bruised lips he was muttering something about the crucifixion of Christ. The crowd stood over the still animal with a feeling of great accomplishment, particularly the man who had thrown the rock.

When Mr. Lamb regained consciousness he was ly-ing on a large marble slab. A group of near-sighted-looking gentlemen were examining him minutely. One of these gentlemen was clad in white. In his hand was a long, thin, and extremely businesslike knife. Mr. Lamb sat up abruptly and looked about him. The room in which he found himself was rigged out as a labora-tory. To Mr. Lamb it had the appearance of a torture chamber. The men seemingly were highly excited. They were staring at Mr. Lamb with deep interest.

"Oh, I say," said one of them in remonstrating tones, "that was really too bad of you."

"How too bad?" asked Mr. Lamb, a trifle giddily.

"Well," continued the man, "a moment ago you were a most remarkable type of animal. Now you're only rather a common-place sort of person."

"You're not so exceptional yourself," replied Mr. Lamb, irritated by the man's manner.

He swung round on the table and addressed another member of the group.

"I wish you would remove the knife from that unreliable-looking individual's hand," he said. "What are all of you trying to do anyway, murder me?"

"No," replied the other. "This is a meeting of scientists. We were just going to find out what manner of animal you were. You seemed to be quite dead."

"Well, I don't seem quite dead now," said Mr. Lamb. "And I'm not an animal. You'll have to stick that knife into someone else, I'm afraid. I want to go home. My head hurts."

"But aren't you going to be that way any more?" one of the men protested.

"Come, come," urged one. "Snap back for us, won't you?"

"All I can say," remarked a third, "is that as you were, you were a great gain to science and that as you are, you are not much of a contribution to the human race."

"Won't you even try?" pleaded a bearded individual. "Come now, make an honest effort. Try hard. Be an animal."

"Yes," urged still another member of the group. "Pull yourself together."

"And you'll pull me apart," replied Mr. Lamb.

"I'd like to cut him open anyway," remarked the man with the knife. "There must be something strange inside him. No one would ever know."

Mr. Lamb slid hastily from the marble slab.

"Everyone would know," he announced. "If you come a step nearer with that horrid-looking knife, I'll let out a yell that will bring in the entire neighborhood, you cold-blooded, long-faced murderer. You look like a horse yourself. Why don't you slit your own hide open?"

Mr. Lamb felt better after this little outburst. He walked to the door with a dignified step, then turned and faced the bewildered and disappointed scientists.

"The next time I turn into an animal," he announced, "I'm going to call in an osteopath."

It was quite late when Mr. Lamb reached home. The house seemed empty. He went directly to his study, and without troubling to switch on the light sat down in his usual chair. He wanted to rest his eyes to see if the pain would not leave his head. Through the doors to his little porch the starlight shone into the room. Presently Mr. Lamb became aware of the fact that a small red light was glowing steadily opposite him. He caught the aroma of cigar smoke.

"Are you satisfied?" came a voice through the darkness.

Mr. Lamb recognized the voice, and his heart began to beat a little more hopefully. He got up and switching on the light, stood looking down at the little russet man. That cheery individual was sitting exactly as Mr. Lamb had last seen him. In one hand he held a half-smoked cigar, in the other a half-consumed highball. His umbrella was neatly arranged on the floor at his side.

"I hope you are," replied Mr. Lamb. "I'm fed up. You've ruined everything for me including the zoo."

The little russet man smiled.

"Well, Mr. Lamb," he said, "you're all through now. It's done you a world of good. Respectability almost had you. You could never have stood the strain."

"I'm not respectable now, God knows," said Mr. Lamb. "I'm the most talked about person in the nation. I'm divorced, disgraced, and forever marked as a freak of nature."

"Do you regret your experiences?" asked the little russet man.

Mr. Lamb thought over the past few months and grinned.

"No," he replied. "Not exactly."

"The world has a short memory," his visitor resumed. "And anyway, you should travel for a while. See something new, Mr. Lamb. As an animal you seemed to have a faculty for getting yourself into trouble. As a man your life should not prove to be so devoid of interest. The best side of you is your bad side—bad, I mean, from the point of view of Mrs. Grundy and her friends. Develop that side. Drink, eat, love, and laugh to your heart's content. Don't worry about people who peer through windows. Don't hurt others, but don't let others hurt you. They'll do it every time if they can get you on the run. The world envies successfully unmoral people. Also it hates them. What your generation refers to as a hangover is not necessarily a mark of shame. There's plenty of room in the world for a decent-spirited drunkard. Sobriety is good for certain persons only. You are not one of them. And, by the way, if I were in your place I'd look up that half-witted chap who tried to help you out. I find him one of the most likeable characters in the community."

Mr. Lamb walked over to a table and picked up the decanter. He was considering the words of his guest. A breeze passed through the room, and Mr. Lamb, turning, saw that the doors to his porch were open. Evidently the little russet man had passed through them, because he was no longer present. Only his umbrella remained beside his empty chair, and as Mr. Lamb stood looking at it the umbrella rose from the floor and moved slowly across the room.

"Almost forgot it that time," from nowhere in particular came the voice of the mysterious little fellow.

Mr. Lamb walked out on his porch and sat down. A small hand slipped through the darkness and came to rest on his. Mr. Lamb sprang up with a smothered cry of fear.

"For God's sake," he complained, "Why is everybody creeping up on me in the dark? I'm as nervous as a bug."

"We'll have to do something about that," said Sandra. "Sit down and keep your shirt on."

CHAPTER XXII

In the Wake

SANDRA AND MR. LAMB WERE TOO MUCH IN THE PUB-
lic eye to get married, so they agreed to play make-
believe. However Mr. Lamb had extracted a promise
from Sandra in the presence of Hebe and Melville Long
to make him an honest man the moment they reached
Paris.

Mr. Lamb had readily consented to go abroad for an
indefinite period.

"If I stay here," he had remarked at the breakfast
table, where the suggestion had first been advanced by
Sandra, "all my friends will be sitting around expecting
me to turn into something for them. As far as business
is concerned, I'm pow. A man who harbors the horrid
fear that at any moment I may become a centipede or
a panther is hardly in a receptive frame of mind to
concentrate on a list of securities. Billings will have to
carry on at the office, and Thomas will stand by the
goods here at home."

"I might run over with a contingent of Boy Scouts
myself," announced Brother Dug. "You'll know when
we get there because we'll all be singing."

"Tell us where you're not going to be," said Hebe,
"and we'll go there."

Douglas grinned amiably.

Hebe and Mr. Long were married. During the last
ten days he had proved himself useful in procuring the
wrong tickets for the right boat or the right tickets for
the wrong boat. The efficient Hebe had at last been
forced to assume the responsibility of getting the party
started. Mr. Long senior had been so pleased at the
prospect of getting his son out of the house for some

time to come that he had disgorged great quantities of money.

"I hope that at least you'll be able to prove yourself a father," the old gentleman had said upon relinquishing the check.

The three young people were now pushing Mr. Lamb up the gangplank. To outwit the newspaper reporters he was wearing a false beard above which his eyes peered out guiltily at the world. Unfortunately the beard fell off half-way up the gangplank. He quickly slipped it into his pocket, leaving part of it sticking out.

"I thought you were wearing a beard, sir," observed his steward when he had placed the luggage in the stateroom.

"No," explained Mr. Lamb. "That was someone seeing me off."

When the steward was about to leave Mr. Long appeared wearing the beard and solemnly shook hands with his father-in-law. The steward departed baffled. Needless to say the party had been well primed for the occasion.

On the table in the Lamb suite reposed a bowl of animal crackers and a large Noah's Ark.

"Don't forget to sing," ran the accompanying note from Brother Dug. "Love and kisses."

The ship was now well under weigh. Several miles up the river two odd-looking characters were emerging from the pier shed—ancient Thomas and the vague-eyed half-wit, both of whom were already missing Mr. Lamb. That gentleman and Sandra were standing in the stern. Sandra was getting very close to him. They were both looking back at the wake of the ship. It was the same ship on which Mr. Lamb had once been such a disturbing stowaway. Sandra continued to cram herself against her companion. Mr. Lamb gave her a pinch of protest.

"Don't hurl yourself at me like that," he complained, looking nervously about him. "You're practically sitting on my chest. I'm not an open subway door."

Apparently Sandra did not hear him. She wedged herself even closer. Suddenly Mr. Lamb pointed to a

weather-beaten old seagull raucously following the
ship.

"See that old devil?" said Mr. Lamb. "Well, I think
I know that gull. He asked me to eat fertilizer with him
once."

"Do you happen to know who's aboard this ship?"
asked Hebe, brightly, suddenly appearing at the rail.

"I hope not," replied her father. "Who?"

"Sapho and Leonard Gray," announced Hebe.

Mr. Lamb stood as if contemplating a rapid descent
into the sea. Sandra seemed highly delighted by the
news.

"Married or not?" she asked.

"Not," said Hebe briefly. "Leonard doesn't know the
meaning of the word."

"A nice ship, this," observed Mr. Lamb.

"Where do you get off?" demanded his daughter.

Mr. Lamb turned back to the rail and gazed along
the trailing wake, where the old seagull and his mob
were scurrying greedily among the waves. A suggestion
of a grin was beginning to gather slowly at the corners
of his lips.

"Well, two can play at that game," thought Mr.
Lamb. "Or rather four . . . and a very amusing game
it is."

Then he addressed himself to his daughter.

"Hebe," he said, "with your usual efficiency, will
you discover if the bar is working yet?"

"Go on, Hebe," urged Sandra. "He's been sticking
his head in and out of the smoking-room so often, the
stewards think he's trying to play peek-a-boo with
them."

And Hebe scuttled away on her edifying quest.